# WHO KILLED
# FATHER CHRISTMAS?

# WHO KILLED
# FATHER CHRISTMAS?

### And Other Seasonal Mysteries

*edited by*

MARTIN EDWARDS

BRITISH LIBRARY

This collection first published in 2023 by
The British Library
96 Euston Road
London NW1 2DB

# CONTENTS

# INTRODUCTION

**M**OST OF US WILL SURELY AGREE THAT CHRISTMAS IS, AS THE song goes, "the most wonderful time of the year". Remember, though, that it's also a time when—in Britain, at least!—there is always a chill in the air. These days, Yuletide stories of mayhem and murder rival Christmas songs in terms of popularity. There's something about Christmas that has inspired crime writers since the days of Conan Doyle and Stevenson and *Who Killed Father Christmas? And Other Seasonal Mysteries* gathers together an exciting mix of stories about people trying to make crime pay, even as others yearn only for peace and goodwill.

This is the fifth anthology of seasonal mysteries that I have edited for the British Library's Crime Classics series. It's hard for me to believe that it is fully eight years since I put together the first of these collections, *Silent Nights*. Compiling that book was a hugely enjoyable experience, but I never dreamed that the anthology would have four successors: *Crimson Snow, The Christmas Card Crime, A Surprise for Christmas*, and now the present offering. The enthusiastic response of readers to the books—not just in Britain but around the world—has far exceeded my expectations.

Clearly there is a huge demand for Christmas-related crime fiction, but eight years ago I'd have assumed that there wouldn't be enough enjoyable stories to fill five volumes. Fortunately, my own continuing researches into potential material have been supplemented by helpful advice from a number of collectors and researchers. Between you and me, I'm even starting to glimpse through a wintry haze the outlines of a sixth collection… time will tell whether this is achievable!

Why are Christmas mysteries so popular? One reason is that crime fans often enjoy combining festive fun with the chance to sit down and read a good book. Another is that a book makes a marvellous Christmas present. Whatever the explanation, crime publishers have long been aware of the demand for Christmas mysteries. This phenomenon dates back many years, but it seems to have become even more pronounced following the British Library's publication of J. Jefferson Farjeon's *Mystery in White* back in 2014. That book rapidly became a word-of-mouth bestseller and there's no doubt that the delightful cover artwork, depicting a train stuck in a snowdrift, contributed to its appeal. Since then, the run-up to December 25 has seen bookshops heaving with all manner of Christmassy titles with snow-laden covers. There seems no prospect of that changing any time soon.

Ultimately, though, a book must be judged not by its cover but on its contents, and I like to think that this anthology stands comparison in terms of the quality of stories with any of its four predecessors. In a collection such as this, variety really does count for a good deal, because different readers favour different types of crime writing. So here we have another story by Farjeon (which I've rescued from obscurity with the help of Jamie Sturgeon; intriguingly, the premise has distinct echoes of *Mystery in White*) as well as contributions by authors as diverse in style and subject matter as Frank Howel Evans, Glyn Daniel, John Dickson Carr, Ellis Peters, and Vincent Cornier. Something, we hope, for everyone.

I'd like to thank all those readers who contact me regularly with their thoughts on the series and who sometimes come up with suggestions of future titles for consideration. In response to some of their comments, we've decided to experiment in terms of the presentation of stories. In previous anthologies in this series, the stories have appeared, broadly speaking, in chronological order. Here, we have tried something different in order to emphasize that all-important element of variety between one story and the next. We welcome readers' feedback on whether it is worth persisting with this approach. I do appreciate the comments that I receive from fans of the Crime Classics and I'm also indebted to the experts whom I consult regularly to see if there are interesting stories that I've overlooked or of which I'm unaware. The help that I have received from, in this case, Jamie Sturgeon, Nigel Moss, John Cooper, Barry Pike, Doug Greene, and Jeffrey Marks, has been invaluable. My thanks also go to everyone at the British Library who has worked on putting this book together. My name appears on the cover, but it's truly a team effort.

So have yourself a merry literary Christmas—and may your path never cross with any criminals except in the pages of a good book...

MARTIN EDWARDS
www.martinedwardsbooks.com

# A NOTE FROM THE PUBLISHER

The original novels and short stories reprinted in the British Library Crime Classics series were written and published in a period ranging, for the most part, from the 1890s to the 1960s. There are many elements of these stories which continue to entertain modern readers; however, in some cases there are also uses of language, instances of stereotyping and some attitudes expressed by narrators or characters which may not be endorsed by the publishing standards of today. We acknowledge therefore that some elements in the works selected for reprinting may continue to make uncomfortable reading for some of our audience. With this series British Library Publishing aims to offer a new readership a chance to read some of the rare books of the British Library's collections in an affordable paperback format, to enjoy their merits and to look back into the world of the twentieth century as portrayed by its writers. It is not possible to separate these stories from the history of their writing and as such the following stories are presented as they were originally published with the inclusion of minor edits made for consistency of style and sense. We welcome feedback from our readers, which can be sent to the following address:

British Library Publishing
The British Library
96 Euston Road
London, NW1 2DB
United Kingdom

# ON THE IRISH MAIL

## Garnett Radcliffe

Garnett Radcliffe (1898–1971) was an Irishman. Born in County Meath, he was educated at Campbell College, Belfast, and then at Sandhurst. He served in India on the North-West Frontier and with the RAF in South Arabia and Socotra, before becoming a civil servant. As a novelist and author of short stories, he ranged from detective stories—in the early 1930s he was a regular contributor to *Detective Fiction Weekly*—and adventure stories and thrillers (sometimes published under the name Stephen Travers) to sci-fi. During the 1950s, he contributed several stories to *Weird Tales*. The online *Encyclopedia of Science Fiction* gives a flavour of his lurid style: "the title novella of *The Return of the Ceteosaurus, and Other Tales...* pits a huge saurian against a Death Ray... The ocean liner threatened by a resident ape... in *In the Grip of the Brute* has some of the lineaments of the Ship of Fools. The task of the heroine of *The Lady from Venus* is to acquire Earth eggs for use back home on Venus as a form of currency."

Radcliffe, then, was an entertainer pure and simple but his story-telling talents were sufficient to prompt Dorothy L. Sayers to include "On the Irish Mail" in the third of her ground-breaking anthologies *Great Short Stories of Mystery, Detection, Horror* (1934).

I T WAS NOT UNTIL FOUR O'CLOCK ON THE DAY BEFORE CHRISTMAS that Dick Fenton knew definitely that he would be able to spend Christmas with his people in Dublin. He was a junior partner in the firm of Rogers and Waberley, chartered accountants, whose offices were in London, and he had had to work against time on the important task of looking into the books of a certain bankrupt firm. He was, however, anxious to spend the great festival with his parents, and by starting at six o'clock in the morning, having a very hurried breakfast and omitting lunch altogether, he managed to have the books balanced and approved by four o'clock.

He slammed the last ledger and hurried to the private office of Mr. Rogers, the senior partner.

"All finished," he cried in triumph. "Now, I hope, I can get off to Ireland!"

Mr. Rogers congratulated him. "You'll have plenty of time to catch the night mail from Euston," he said. "That means you will arrive at Kingstown about seven on Christmas morning. Well, I mustn't delay you. Good-bye, and I hope you will have a very merry Christmas."

Fenton thanked him. Then he tore off to wire the good news to his parents and to pack some belongings. He dined comfortably and sauntered into the station three-quarters of an hour before the mail was due to start, as he anticipated there would be a rush of last-minute travellers hastening back to spend their Christmas in Ireland.

The porter who carried his suit-case confirmed his suspicions.

"There'll be a big crowd tonight, sir," he said. "First class, sir?"

"Yes," said Fenton, who was a rather opulent young man.

The porter hurried down the long train and found him a corner seat in a smoker. Fenton opened a novel and composed himself to read until the train should start. For about twenty minutes he had the carriage to himself, then it began to fill.

The first to enter was an Irish priest, who took the seat opposite to Fenton, said "Cold evening" and began to read a newspaper. He was followed in rapid succession by a well-dressed business man wearing a fur coat, an elderly man with spectacles, and, last of all, a big man with heavy boots who had something vaguely official in his bearing. Fenton covertly took stock of each as he entered and decided that his fellow-passengers were not particularly interesting. On the other hand they were not objectionable. He returned to his book which was enthralling. When the train started he was so immersed that he hardly noticed it.

For the first half-hour no one spoke. The priest was busy with his newspaper, the business man was writing a letter, the elderly man was staring out of the window, and the big official-looking man was gazing at a small hand-grip that one of the passengers had deposited upon the luggage-rack. Suddenly he rose to his feet and taking the hand-grip from the rack examined it minutely. No one paid any attention.

"Jim Dawson, you're spotted," he said. "Come now, you may as well give yourself up."

The other passengers in the compartment exchanged glances, but no one replied. Each was waiting for someone else to speak.

"Gentlemen," said the big man, "I am sorry to interrupt you. Three of you are innocent men, but one of you is a crookster known as Jim Dawson. This bag was snatched this afternoon from the counter of Coulter's Bank. It contained two hundred pounds. It has been proved that the robbery was the work of Jim Dawson. Any one of you may be Jim Dawson in disguise. The presence of this bag proves conclusively that Jim Dawson is in this compartment."

The Irish priest was the first to recover from his astonishment. "Well, I can easily prove my identity," he began, but the business man interrupted.

"One moment," he said. "Before we go any further, may I ask who *you* are and by what authority you are questioning us in this way?"

"Certainly." The big man produced a badge and a slip of paper. "As this badge will show you, I am a Scotland Yard detective. My name is Sullivan. This paper is a warrant for the arrest of Jim Dawson, alias Ned Harper, alias William Ferguson..."

The business man took the badge and the piece of paper and examined them carefully. "Yes, they are quite in order," he said. "But look here, Detective Sullivan, you can't arrest all four of us on suspicion. Your warrant only authorizes you to arrest Jim Dawson. I am not a legal expert, but I am sure you will be exceeding your powers if you arrest three innocent men simply because they happen to travel in the same compartment as a thief!"

"Quite," Fenton agreed. He had already decided in his mind that the elderly man seated on his left was the guilty party. Now that he observed him closely he thought that there was something palpably false about his beard. What a tale this would make to tell his parents!

Detective Sullivan glanced with shrewd eyes from one face to the other.

"As you say, it is impossible for me to arrest you all," he said. "What I shall have to do is to detain you at Holyhead until you can furnish proof of your identities..."

The priest uttered an exclamation. "That means that we miss the mail boat and cannot get to Ireland for Christmas Day! I really must protest. I have promised to take a service in Armagh Cathedral and it is most essential that I get there in time..."

"And my parents are expecting me," Fenton broke in. "They will be terribly disappointed if..."

Detective Sullivan shrugged his shoulders. "I'm very sorry, gentle-men," he said, "but you will understand how impossible it is that I should run the risk of allowing Dawson to get away to the Irish Free State. Once there he could easily get to America as this warrant is not valid in Ireland. It would have to be renewed in Dublin and that would cause delay. For the benefit of the three of you who are innocent I may as well say that it is not only for the robbery in Coulter's Bank that Jim Dawson is wanted. There are other and graver charges against him."

The elderly man spoke for the first time. "It's utterly preposterous," he said in a falsetto voice which Fenton was certain to be assumed. "I am not an Irishman, so have no sentimental reasons for wishing to be in Ireland on Christmas Day. On the other hand, I have an important engagement. Furthermore, I have letters which can conclusively prove that I am not the person you call Jim Dawson. I absolutely decline to be detained at Holyhead." The other passengers murmured concur-rence, but the detective was adamant.

"Letters and proofs of identity can easily be forged," he said. "Jim Dawson is the very person to be well provided with them. When we get to Holyhead those of you who are innocent will have no difficulty in proving that you are bona-fide travellers. It should not be necessary to detain you for more than three hours at the most. If any pecuniary loss is entailed you will be able to claim reasonable compensation."

For a few minutes there was silence. Fenton saw the priest eyeing him suspiciously, and despite himself began to flush. It was not an agreeable sensation, this being a suspect. He knew that he was inno-cent, but he also knew that it would take some time to prove it. Then he wondered how on earth he was to spend his Christmas Day in Holyhead and cursed his luck in having chosen that ill-fated compartment.

Detective Sullivan lounged against the door, one hand thrust neg-ligently into a side pocket. Through the window Fenton could catch glimpses of snow-covered fields and endless telegraph posts rushing past. Occasionally he saw the lights of villages and towns.

The business man in the fur coat suddenly spoke with the air of one who has been struck by an idea.

"Why don't you open the bag and see if the money is still inside?" he asked.

"It doesn't matter a straw if the money is inside or not," Detective Sullivan replied. "The point is that it is the stolen bag, marked T. H. B., the cashier's initials. However, if it will give you any satisfaction I will open it." He undid the catch with one hand, thrust his hand inside and drew out a wad of bank-notes.

"That's a pretty conclusive proof," he said, counting them rapidly. "Yes, there are twenty ten-pound notes. Whichever of you is Jim Dawson must have felt pretty safe from pursuit! You've had a nasty surprise, haven't you, Jim?" His quick eyes darted from face to face, but all stared blankly back. Fenton, who was of a rather nervous disposition, actually found it difficult to meet the detective's accusing gaze, secure as he was in his own innocence.

Detective Sullivan sighed. "You bluff it out well, Jim," he said, "but you may as well own up. You're bound to be caught at Holyhead, and you're only causing a lot of inconvenience to three innocent men. Come, Jim, be a sport!"

No one answered, but presently the elderly man in spectacles said, "Does the fact that the bag was left in this compartment necessarily prove that Jim Dawson is here? It seems to me that it is quite possible that he left the bag here, then got frightened and slipped off to another carriage while the train was at Euston. If you really wish to make sure of his capture you ought to detain everybody on the train!"

For a moment Detective Sullivan seemed taken aback. "Who was the first to enter the compartment?" he asked, sharply.

"I was," Fenton said.

"And did you notice if the bag was here when you came in?"

"I am absolutely certain that it was not here. I looked round carefully to see if any of the seats had been taken. They had not, nor had any luggage been left on the rack."

"And while you were sitting here did anyone come in, leave a bag and go away?"

Fenton shook his head. "Not that I remember. I was reading, but I am sure that if anyone had come in I should have noticed it."

The detective gave a grunt of satisfaction. "That proves that one of you four must have brought it in," he said. "I'm afraid, gentlemen, that you must reconcile yourselves to the prospect of spending some of your Christmas Day at Holyhead."

There was another silence. Suddenly the train slackened speed and Fenton, peering through the window, perceived that they were stopping at Crewe. He turned to the detective.

"We stop here for a quarter of an hour. May I get out and see if there is any possibility of leaving a telegram to be sent to my people in the morning?"

Detective Sullivan shook his head. "Sorry. No one leaves this carriage until we reach Holyhead."

"Well, of all the rot I ever heard!" It was the business man, exploding into sudden wrath. "Look here, Mr. Detective Sullivan, in my humble opinion you are exceeding your powers. It is preposterous that three innocent travellers should be put to such inconvenience because you are too inefficient to be able to spot a well-known criminal. It practically amounts to illegal imprisonment. If I demand bail, can you refuse it?"

"In this instance bail would be two hundred pounds in ready money," the detective replied. "If you can produce that sum you can go free. I don't suppose you have that amount of money on you, have you?"

"Then you suppose wrong, my fine fellow," retorted the fur-coated man. "As it happens I have nearly five hundred pounds. Now, I'm going to take you at your word and bail myself out for two hundred. Here you are…" He produced a wallet, counted out forty five-pound notes, and handed them over.

"I want an official receipt," he snapped.

The detective hesitated. "I am not sure…" he began slowly.

"I want an official receipt," the fur-coated man repeated. "You fixed bail at two hundred pounds and you can't go back on your word. What's more, I intend to charge you interest on that two hundred!"

Detective Sullivan reluctantly wrote out a receipt on an official form. Before he handed it to the fur-coated man he scrutinized each note carefully.

"You are allowed to proceed to Ireland on bail," he said at last. "But I warn you that I shall telegraph your description to Dublin and that you may be under surveillance for some days."

The fur-coated man chuckled. "Hang your surveillance," he said. "All I care is that I get to Ireland for Christmas Day. I'm sorry for the rest of you though"—he looked round the carriage—"that is to say I am sorry for *two* of you."

"I am quite resigned to my fate," the priest said. "I shall telegraph to Armagh that I am unable to take the service. By the way, can one send a telegram on Christmas Day?"

"Up to twelve o'clock," Fenton said.

"Thank you. In that case my absence will not greatly matter. There is an excellent curate, who will doubtless preach a much better sermon than I could. As for myself, I shall seize the opportunity of visiting friends who live near Holyhead… I am quite content." He turned over in his corner and went to sleep.

The fur-coated man produced a cigar-case and handed it round, omitting the detective.

"It's a devilish interesting situation," he said cheerfully. "One of us four is a criminal and we don't know which. However, according to law a man is innocent until he is proved guilty. I *know* that I am innocent and I'm inclined to think that our clerical friend is also—no guilty man could sleep so placidly. Therefore the choice to my mind lies between you two"—he looked at Fenton and the elderly man. "No offence meant, of course. One of you is innocent and the other guilty. The question is which?"

"I can easily prove that I'm innocent," Fenton said eagerly. "My name is Richard Fenton and I'm junior partner in the firm of Rogers and Waberley. My home is in Rathmines, Dublin. I've any amount of letters here…"

"So have I," the elderly man with the spectacles interrupted. "I am a secretary of the Southern Irish Loyalists' League. My name is Featherstone and I was crossing over to attend a committee meeting. I am quite well known and if I were allowed to leave the compartment I believe I could find someone on the train to identify me. In any case, surely these documents…?" He produced some papers and thrust them under the detective's nose. Detective Sullivan waved them away.

"Jim Dawson is the most expert forger in Europe," was all he said, and the spectacled man subsided with a grunt of disgust.

The train entered Chester, stopped for a few minutes and proceeded.

"I've got an idea," the fur-coated man said suddenly, leaning forward to flick the ash off his cigar. "Suppose you two gentlemen both show me your evidences of identity. I shall examine them and satisfy myself which of you is innocent. I'm willing to bet that no forgeries will deceive me"—he darted a withering glance at the detective—"then, when I have decided, I shall cash the innocent man's cheque for two hundred pounds and he can pay his bail. Will you agree to this?" He looked at the detective.

"I shall have to," Detective Sullivan answered. "But I warn you that although you are on bail you will still be under supervision. Also you will have to take the risk of the cheque being genuine."

"Well, personally, I shall be very glad to avail myself of your kind offer," Mr. Featherstone said. "Here are my proofs of identity. I bank with Lloyds, and I don't think that you need have any fear that my cheque will be refused."

The fur-coated man took the papers and examined them carefully. Presently he said, "You're all right, Mr. Featherstone. Now, what about you?" He turned to Fenton.

Dick handed over his letters and the fur-coated man went through them one by one. He looked puzzled.

"I believe it must be our clerical friend after all," he said in a low voice so as not to disturb the sleeping priest. "Mr. Fenton, you are as innocent as Mr. Featherstone and myself. But this puts me in a quandary. Which of you two gentlemen am I to bail out? If I could I would be very pleased to oblige both of you. Unfortunately, I have only another two hundred pounds to spare."

"Bail me out." The elderly man craned forward in his eagerness. "I assure you that it is most essential that I should attend the Christmas meeting of the board. Perhaps, sir"—he turned to Fenton—"perhaps you will be kind enough to waive your right?"

"I'm sorry," Fenton replied, "but I also am desperately anxious to be home for Christmas. It is more for the sake of my parents than myself."

The fur-coated man looked from one to the other, then he turned to Detective Sullivan.

"Which shall I choose?" he asked.

"Toss for it," the detective answered. "It doesn't matter to me which goes so long as the bail is paid. But I warn you again that your descriptions will be telegraphed to Dublin and you will be under surveillance."

"That's quite fair," Fenton said. "Let's toss for it. I promise that I will abide by the decision."

"And you?" the fur-coated man asked Mr. Featherstone.

"I suppose I shall have to," he replied.

The fur-coated man produced a match. "I shall break this into two uneven pieces," he said. "Whichever of you draws the longer piece I shall bail out…" He broke the match, then put his hands behind his back for an instant.

"Now draw."

Fenton chose the piece nearer to him. It was the longer, and he held it aloft in triumph.

"Congratulations!" the fur-coated man said. "Detective Sullivan, here are two hundred pounds to bail out Mr. Fenton."

Dick produced his cheque-book. "Who shall I make it payable to?" he asked.

"Charles Mannering." The fur-coated man took the cheque and glanced at it. "That's all right. I shall cash it in Belfast on Boxing Day. Well, Mr. Fenton, I am very glad to have been able to assist you."

"I'm more than grateful," Dick answered. "I'm very sorry for you though, sir." He turned to Mr. Featherstone.

"Oh, it can't be helped. I shall have to make the best of a bad job. I daresay my detention at Holyhead will not be of very long duration. Ah! here we are."

The train glided into Holyhead and drew up alongside the steamer. Detective Sullivan, who had been writing down descriptions of Fenton and the fur-coated man, opened the door.

"Will you come along with me, please?" he said to the priest and Mr. Featherstone. "All right, you other gentlemen are free to proceed on your journey. The bail money will be returned to you within a week, I *hope*." He hurried off with his captives and Fenton heard him asking a porter if there was a policeman on duty on the quay.

The fur-coated man began to laugh.

"Well, this is the queerest journey I've ever had," he said. "Gad! I'll be curious to know which of those two chaps really is Jim Dawson! Which do you think?"

"Certainly not the priest," Fenton said emphatically.

"Then you suspect Mr. Featherstone?"

"Yes."

They shook hands and parted with mutual expressions of goodwill. Fenton, being a bad sailor, stayed in his cabin during the crossing and they did not see each other again until next morning at Kingstown, where they had a few words at the Customs.

"Don't forget you're under police surveillance," was Mr. Mannering's final, laughing injunction.

Dick Fenton enjoyed a roaring Christmas in his home at Rathmines. He had to tell the story of how nearly he had been detained at Holyhead again and again. The more he thought the matter over, the more certain he became that Mr. Featherstone was the thief.

"I spotted him at once," he said to his admiring circle of relatives. "You just keep an eye on the papers and see if I wasn't right."

Two days after Christmas his elder brother returned from London, where he was employed in a business firm. He arrived when the family were having breakfast, and the mother rushed out into the hall to welcome him.

Above the barking of dogs and the mother's incoherent welcomes, Dick heard his brother's loud, cheery voice:

"Hallo, mater... Yes, had a jolly good journey... I was devilish nearly arrested in the train though... A detective wanted to detain a priest, an old chap, a business man called Mannering and myself at Holyhead... Bank robbery, or something... The 'tec spotted the bag in our compartment... Mannering bailed me out... Jolly decent of him..."

It was then that Dick realized that he and his brother had been the dupes of an uncommonly astute gang of confidence-trick men. Needless to say, Scotland Yard did not repay the money spent on bail.

## THE CHRISTMAS THIEF

# Frank Howel Evans

Francis Howel Evans (1867–1931) was, to quote the National Library of Wales, "a writer of short stories and crime fiction under the names Frank Howel Evans and Howel Evans, and apparently also novelettes under the nom-de-plume Atherley Daunt." Another pen-name was Crutchley Payne. He was a prolific contributor to publications such as *Chums*, *The Boy's Own Paper*, *Hutchinson's Mystery Magazine*, *The Detective Magazine*, *Murder Mysteries*, and *Clues*. Like many other journeymen writers, he tried his hand at Sexton Blake stories, contributing half a dozen to *The Union Jack* and *The Penny Popular*.

Today, Evans is most widely remembered as the creator of Monsieur Jules Poiret, "late of the French Secret Service", but based in Britain. Poiret came into being more than a decade before Agatha Christie created a rather better-known Belgian with a strikingly similar surname. This has prompted one or two people to suggest that Christie "stole" the concept of the character from Evans, but this argument seems to me to be lacking in both evidence and credibility; coincidence is a much more likely explanation. This seasonal story first appeared on 9 December 1911 in *Chums*, a popular boys' newspaper which was published in various formats between 1892 and 1941 and remains highly collectible to this day.

"WELL, LET'S GO AND SEE THAT THE DINING-ROOM'S NICELY decorated, and if the turkey's not arrived I shall give that poulterer beans. And the plum-pudding must be nicely set alight. Come along, Harry!"

Two boys stood at the top of Marshall Street, which ran from the Strand down to the Embankment—tall, well-set-up, good-looking lads of sixteen and seventeen years of age, one with dark, curly hair and firm, well-set features, a little taller than the other, a fair-complexioned boy with close-cropped, reddish hair, a snub nose, round chin, and a comical mouth.

It was the latter who had spoken of attending to the decorations of the dining-room, and the dark one turned to him with a smile as he tightly buttoned his thin, shabby coat round his broad, well-shaped frame.

"There's nothing like looking on the funny side of things, is there, Tommy?" he said. "But, personally speaking, I don't quite see the humour of Christmas Day on the Embankment, with a free ticket for soup and a seat afterwards on the bench to warm our hands in front of the Thames, which, by the way, looks as if it were going to be frozen over."

"Well, cheer up, old sport!" was the reply. "It's a long lane that has no turning, even if you have to walk miles to find it. Come on, let's go and find out the softest seat, and stick a placard on it: 'Engaged for Christmas Day by Harry Marchbanks and Thomas—generally known as Tommy—Harrop.' Anyway, let's get out of the Strand, where every-body seems to have plenty of money and the sight of the motor-cars and the warm coats makes me feel inclined to commit murder or bigamy or whatever they call it. But, seriously, old sport, we might pick up a dinner ticket for Christmas Day down there. There are a lot of charitable people about. Come on!"

The two lads, neither of them with overcoats, and in shabby though well-kept garments, resolutely turned their backs to the Strand, which was crowded with those intent on Christmas shopping. Buses, motor-cars and cabs rolled along, most of them containing happy faces and well-clothed, well-nourished forms. Holly decorated most of the brightly illuminated windows; advertisements of pantomimes and music-halls allured, attracted; the restaurants were doing a busy trade; the spirit of Christmas hung over everything, and the two lads, without a solitary penny in their pockets, tried to put a cheerful face on it and think that they were not next door to starvation.

Harry Marchbanks and Tommy Harrop were old school friends; by chance they had met again in London after a few years' separation, and being both employed in commercial life in the City they had set up rooms, together, and had got situations in the same office.

But by one of those hard tricks which fortune sometimes deals out, the firm by which they were employed had gone bankrupt; a wholesale reduction of the staff was necessary, and three months ago they had both been thrown out of a berth.

They were of more than the average intelligence; they chafed some-times at the restrictions which clerical life involved, and they both had ideas of a larger sphere of work. Still, they were obliged to be content with what the present sent them, and could only speculate hopefully as to the future. But, alas! The market of clerkdom is overstocked; try as they would, they could not get other work.

Tommy Harrop was an orphan; Harry's parents came from a small farming stock in the North of England. It had been a struggle for them to educate him and start him in London, and sooner than appeal to them for help he preferred to write cheerful letters home, implying that things were going well with him and sharing the bad times with his bosom friend Tommy.

And now it was within two days of Christmas Day; they had had nothing to eat for the last twenty-four hours. Fortunately their rent was paid for the ensuing week, but when that time had elapsed, what were they going to do? Tommy had friends—far, distant friends—in the country, but none of them had thought of the poor, lonely lad in London. And Harry had received a letter saying that an epidemic had broken out in the village where his parents lived, and instead of going home for Christmas they would ask him to wait until the New Year. He had sent a cheery letter in reply, saying that he would have a good time in London with his friend. He was not going to show the white feather to his people.

And now it looked as if there would be no Christmas of mirth, of jollity, of food and fun for them, but simply blank days of despair, and perhaps starvation.

"I'll bet they're going to have a good time in there!" said Harry, as they walked down the little street, meeting the icy blast which came up from the Embankment, and pointing to a big hotel on the right, in every window of which shone a light. "My word, isn't it cold!"

"Parky isn't the word!" replied Tommy. "I shouldn't be surprised if we met Nansen down here. It's just about the sort of climate he'd revel in, I should think."

"Well, personally, I should imagine the North Pole would be warm compared to this," said Harry. "But, I say, look there. What's that? Those chaps are trying to hustle that fellow. Let's take a hand. It'll keep us warm, anyway."

It was growing dusk, and the light was not too distinct, but a few yards ahead of them they saw a tall, well-dressed man in a fur-trimmed coat being hustled up against the railings by a couple of rough-looking men who had suddenly emerged from a side turning. The street was practically deserted, for not many foot passengers made use of this thoroughfare. But the boys plainly saw one of the roughs aim a blow at the well-dressed man, who was standing with his back to the railings endeavouring to protect himself. He ducked, and the blow went harmlessly over his head, and something glittered in the other rough's hand.

Almost simultaneously the boys tore ahead, and smack, crack, smack, the man who had struck out with his fist went reeling backwards, and the other ruffian's right hand was clasped in Harry's grip, and a knife went tinkling to the ground.

The man half stooped, as if to recover his knife, and Harry, with an upward sweep of his arm, uppercut him with his clenched fist, sending him reeling back with a nose that felt as if it had been broken.

In the meantime the first rough had recovered himself from Tommy's smart blow between the eyes and advanced threateningly, and as he came near he lowered his head as if to butt the boy below the chest. But Tommy simply stepped on one side, the man went floundering past, and received a precise and powerful kick behind which sent him sprawling on his face, and Harry put his fingers between his lips and whistled loudly, as if for the police.

In an incredibly short space of time the two men had pulled themselves together and bolted for dear life down the turning up which they had come.

"Are you hurt, sir—are you hurt?" asked Harry of the man, who, tall, bearded, and rather stout, was leaning back against the railings puffing for breath.

"No, no, I am not hurt, I thank you. But you are brave boys! The rascals, they nearly had me—yes, it is safe? Yes. That is good!"

He spoke in English, but with the accent of the well-educated foreigner, and heaved a sigh of relief as he felt anxiously in his inner breast pocket.

"You are good boys, yes. Stay, I would like to reward you, but one does not pay for bravery, no. But still, when I was young, a young lad, I did not refuse a piece of gold, no. So, you will take this, please. Also my card of address. If at any time I can do some things for you, you shall come and see me, please. I shall be here for the next few weeks, is it not? Now, quick, I must hurry me, I must go, I have appointments. Here is a little gold piece for each of you."

He dived into his pocket and handed each of the boys a sovereign, and to Harry he gave a visiting card on which was engraved simply "Monsieur Naumont." And underneath the name he scribbled the words, "Hotel Reutz."

"You must see me again, is it not? I must now say the good-day."

He buttoned up his thick coat, after feeling again at his breast pocket, took off his hat with a foreign gesture, and hurried away, leaving the boys staring each at an open hand in which had been deposited a sovereign.

"Well, if that doesn't take it!" said Tommy. "It's like a fairy tale. A biff, a smack, a crack, a nice foreign gentleman—French, I should think—with a big fur coat and a polite manner, and a glorious golden quidlet in each right hand! Harry, after all we shan't have to look at the decorations on the Embankment dining-room. We'll now go and have a preliminary canter with some good, old-fashioned English roast beef, and on Christmas Day we'll—well, my word, if that turkey, wherever he is, only knew what is waiting for him when we start on him! Advance, my brave buccaneer, towards the shop of one Johnson, who sells good meat and the potatoes that are floury, to say nothing of the bread and cheese and celery! To the front, my warrior bold!"

And Tommy, skipping and dancing in his delight, took Harry by the arm and turned him back towards the brilliantly lighted Strand; already the thought of a good, square meal seemed to make both the lads stronger, and their spirits rose.

"You'll excuse me, young gentlemen," said a voice behind them, "but could I have a word with you?"

They turned and saw a well-looking man of about forty-five, decently dressed, clean shaved, and with a strong but rather repellent face, looking down at them.

"Would you mind telling me exactly what happened?" he went on. "I'm rather interested. I just caught sight of what appeared to be the end of a struggle, and of the man you rescued speaking to you. Would you mind telling me exactly what took place? I have reasons, and perhaps I might say authority, for asking. Here's my card."

And he in his turn handed the boys a card, on which was engraved: "Chief Detective-Inspector Frande. Scotland Yard."

Harry looked at him, and Tommy looked at him, for they knew the name of Chief Detective-Inspector Frande well as one of the foremost detectives of the day. They had on one occasion seen his portrait in the paper, and again had seen him giving evidence in a case at Bow Street. For during their idle days they had taken to the inner study of crime, which had always attracted them. And, besides, the police-courts, if stuffy, were, at any rate, warm when the wind was biting outside.

"I don't think—" began Harry.

But Tommy trod on his friend's foot with a pressure that silenced him at once.

"Certainly, sir. Glad to see you," said Tommy. "But you'll excuse us, won't you? We've got an appointment with a joint. If you'd call on us tonight we should be very pleased to see you and tell you what we can. Our address is 72 Hare Street, Borough, S.E., which, being interpreted, meaneth that if you walk over to the other side of the water, and then inquire for the Borough, and walk on until you nearly drop, then you will come to Hare Street, and No. 72 is where we hang out our flag. And so, sir, as they say in the classics, a friendly but speedy adieu."

The man seemed taken aback for a moment, and then replied with a smile:

"Oh, very well, I'll call on you tonight."

"What on earth made you shut me up like that, Tommy?" asked Harry, as they sat together over a good round meal at Johnson's Restaurant, famed for its good, old-English cooking.

"Dear old chap," said Tommy, "I don't believe that fellow's Chief Detective-Inspector Frande any more than I am. Frande, when we saw him, had a moustache. Certainly in build and height and shape of features he wasn't unlike this man, but I don't think he's Frande."

"But, old man," argued Harry, "Frande might have shaved his moustache off for purposes of his own. You know it makes a great deal of difference to a chap when he gets rid of his hair, whether it's on his face or his head."

"Quite so. And that's why I want to be very certain before I tell Mr. Frande anything, or the supposed Mr. Frande. It looks to me as if we were in what the novelists might call a good, juicy, fruity mystery. We'll have a dig at it, Harry; it'll give us something to think of over Christmas. And now let us go forth to buy wood, coal, the oil that illumineth the lamp, the turkey that shall on Christmas Day rejoice our hearts, and the pudding that maketh glad the heart of man. Forward to the jocund glades of Hare Street, Borough."

In a little, top, double-bedded room in a dull but respectable street off the Borough lived the two boys. Formerly they had been able to hire a sitting-room, but with the reverses of their fortunes they had ascended to the top floor, and here they had every night sat and shivered without a fire after the day's hunt for employment, trying to keep a cheerful heart in spite of everything. They had not been able to afford a fire; their sole source of warmth had been the free library, and often they had gone for a day without food, the next one perhaps only having a sausage between them and a bit of stale bread.

But now the little room seemed quite cheerful. A fire crackled in the grate. The landlady had promised to cook their Christmas dinner for them, and they sat there, with some warm coffee, talking over the events of the day.

"I liked the look of the fellow we got away from the roughs," said Harry; "nice, genial sort of sport he was. But I didn't care much about the other chap with that peculiar look in his eye and the twisted mouth. I'm beginning to believe that you're right, Tommy, and it wasn't Frande after all."

"Well, we'll soon find out," answered Tommy. "Wait a minute. How much have we got left? Let's count it up. Thirty-two shillings. Yes, I dare say that'll do. Half a mo', I shall be back in a minute."

Tommy bolted out of the room, and Harry sat down to enjoy a read at his favourite weekly paper, a treat he had not had for a long while, and in a few minutes his friend returned bearing a small, square, black box.

"Old Jenkins hummed and hawed a bit at first," he said, "but as I was such a good customer in the old days he's hired it out to me for two shillings from eight till ten, and thirty shillings deposit. Now, then, let's set it up on the noble oak sideboard."

There was a little rough piece of furniture—half bookcase, half chiffonier—at the side of the room, on the top of which were a few books, and Tommy arranged the black box on it, building the books round it so that it was not conspicuous.

He had hardly finished when there came a knock at the door, and the landlady announced that there was a gentleman to see them, and close on her heels followed the man who had announced himself as Chief Detective-Inspector Frande.

"Now, then," he said, "I'm here to ask you boys to help—to give me what information you can. And if asking isn't sufficient I shall be obliged to use the authority which the law has placed in my hands. Now, will you kindly tell me exactly what happened this evening?"

Again Harry felt the warning pressure of Tommy's foot, and the latter told the inspector exactly everything that had happened, and the man drew a breath as of delight.

"Ah, yes," he said. "Gave you his card, did he? Let me have a look at it. Monsieur Naumont, Monsieur Naumont! Very interesting. And he felt in his breast pocket, did he? Ah, then he has them on him! That's what I wanted to find out. Now, then, boys," he went on, his voice assuming an impressive note, "I'll confide in you. That man who describes himself as Monsieur Naumont is nothing more nor less than the Grand Duke Leo of Russia. Yes, you may well look surprised! I'm acting under instructions from both our own and the Russian Governments to obtain from him certain papers which he has long been believed to have in his possession. All grand dukes of Russia, as you may be aware, are entitled to receive from the State a sum of money annually equal to a quarter of a million sterling; but many of them are notoriously wasteful and improvident, and even grand dukes may get hard up at times. Now, this certain grand duke has in his possession the particulars of an enormous, a colossal swindle which he and many associates are endeavouring to work here in London. It concerns high finance and the flotation of an alleged gold mine, together with false notes of credit, and other efforts into which I need not go now. If we suspect him, you will rightly say why not arrest him at once and see if he has the documents in his possession? But, my young friends, that is impossible, for the person of a grand duke of Russia is sacred; he could not be arrested according to the laws of his own country, and ours wouldn't touch him. But if once we can get from him the names of those who are associated with him—all particulars, in fact, as to how this swindle is being worked, we can use persuasion—merely gentle persuasion; he can be threatened with exposure and so on. So that all we want to do is to get hold of these papers, which it is evident he carries with him. For a long time we've been trying to get at him to find out exactly where they were, and now it seems as if chance had put this information in my way. He evidently had the papers on him when he was attacked, for you say you saw him touch his breast pocket, and that he said, 'Ah, they are safe!' That is good news to me, and I think—no, I am sure—that you can help me. Now, will you?"

"But," put in Harry shrewdly, "who d'you think were the two men who attacked him? Were they after the papers too?"

"Good point, good point!" said the man approvingly. "I don't think they were. I saw the two fellows a few minutes before—simple roughs, they were, that's all; they were out for a gold watch or something of that sort. I had been tracking my gentleman from the City, and took no notice of these fellows, and I was only just in time to see the end of the struggle and the rascals running for their lives. Otherwise, of course, I should have stepped in, and it would have been my chance. But now, look here."

He leant forward and spoke in a half-whisper, as if fearful of being overheard.

"You say this Monsieur Naumont, as he calls himself, asked you to go to his hotel, and said that if there was anything he could do for you he would. Now, what I propose is this. You go and tell him a fine tale, possibly a true one, that you're hard up, that you want work; interest him in yourselves; if possible, one or both of you try and attach yourselves to his service in some way or another, his personal service, or, at any rate, contrive that you're in his rooms as much as possible. In fact, do anything you like, only"—he leant forward still nearer—"*get hold of those papers*, and I, on behalf of the Government, will pay you a thousand pounds. You can divide it between you, or do what you like with it. Providing I get the papers there's one thousand pounds for you. A thousand pounds isn't a bad amount for a couple of lads who, well"—he looked round the room—"might perhaps want it."

Harry caught Tommy's look and kept his mouth closed.

"All right, we're in it," said Tommy, walking over to the chiffonier, where the inspector had deposited his hat. "We'll try it, at any rate. But now you'll forgive us, won't you, but we have an appointment. Your hat!"

He handed the hat to the inspector, who took it, and with a few words of final caution was about to take his leave, when Harry put in a question:

"Where shall we communicate with you? To the Yard?"

"Oh, no—oh, dear, no! Let me see! Oh, perhaps it would be better to my private address, The Laurels, Cedar Avenue, Wimbledon. Yes, that'll be the best plan. Write it down, will you? And you'd better call on Naumont as soon as possible—tomorrow morning, say; pitch him a good tale, tell him you're starving, that you want something to do, however small; say that you've got no lodgings, that you've been turned out, that his sovereigns came too late, and that you're just living in a common lodging-house. Tell him any tale you like, but keep him interested in you, and keep your eyes open all the time you're there to see if there's any particular packet of which he takes great care—just a few papers, that's all they'd be. Lead up to them by degrees, ask if his goods were all safe, if the men had taken anything from him; find out where he keeps them, where they are, that's all. Then, if you can't get at them yourselves, let me know; and if I get them through your information, even if I have to get them myself, the thousand pounds is yours. Now, don't forget that! I know I can ask you this, because I remember when I was a lad how detective work appealed to me. Goodnight. And don't forget—The Laurels, Cedar Avenue, Wimbledon."

"Yes, indeed," said Tommy, removing the books from around the square, black box, "detective work does appeal to us! Now, then, Harry, out with the lamp. Let's get the dark room ready."

"What's your game, Tommy, what's your game?"

"Oh, my dear old fellow, I took his photograph, that's all. You recognized the apparatus when I brought it in, didn't you?"

"Yes; but I wondered what you were going to do with it all the same."

"Well, I hired it from old Jenkins, as I told you, for two shillings and thirty shillings deposit, arranged it here with the little bulb behind, so that I could work it, and when I saw old supposed-to-be Mr. Frande right well in the focus I went up and got his hat, squeezed the bulb at the same time, and, unless I'm mistaken, there ought to be a pretty good photograph of him inside. And now to develop it."

The two boys had always been devoted to photography, and the little ingenious tricks and ways in which snapshot photographs can be developed without enormous expense and tricky mechanism were well within their knowledge; and the next morning Tommy, after breakfast, produced a very fair photograph of Chief Detective-Inspector Frande.

"And with this," he said, "we'll go and call on Monsieur Naumont."

## CHAPTER 2
### In the Den of Thieves

"Ah!"

Monsieur Naumont, who had received the two boys cordially, sat with them in his sitting-room at his hotel and listened intently to their tale.

"Ah!" he said, looking at the photograph which Tommy had handed to him, "that is my proof, then! Now, then, my young friends, you see me! Which of the two of us do you love?—like, I should say; your English sometimes puzzles me. Which of the two of us, then, would you like to help, the gentleman here with the bad face, or the gentleman here?"

And he touched himself with his finger on his broad chest.

"Well, sir," said Harry, smiling, "we should never have come to you and told you all our tale if we hadn't mistrusted the other man. Besides, we had a sort of friendly feeling towards you, if we may say so, for without your having got in the way of those roughs, we shouldn't have been able to help you, and we shouldn't have had any Christmas dinner."

"No Christmas dinner! Name of a pipe, but this is serious—this is indeed a bad thing to hear! Tell me now, come! Leave me myself alone and the other men for a little; I would like to hear about you, and how you come to be—what is it?—so hard up."

Tommy and Harry between them told him their tale, and the Frenchman's eyes filled with tears.

"My poor children, my poor boys!" he said. "You have no work, you have but a little money! Oh, dear, but we will soon put that right!" He snapped his fingers. "Tomorrow you shall Christmas with me and with Madame Naumont and with the little children Naumont. Oh, we'll be happy! It is a great feast, this Christmas, is it not? Stay, we will go out and buy many warm overcoats, new boots, and all those things which make one feel happy, rejoicing; and after Christmas is over, then it is Naumont who will find you some work. Oh, yes, he knows many, does Naumont. But, stay, now! Ah, I have it!"

In his excitable, foreign way he skipped as if delighted.

"A thousand pounds for you would be a nice box of Christmas, eh? And it is Mr. supposed Inspector Frande who shall present it to you! See, the papers that he requires, they are here!"

He felt in his breast coat-pocket.

"I carry them about with me always; I leave them nowhere; I like to have them on me, except one that I have here." He touched his forehead. "I learnt him by heart, and then I burnt him. Without him the other papers are useless. Mr. Frande can have them. They are useful, certainly, but I can remember them. Shall I give them to you?"

He took a large, thin envelope out of his pocket and handed it to the two boys.

"Behold, see, I trust you as you trust me. Take it, then, to Mr. Chief Detective-Inspector Frande at his own, no doubt, beautiful house. You will see the seal has not been tampered with at all. He will see the papers are there, and he will think that I am—what do you call it in English? I know—spoofed, but I shall have him just the same! Ah, pardon, one moment."

With astonishing agility for so stout and big a man he leapt across the room and flung open his sitting-room door.

"I did think me I heard someone at the door, but it was only that waiter, who is a pig's head all the time, and of whom I shall make a complaint to the management. I thought it was someone listening, but it was only that fool's head, who fumbles with the door handle. Give it to me, you imbecile! He irritates me always; he is so slow!"

A solemn-looking, sheepish, youngish man, in the ordinary waiter's dress, with a peculiarly vacant look on his face, stood in the doorway with a salver, on which were some letters for Monsieur Naumont.

"He has been nearly a quarter of an hour in bringing up my post! Va, done! Quittez, done!"

And he pushed the vacuous-looking youth out of the room. He glanced through his letters, and then turned to the boys and went on with his suggestions as to their visit to Mr. Frande at Wimbledon.

A telegram was written saying, "Papers in hand. Calling tonight eight," and it was signed "Two young friends."

"Now we send that," said Naumont. "That will give him time for your reception and time for him to send a telegram to your lodging, of which he have the address, if it is not possible to see you tonight. If no telegraph, you go down in my motor-car; I lend you one. You hand him the papers, you take his one thousand pounds, you come back to me, and we have a merry Christmas together. Yes, it is a good idea!"

"But I'm not sure whether we ought to take the man's money," said Harry. "I suppose it's honest enough, but it seems rather a funny sort of thing to do."

"It's all right," said Naumont. "You take his money, and if all goes well there will be another thousand for you from Naumont's friends, you see. Now, come along, we go to buy some boots and some coats."

The telegram was sent from a Strand post office, the good-natured Frenchman, whom the boys found so pleasant and amiable, drove them round in his magnificent motor-car and fitted them out with clothing of all kinds. He made them lunch with him at one of the best West End restaurants. Then, in the afternoon, when there would have been time for Frande to have replied to their telegram, they called at their old lodging, to find that there was no message for them. Then back they went to the Hotel Reutz, had an early dinner with Monsieur Naumont, and a little before eight found themselves in Wimbledon, where, leaving the car with the chauffeur at a garage, they made inquiries for The Laurels, which they found was situated about half a mile outside the town, in what was almost a rural district.

"We won't take the car out there, Tommy," said Harry. "It would look fishy, and it might make them smell a rat. Now, let's see if I've got the papers all right."

Harry felt in his pocket.

"Yes, they're all right. And now it only remains for us to tell our tale properly, get our thousand pounds, and then back to Monsieur Naumont and a merry Christmas waiting for us tomorrow. But, I say, Tommy, I hope we're not lying or doing anything deceitful. If I didn't think old Naumont was a really good man I wouldn't take it on. I wonder what the mystery at the bottom of it all is? In spite of his chatter, old Naumont's a pretty close fish; he doesn't let out much, does he?"

"You bet he's all right!" answered Tommy. "A good-hearted fellow like that wouldn't send two chaps like ourselves on a rotten errand, I know. Now, here we are! Third house up. Is this it, I wonder?"

Tommy struck a match, examined a gate-post, and saw painted on it "The Laurels." The gate swung open easily, and led through a dark shrubbery, up a drive of about four hundred yards, to a large, stone, square house standing in its own fairly spacious grounds. It was in pitch darkness; not a light was to be seen in any of the windows, nor through the fanlight. After striking another match they found the bell-handle, the sound rang tinkling and hollowly far away at the back of the house, with that peculiar note that tells that a house is empty of furniture.

"It sounds quite ghostly, doesn't it?" said Tommy. "Can you hear anybody coming, Harry? I believe the place is deserted."

They listened, but not a sound could be heard, human or animal, and again they pulled that tinkling bell, this time a little harder.

It was a pitch dark night, the only relief being the snow which had fallen lightly during the day, and which still lay in a thin carpet, and the boys both involuntarily gave a little shiver; they were not frightened, but there was something eerie about this silent house and its quiet, gloomy surroundings.

Again they pulled the bell, and at length they heard footsteps coming over what were evidently uncarpeted boards, and there was the noise of bolts being withdrawn. At length the door was opened, and they saw dimly the figure of a man standing in the unlighted hall.

"Who are you, and what's your business?" came a voice which they recognized as that of Frande.

"Two young friends about some papers," answered Harry.

As he spoke a strong light flashed in his eyes, and he saw that Frande was holding an electric torch.

"All right, come in; I see, it's you. Follow me. Let's bolt the door first."

Strange, thought the boys as they stood in the empty, dark hall while Frande fumbled with the bolts, that they should be received in what appeared to be an empty house in perfect darkness, and rather doubtfully they followed Frande through a long passage, who just flickered the electric torch now and then to show them when to turn a corner.

At length he paused in front of a door, knocked twice, then once, and afterwards whistled. The door was thrown open, and a sudden blaze of light struck upon the eyes of the two boys. They found themselves pushed inside and the door slammed behind them.

When they had recovered from their astonishment, they saw that they were in a magnificently furnished room, electric lights everywhere, a table smothered with delicacies of all kinds, and round the table, smoking and drinking, sat at least twenty-five or thirty men. They were men of all kinds and classes, some in evening dress, some in coarse clothes, and the two boys found themselves the centre of observation, and they felt rather uncomfortable as each man turned in his chair and fixed a pair of eyes upon the new-comers.

"These are the lads I told you of, comrades," said Frande. "Now, have you got those papers, my boys?"

"Yes," said Harry coolly. "Have you got our thousand pounds?"

A roar of laughter went up, and Harry at once recognized two of the men as the roughs who had assaulted Monsieur Naumont. Then the old Frenchman was right! This man was a scoundrel! But they, the boys, were they trapped, or what? But, anyway, even if they did not get the thousand pounds, they were doing Naumont a good turn, a turn for the good-hearted man who had been so kind to them.

"Don't you talk any nonsense about a thousand pounds," said Frande. "You hand over the papers, and think yourselves lucky that you get out of here alive."

"It would be useless, of course, to refuse to hand over the papers," said Harry frankly, and speaking out boldly, while Tommy stood by him shoulder to shoulder, "for there are enough of you here to take them from me, so there you are. And now, perhaps, you'll let us go?"

"Oh, wait a minute, wait a minute, my young friends!" said Frande. "We don't do things in such a hurry as that, you know. Of course, the first thing you'd do when you got outside here would to go and tell the police. That would be your natural thought, wouldn't it? But don't forget, my little cocks of the walk, that if you did give information to the police you'd only brand yourselves as thieves for having robbed Monsieur Naumont. So you'll simply just walk outside here as you came in, and do what you like, and the next time don't be so easily taken in."

Harry and Tommy looked at the man and laughed in his face.

"You don't know what you're talking about!" said Harry. "My word, this is a joke, if you only knew!"

They were thinking of the envelope, which contained one paper short, though Frande did not know it, for he had broken the seal and was rapidly examining the contents. He took out several pieces of blank, crackling paper, and then appeared to be looking for another one.

"Yes, yes," he said, as he did so turning to the men at the table, "we shall have to alter our plans. Confound it! I wonder how he got the information? Hallo, hallo, who's that? Wait a minute, I'll see who it is."

The telephone in the corner rang, Frande took up the receiver and listened intently for seconds, minutes, and then spoke back.

"All right," he said, "I'll bring the chloroform with me. Yes, I can get in by the balcony. You leave the window open, I'll do the rest. What time did you say he goes to bed? About half-past eleven? All right, plenty of time. I'll be there just before twelve."

He slammed back the receiver, and then turned to the company with glittering eyes and an evil frown on his face.

"Spies!" he said, pointing to the two boys. "Spies, that's what they are! Jules—you know, the waiter at the Reutz, one of us—overheard everything; he listened at the door. These boys are on Naumont's side. All the papers save one are here; Jules couldn't overhear where that was. But these boys are here to spy on us! What are we going to do with them? No, no, we don't want any shouting; we don't want any noisy deaths," he said to the men, who had nearly all sprung to their feet. "Let me think!"

So, thought the boys, the waiter, the vacuous-faced waiter, was, after all, in league with Frande. It was no good denying anything. The only thing was for them to try and think of some way, some means of escape.

There was no window in the room, only a ventilating shaft. The door behind them Harry furtively touched and found that it was made of steel or iron, and that it closed with a clink that seemed to shut it flush in with the wall.

"I know!" said Frande at length. "We'll leave them here. Turn off the air, and there you are!"

"But what are you going to do then, Frande?" put in one of the men.

"I'm going up to the Reutz tonight. Where are your brains? Didn't you hear me talking at the 'phone? I'm going to Naumont's room, and I'm going to chloroform him. Jules will see to it that the sitting-room window is left open, and I can get in that way, and then through to the bedroom. I'll have that paper tonight if I have to eat my hat!"

"If you ate a shop full of hats you'd never get that paper!" broke in Harry.

"Ah, you're being funny, my young man are you?" said Frande. "D'you know what's in store for you, both of you? This is an underground, secret chamber, air-proof when the ventilator's shut. You see, underground rooms don't have windows as a rule. The door, walls, everything is air-proof. Now, then, are we all ready? There's no time to waste. We've got lots of arrangements to make."

The men all rose, and began putting on their coats and hats. Harry and Tommy stood blankly against the wall, knowing that it was useless to put up a fight. What could they do against so many? It was hopeless making a dash for the door when it was open, and one by one they watched the men file out, Frande standing by all the time with a revolver in his hand.

"Now, listen," he said. "Keep quiet for a moment."

There was a faint, whirring sound, and Frande pointed to the ceiling.

"That's the ventilator," he said. "One of my friends outside will shut it in a moment. There! See, it's stopped."

The whirring noise suddenly ceased.

"That means that the air supply for this room is cut off. It'll take you about, I should think, twelve hours to exhaust it all, so just about breakfast-time tomorrow, when you expected to have been opening your Christmas cards, you'll be dying what I'm told is a very unpleasant death, and it seems to me to convey a warning that used to be given to me when I was a child, 'Little boys should be seen and not heard.' Now, you've both seen and heard too much, my young friends, so now unkind Fate overtakes you. There's plenty of food for you, and I'll leave the light on; but, by the way, I shouldn't eat too much, for they tell me it's very bad for you when you come to die for want of air. Good-bye, and a merry Christmas to you!"

The door slammed to, and there were the boys left in this brilliantly lighted room, with the remains of a feast on the table, amidst a perfect, dead, ominous silence, and—though in imagination only—they could feel the air getting scarcer.

The ventilator was in the ceiling, in a sort of narrow, dome-shaped opening, from which also depended the electrolier; escape was impossible that way. The door was, as it were, hermetically sealed. Deliverance was hopeless, impossible, improbable. They both examined the door

again and again—but no, it was impossible to open it. In one corner
a piece of the material had been worn away, and Tommy tried the
material beneath it with his knife.

"Wood covered with steel," he said. "See, there's the lock! If we
could only get through that inch of steel, we could pick the lock easily
enough and get out! Well, we'll have a try."

They tried with every blade in their knives, blunting them and
cutting their fingers, but they could, of course, make no impression,
and after an hour's work they were obliged to give it up, while the
perspiration stood on their brows and a haunting oppression was in
their hearts.

Suddenly Harry, who had been sitting near the table and examining uninterestedly some of the things the men had left behind them,
jumped to his feet with a shout that rang through the room.

"I've got it, Tommy—I've got it!" he said. "See here! Look at this—
an electric cigar-lighter!"

He held up a long, thin piece of metal attached to a flexible wire,
which, upon being pressed, emitted a steady glow of heat, from which
it was possible to obtain a light for a cigar.

"Thank goodness I learnt electrical engineering! Yes, I've got it!"

"What on earth do you mean?" asked Tommy.

"Don't ask me what I mean, help me. Now, first of all let's fasten
this wire up to the electrolier. I want to concentrate the whole of
the current on to the end of this lighter. Help me disconnect it for a
moment. Ah! here we are! Now I've got it! Now then, turn that off,
Tommy, and that other one on. That's it. I believe I've got it now!"

Harry had been standing on the table, and with nimble fingers
twisted wires here and there disconnected the current, then turned it
on again, and at length, with the cigar-lighter in his hand, connected
by a long piece of flexible wire with the electrolier, he stood before
the steel-plated door.

"I'm running all the current I can to the end of this lighter," he said. "It's a sort of forlorn hope, but it might work. I want to cut a ring into that steel by melting it by the aid of the current so that we can unpick that lock."

A little glittering point of light, with an immense force of electric current behind it, was directed on to a little circle traced by Tommy with a pencil round the spot where they could discern the patent lock. For a long time the heat appeared to have no effect, but at last there was a little, tiny sign of melting; it gradually grew bigger and bigger, little drops of molten steel fell to the ground and then, after strenuous work and patience, they accomplished their object.

"Now this is where I come in!" said Tommy. "Mechanics have always been my hobby. I think I ought to be able to pick that lock."

With his useful knife and several pieces of wire snipped from the electric cords, Tommy worked away, until at length he gave a pull at the door; there was a little rattle and tinkle as the bits of the picked lock fell to the ground, and the door was open.

"By Jove, it's nearly half-past eleven!" said Harry, astonished. "Come on, Tommy, run for it! Turn to the left, don't we, if I remember rightly? Yes, that's it—the left, and then straight along. We shall have to chance our luck. If there are any of 'em about, go through 'em, for that's our only chance. Here, thank goodness they've left those behind them."

There were two or three stout sticks standing in a corner; each of the lads seized one, and, leaving the door wide open, the electric lights blazing in spots, they accustomed their eyes to the gloom, and, aided by the light shining through the door, managed to see their way through the passage, both of them gripping their sticks tightly, ready to land out at anyone who might try to stop them.

But no, the house was deserted; the men had evidently all gone, and, after fumbling with the bolts, they were soon outside, and tore down the long drive out into the road into safety, into civilization, and without waiting to take breath they covered the half-mile that separated them from the chauffeur and the waiting motor.

"The Reutz! Back again as quickly as you can!" said Harry. "We've got barely a quarter of an hour. Never mind about your licence, fines, or anything Monsieur Naumont will gladly pay for anything!"

Five minutes before the stroke of twelve they stood at the door of the Hotel Reutz, only to find themselves barred by the porter.

"Monsieur Naumont has sent word that he can't see anyone tonight; he isn't well, and he's gone to bed."

"But surely he's taken rooms for us here? We were to stay with him for Christmas!"

"I can't say. My instructions are that no one is to be admitted tonight under Monsieur Naumont's name. You must go."

The porter did not add that he had been given a sovereign by Jules to deliver this message to anyone who might happen to wish to see Monsieur Naumont. Jules said that the sovereign came from Monsieur Naumont himself, as it was most important that he should not be worried by anyone that night.

"There's only one thing for it," said Harry, his breath coming and going. "We can't stop to argue with that fellow; we shall never get in! It's just on midnight. Remember, that brute of a Frande said he'd be there, and that he'd get in through the window. I bet anything that he's been in the hotel, and that Jules has let him out on to the balcony, or somewhere like that. Come on, there's only one way we can get up. We must save Naumont if possible. Never mind about bringing your stick; we shall have to trust to luck. Come on, this way round to the back. Monsieur Naumont's rooms are on the fifth floor, and the fire-escape ladder is just below his bedroom. I know that, for I looked out of the window this morning."

A fire-escape ladder is not the easiest thing to climb in the dark; it is easier going down, and it wants a nerve to climb five stories up just upon midnight, to meet perhaps one or two desperate men.

But up shinned the boys, their hearts not unnaturally burning to be revenged on Frande, and at length they reached the little balcony which ran beneath Naumont's suite of rooms. In the bedroom there was a light. The boys crept cautiously on to the balcony, and Harry just raised his face to the level of the window, bobbed down again, and whispered to Tommy:

"Frande and Jules are in there searching Naumont's clothes. He's lying on the bed in his pyjamas; evidently they've drugged him. There's only one thing for it, Tommy! I'll smash the glass in, get hold of the hasp of the window and pull it back; then in we must bolt, yell at the top of our voices, ring bells, do anything. The window opens sideways. Now, when I say 'go' let me go first, and you follow."

Harry took off his cap, wrapped it round his hand to prevent the glass doing any injury, waited for a moment to collect himself, and then, below his breath, he said to Tommy:

"Now, go!"

Up he sprang, dashed his hand through the window, caught at the hasp, tore it open, jumped into the room, followed by Tommy, and with a shout that would have made a Red Indian jealous they flung themselves upon Frande and Jules. There was a brief struggle; the two men were taken completely by surprise; the boys' yells were easily heard outside the room, and in a few minutes waiters and the manager and all sorts of people had appeared in the room, Frande and Jules were securely held, while the two panting hoys pointed to the chloroformed figure of Monsieur Naumont as evidence that there was foul play somewhere.

At nine o'clock the next morning, instead of being suffocated in the underground chamber at The Laurels, the two boys were seated by the bedside of Monsieur Naumont, who the night before had been quickly brought to by the hotel doctor. In the meantime the two men, who, as well as the boys, had been held under arrest by the hotel management until Monsieur Naumont had recovered, were, when he was able to speak, at once removed to the police station, while the boys were set free. And from Monsieur Naumont's own lips they heard the solution of the mystery which had so puzzled them, and with which they had become so involved.

Naumont was not the Frenchman's real name, but of that no matter. But he astonished the boys beyond measure by telling them that he was in reality a celebrated French detective. He had been "lent" by his Government to ours under circumstances which were causing the greatest anxiety. Forged Bank of England notes were being placed upon the market in such quantities as to cause the greatest alarm and uneasiness in financial circles. The notes were such magnificent imitations that the Bank of England's own printers declared that the paper must have been stolen from their own mills, and that the notes would deceive anybody. All the best English detectives were put on the trail, but it was evident that somebody who knew them all was at work circumventing them in every way, and it was for this reason that Monsieur Naumont had been called in. He had never set foot in England before; his face was not known to any of the English criminals or swellmobsmen, and he was more successful. He found out that the paper was being stolen from the mills where it was made. Gradually, patiently, and with infinite cunning, he began to track down man after man, but he never found out where the notes were made.

But slowly and surely was he casting his net. All that he now wanted to do was to find the principal, the guiding brain, and then he would close in and snare them all. But he was fighting against a man almost his equal in brains, the man behind the gun, as it were—the man Frande. He had—to his everlasting shame be it said—been once connected with Scotland Yard, and it was Frande who had discovered that Naumont was on the track. He knew the face; he had seen it when he had been over in France. Naumont! Yes, Naumont must be on the trail! Certain indications, certain small happenings, told him that suspicion was being aroused, and from that moment Naumont was a shadowed man.

The paper really was stolen from the Bank of England mills by a dishonest employee, who did it in such a clever manner that he could not possibly be traced—for, of course, a very careful record is kept of every scrap of bank-note paper that is made. Unknown to the authorities, this employee had corrupted others with lavish bribes, and they were gradually making regularly more paper than could be accounted for, and this was sneaked out of the mill and handed over to Frande.

But one day there was a panic in the camp. A small parcel of plain bank-note paper, which should have been delivered to Frande by a trusted messenger, did not arrive, though the messenger did, explaining that he had been held up in a quiet street by a big, bearded man, who in some miraculous way came behind him, got hold of his arms, held two wrists with his own left hand, so preventing him from struggling or crying out, while with his other hand he felt in every pocket till he took out the little parcel, which he kept, and then dismissed him with a hearty kick.

That was Naumont, decided Frande, and one of his gang, Jules, was placed to watch over the French detective, and he reported to Frande that he had seen Naumont examining the blank paper that he always kept on his person, and in the same envelope he also kept another paper on which was much writing; and this envelope was what the two roughs were after. And that was the beginning of the end. The authorities evidently wished to see if the paper was their own, if it was genuine. They had found out how it had been procured, and the

wily Naumont was only waiting to pounce. Inside that precious envelope which he kept to himself the writing might mean anything—the
names and addresses of those he wished to arrest, and so on—and so
the gang had instructions to get it from Naumont at any cost, even to
kill him if necessary; but this latter was not to be attempted except as
a most extreme measure.

Various attempts having failed, Frande had told off two of his ruf-
fians to make the final attempt and get possession of the envelope at
any cost, and he was looking on from a safe distance when the two
boys intervened.

All this came out at the trial afterwards. The Laurels at Cedar
Avenue, Wimbledon, was an old house which had been bought by the
gang which comprised many men of wealth. The underground room
had been built, and here in the air-proof chamber the forged notes
were made by machines so wonderful, so delicate, that they evoked
the admiration of experts. The room could be made air-proof—when
necessary—for while the bank-notes were being made, at certain stages
in the process it was essential that there should be no air in the room
at all. At other times the room was used as a meeting and dining place
for the gang.

Frande had, as suspected, arrived at the Hotel Reutz as a visitor,
and had been concealed by Jules, who had stolen a pass-key to the suite
of rooms, and, sneaking off the balcony in through the sitting-room
window, he had successfully chloroformed Naumont as he slept, only
to be defeated at the last moment by Harry and Tommy.

"And now," said Monsieur Naumont when his part of the tale was
finished, "I get me up. I feel better, though the chloroform is nasty
sickly stuff. And we go to spend Christmas with Madame Naumont
and the little Naumonts. They live not here. Oh, no; when I am in
business they live at another hotel. It would be dangerous for them to
be with me perhaps."

And in the private sitting-room of another West End hotel, at the close of a lively Christmas dinner, a huge "plom poodin," as Naumont called it, was brought in gloriously alight, and when all the plates were filled the old detective rose to his feet. There were tears in his eyes, and he spoke rapidly in French to his wife and their four children, and then in his quaint English he spoke to the boys.

"I have told them again yet a time what they know already, that but for you Papa Naumont would not be here. We love you for it, and we thank you. May the good God bless you!"

"May the good God bless you!" repeated Madame Naumont and the little ones in quaint accent.

And the boys half-smiled through their tears, for they saw that this was a home of love where they were indeed welcome.

And at the same moment Frande and Jules were feasting on gruel and dry bread in their cells, and others of the gang were already being tracked.

"And now," went on Monsieur Naumont, "although it is the day of Christmas, I already have been to work with the telephone to my principals. They are overjoyed; they are pleased. To the two boys who found out so much there will be given a little work place at the Bank of England at three hundred pounds a year each, and in their names will be made an investment also of two thousand pounds. So after all it is a good Christmas, is it not?"

"Yes," echoed the boys; "it is indeed a good Christmas!"

## THE CHRISTMAS SPIRIT

# *Anthony Gilbert*

Anthony Gilbert was the main writing name of Lucy Malleson (1899–1973), who also published as J. Kilmeny Keith and Anne Meredith. Although (perhaps because of that male pseudonym) she is not commonly spoken of as one of the Golden Age's "Queens of Crime", she enjoyed a long and successful literary career. *Murder by Experts* (1936) introduced her most famous detective character, Arthur Crook, a cigar-smoking solicitor known as "The Criminal's Hope"; his methods are sometimes dubious but almost invariably effective. Her 1933 novel *Death in Fancy Dress* has been republished in the Crime Classics series in an edition which includes two short stories.

In addition to her sixty-five novels, Gilbert wrote more than twenty plays for radio and at least sixty short stories. A posthumous collection of her short stories edited by John Cooper, *Sequel to Murder*, displays her professionalism as a mystery writer. As Cooper says, she was "noted for vigorous characterization, much humour, and adroit plotting". This story first appeared in the 1964 Christmas issue of the *Illustrated London News*.

I HADN'T SEEN CHARLIE SEDLEY FOR SIXTEEN YEARS BEFORE THAT gloomy November afternoon, and the last place I'd have looked for him would have been a remote pub in East Anglia with a cold wind blowing off the sea, and not a tree between you and Siberia. I'd been his navigator in the R.A.F., where he'd gone through more lives than a basketful of black cats, and I'd always imagined him hunting for the lost gold of the Incas or living in a house under the sea, something a lot more spectacular than landlord of The Green Girl at Dunscombe.

But even before I knew about him I was enchanted—note the word—by the inn-sign, which showed a girl who seemed to have the quality of eternity; she blazed with vitality, I don't know how old the sign was but it might have been painted the day before, and to look at her was to catch a radiance as brilliant as the sun. She wore a tight green bodice and a great emerald hat over chestnut curls. What she was doing in this bleak landscape was anyone's guess.

"Darling," said Christine's voice in my ear, "do you think it could be your Charlie Sedley?"

"My Charlie…"

"Yes. Look. Charlie Sedley, licensed to sell…" She rang the bell. "I'm going to ask if they'll give us some tea."

The woman who answered the door wasn't the least the type I'd have expected Charlie to bed down with, remembering the beauties who used to hang round his neck like a flight of albatrosses; she was a big tranquil woman—you'd never think of calling her a girl—but she had the kind of serene beauty the years can't spoil. I was prepared to find him changed, but I needn't have worried; he was the same red-haired Goliath of a man, who looked ready to set out for the moon at ten minutes' notice.

"Lou and I took this place as a challenge," he told us later over the sort of tea our sons would have described as "smashing" and he gave her the sort of glance many wives don't get from their husbands in a lifetime. "It had a bad name, no one ever stopped, it was too remote, there were queer stories, off the map, they said. Well, we've put it on the map. Concentrate on weekend trade," he added. "If a driver can get his car up Heartbreak Hill he won't much mind what he pays for a decent meal. And when he's been once he comes again. It's not surprising so many great men have married their cooks."

"You were always the luckiest chap I knew," I said. Still, looking at Chris, I didn't think I'd done too badly myself.

"Mark's fallen in love with The Green Girl," Chris told them.

"He wouldn't be the first, but it won't do him any good. Anyone round here will tell you that."

He didn't say any more but went on to tell us they were laying on Christmas *en fête*. "Four days without having to see your own stove or sink," he boasted. "And chaps don't seem to mind what they pay at Christmas. Staff 'ull be our main headache. Anyone not wanted by the police and able to stand upright can name his own price hereabouts."

I thought of that desolate landscape, the woods stretching to infinity, the long quiet nights with only the owls calling and wondered who on earth would come.

"What will you do with them for four days?" I wondered.

"Well, of course we hope they'll spend a good part of the time eating and drinking—to our profit. Then there's the Meet on Boxing Day, panto at Earthenshaw in the evening—that's quite something—Mystery tour—I've got the charas laid on—and a grand fancy dress ball for the last night. Might try and get a TV personality to give away the prizes."

"He hasn't changed a bit," I told Lou. "He was always one size larger than life."

"Is there anything we haven't thought of?" Lou asked. "You're the public, you know what you want."

"Why not lay on a ghost?" I suggested. "It's the right part of the world for it. Weren't the last witches and warlocks ever seen in Britain found in these parts?"

"It's a grand idea," Charlie agreed, "and I'm sure the guests would go for it, but—Lou likes everyone to have a good time, including the ghost."

"We shall have our hands full with flesh-and-blood visitors," said Lou, and to my surprise she wasn't smiling. "Let the dead rest in peace."

"Why don't you come along?" Charlie proposed when it was time to go. "We'll see you get a room in the pub. whoever else has to sleep out."

"We have commitments," Chris explained. "Two boys, Luke and John."

"Well, if you should change your mind, send a wire."

"I think I'm glad we have got commitments," said Chris thoughtfully, as we drove away. "Did you notice neither of them told us who the Green Girl was?"

"Probably Charlie doesn't know."

"He may not but Lou does." Charlie's not the only man to have a sensitive wife.

We sent that telegram, after all. Some oaf knocked Chris down with his motor-cycle a couple of weeks later, and by the time she left hospital it was obvious she wasn't going to be able to cope with our rumbustious household, so I closed with my brother-in-law's offer to take our sons along with his three, and we drove down to Dunscombe on Christmas Eve. There'd been snow for three days followed by a bright frosty wind, and the landscape sparkled like a Christmas cake. The Green Girl looked like something out of Dickens; I don't know how Lou managed it, but she actually contrived to reproduce an atmosphere of more than a century ago. There were Christmas trees blazing at the door, and candles filling the house with a lambent light. I don't know whom Charlie had turfed out to give us a room at the inn, but it was a very nice one. I needn't have worried about who was coming, he could have sold every room twice over; as it was he'd rented every vacant corner in the neighbouring cottages, and in addition there was a group who'd sleep at home and come up every day for the jollifications.

Actually there was more room inside than you'd have guessed. The place had been a hunting lodge to Dunscombe Hall, and though it was built on two floors, with a couple of attics and a hot-water system under a saucy little gable, the passages seemed to stretch in all directions. The rooms of the resident staff on the same floor as ourselves stretched away like the outstretched leg of a fowl. Charlie said he could have let all their rooms twice over, but in that case he and Lou would have had to cope single-handed. The non-resident staff had been recruited by the Labour Exchange and varied in age from eighteen to about eighty.

On the square half-landing hung two immense oil paintings—The last of the Dunscombes, Charlie introduced us. They represented a hatchet-faced fellow in full regimentals, with eyes as blue—and cold—as the sea, and his lady wife, with a stony face and an immense bosom trapped in blue velvet. I wasn't surprised to know the Colonel was the last of his line; any child would have frozen to death on that rocky breast.

"But where does the Green Girl come in?" Chris wanted to know.

"Oh, she was the second Lady D., and a living disproof of the axiom that second thoughts are best."

"No painting of her?"

"Only on the inn-sign. And here's something rummer still. You'll find the records of her birth and marriage, but no name on a grave-stone here or, so far as is known, anywhere else. She vanished one day, and was never seen again—at all events not in the flesh. It's a pity Lou put a stopper on ghosts, seeing we have a winner on the premises."

Then Lou came in and we changed the subject.

The party collected for the festival was a fair cross-section of the com-munity, with rather more emphasis on brass than breeding as you'd expect. There was a fellow called Blair (with a young woman named Peggy who may or may not have had a right to her wedding-ring), a natural leader, the inn might have belonged to him; a sprinkling of elderly locals, all well-cushioned—I hoped Charlie was adequately insured—if their jewels were anything to go by; a good many couples, as you'd expect, and a few singletons, thankful not to be on their own at this time of the year. All the women had brought their glad rags; between them they could have stocked a fair-sized mink farm. Of the singletons the most noticeable was a tall thin fellow called James, who looked remarkably like a ghost himself. I wondered if he might be a house detective, he didn't seem to mix much, and could be found prowl-ing in odd places, but Lou said Charlie wouldn't hear of engaging one.

"He was always as mad as a hatter," I told Chris. "What's to prevent the real articles coming along to this fancy dress affair with stockings over their faces and black tights and making a kill?"

"I wouldn't bother," said Chris, "they'd have to get past Charlie, and I'd as soon tackle a Messerschmitt. Anyway, no reason for us to get ulcers. They wouldn't pay their fares back to town on what they'd get from us."

The servants were, as he'd warned us, a pretty rumty-ti-foo lot, a few students anxious for a square meal and a spot of cash, a few old totterers who looked as though they'd turned out of their coffins for the occasion, chaps I wouldn't have trusted with a penny bank. A little fellow called Joseph seemed to wait on us, willing enough and no gabber, but if ever he'd been an indoor servant I'm the Duke of Bedford. His eyes were everywhere and he had a mysterious way of surfacing when you thought he was a quarter of a mile away.

"I think he's an out-of-work actor," said Chris. "Well, even actors have to eat."

Charlie and Lou must have worked like blacks, the whole holiday went as merrily as the proverbial marriage bell and we were on the verge of its crowning achievement, the fancy dress ball. It had been arranged that the hotel guests should all dine together at one long table in the main bar; the dining-room was being prepared for the dance. Blair had come in a gold and white satin suit as Henry VIII, in which he looked rather distinguished, Peggy was a fairy queen, James came in a white sheet.

"Who are you?" Peggy demanded.

And he said, "Oh, I'm the ghost."

I thought Lou gave a bit of a start. "Oo," said Peggy. "You won't suddenly disappear, will you?"

"That's all right by me so long as you don't disappear at the same time," Blair told her. "I was thinking, Sedley, the one thing that was missing was a ghost."

One of the bediamonded carrion crows near the foot of the table said. "But I thought the ghost was a young woman, the Green Girl. Not that I ever set eyes on her... but there are stories."

"You must tell us," said Charlie, heartily. "We never set eyes on her either, did we, Lou?"

Laughing, we turned to Lou, and stopped like the famous greyhound in his leap. For here was the face of a woman who was—initiated was the word that came into my mind. No one could mistake it;

James's eyes were burning. He spoke to her as if he and she were the only people in the room.

"So—you knew, Mrs. Sedley?"

She said quickly, "I've heard stories, of course. But I never saw—or heard—..."

"You *knew*," he insisted. "What did you know?"

She answered like someone under a spell.

"Only that, even when the staff were off duty, when my husband might be out and only I was in the Green Girl, I wasn't alone. It was a sensation, a conviction..."

"A conviction of what?"

In a trice the whole atmosphere had changed; the jollity had gone out of it. I glanced round the table to see faces scornful, fearful, compassionate, but none indifferent. We were in the presence of something we didn't understand and most of us didn't like it.

"Of a grief I couldn't describe, a seeking, a—it's no use, there are no words. It was only now and again, I never had any warning, I've never spoken to anyone—Mr. James, you know about her. Who was she?"

"The Green Girl? The Colonel's second wife. Her father was a tenant farmer, a dour man by all accounts. The Colonel must have been past fifty and she in her twentieth year; he'd been widowed quite a while. Perhaps he hoped to breed sons of her, he being the last of the line. At all events he married her—and the county never forgave him. No one called, no one spoke to her when she went out. Imagine it—when her husband was away on his country's business she was alone in a house as big as a prison and as cold. She'd no sisters and no friends who'd be encouraged to call. The household was run by a witch of an old woman—so she took to taking long walks through the countryside as she'd done when she was a girl, but he soon put a stop to that. She was a person of consequence now, he said. He bought her a black mare, and he took her riding, just the two of them, through this harsh countryside. He couldn't even give her a child. When he was away she might ride with the groom, but never alone. Any man but the Colonel must have foreseen what would happen."

"She took a lover?"

"Say rather she discovered love, probably for the first time in her life. They say during those few months if you met her you had to turn aside, it was like looking into the face of the sun. This was their rendezvous, that's why she haunts it now, perhaps, because it's the one place where she knew happiness."

"No," said Lou in her deep voice. "This wasn't a happy ghost."

"The happy ghosts are those who don't return. Well, consider. If Death, no matter how swift or kind, is an agony as it must be, a bursting of barriers, an abandonment of the familiar, a leaping into the dark, surely the return journey must imply a similar anguish. They come back because they must, not because they will, of that I'm certain. And they come for help from the only people who can give it them, the living."

"I would help her if I could," said Lou.

I felt my flesh prickle: I'd seen death enough in my time, and I no more believed in ghosts than I believed in Santa Claus. I could see Blair at least was of the same mind. I wonder if this was Charlie at work, over-reaching himself, horrified now to see what he'd done.

"But what happened to her?" Peggy Blair asked. "You don't think she'd come back tonight?"

"I never heard ghosts were famed for their good sense," observed Charlie, "but if the young woman has the wits she was born with she'll stay out of the limelight. Think of it, half the county here, and most of those as full as they've any right to be on arrival, four days of jol-lification—why, they'd hunt a ghost as readily as they'd course a hare."

"I challenge you to produce her, Sedley," called Blair. "She'll have a warm welcome for all it's cold outside." We glanced instinctively through the uncurtained windows; and saw an enchanted world. A moon rode in a sky as smooth as soap; stars prickled, even the snow glowed. I believe if the ghost had appeared then no one would have been surprised.

One of the elderly women spoke. "Let her stay in her grave," she cried.

"But some there be which have no memorial," quoted James. "What are they to do if even the grave's closed against them?"

"She must be buried somewhere. Or are you suggesting she's been living these last 130 years?"

"All we know is what the Colonel chose to tell. The lovers became careless, confident, and confidence is a poor bedfellow for caution. Perhaps horses were seen here at a time when the place was presumably closed; or it could be her very radiance... At all events the Colonel got wind of the story. It must have hit him hard; they thought a lot of pride in those days, it was shame enough to be cuckolded by a gentleman but to have the horns put on you by a fellow from your own stables... Oh yes, it was the groom. At all events he came spurring up to this place and presently he went back and said to the old woman at the Hall, Your mistress 'ull not be coming back. You can pack her finery and put it on the next coach for London. She's gone there and you'll not need me to tell you the name of the man who's gone with her. The old woman said she shook for her own life. He only spoke his wife's name once more, and that was to say that if ever she should return, back door or front, the bolts were to stay fast."

"But she never came back?"

"Not to the Hall. The old man became a hermit after she disappeared, and died a year or two later, and it was after that that the stories started. Travellers saw someone moving through the grounds of the Lodge, there were tales of someone looking through the windows, knocking on the doors. The Hall was sold—it's a girls' school now—but this place fell into disrepair. And the questions spread like ripples. How was it that no one ever recalled seeing the pair? Why was the baggage never called for? What happened to the groom's horse? Well, there was an answer to that; he was found, what the carrion crows had left of him, deep in the woods behind the lodge, having been ridden to death. Then the rumour ran that the groom had lost his head and escaped, leaving her to her husband's wrath. They even had a man down making enquiries, but nothing came of it. The unfaithful wife is never a sympathetic figure. In ancient Jewry adulterous wives were buried in the sand and stoned to death; and in your time," he nodded to Blair in his Tudor finery, "they could be burnt at the stake. Don't they say even Anne Boleyn quaked…? If it's true they escaped through the woods it's little surprise if they were never seen again. There are pits there, ancient workings, even bogs…"

An unearthly cry disturbed him. Peggy was on her feet pointing into the grounds, as white as the snow beyond the glass.

"No," she cried in an inhuman squeak, "don't let her come in, don't let her in."

We all turned, like feeding cattle; it seemed almost too pat to be true. There, under the crystalline trees, a figure moved, a slender green apparition, her face half concealed by the sweeping hat, the chestnut curls gleaming in the moonlight. I must make it clear that she wasn't only seen by the compassionate, Chris, Lou, James himself, but by everyone present. She seemed to move as though she had wheels instead of feet, she glided. And though the windows were closed and she didn't make a sound there was a terrible sense of chill, as if a wind had blown her in through the Gates of Death.

Charlie saw panic would be among us in a moment. He sent Joseph for a fresh supply of wine, and said, "Ladies and gentlemen, keep your places and your heads. I don't know whose idea this is, but it's not mine."

"Too bad," said Blair. "I was thinking—I like an enterprising chap—still, let's have the young lady in and hear what she has to say for herself."

He went confidently towards the big window opening on the grounds, but James was before him.

"In God's Name," he said, "have you no pity?"

"You do it very well," Blair told him. "As for pity, I'm only inviting her to come in and have a warm. What's happened to that wine, Sedley? Or is that chap of yours drinking it all himself?"

Blair next banged on the glass and beckoned with an immense hand; but the ghost only floated out of sight round the side of the house.

"If the servants see her we'll be getting our own supper," prophesied Charlie grimly.

"Did you see?" whispered Chris, "she was wringing her hands. I thought it was only ghosts…"

"She shouldn't have come," burst a voice behind me, the herald of a general hysteria. "It means a death to see a ghost. Who saw her first?"

"I did," wailed Peggy. "Arthur, take me home. I'm frightened."

"I was never yet frightened of anything flesh-and-blood," said Blair, coolly. "It'll take a lot more than a professional ghost to scare me. Besides, if it's true, I'd like a word with the lady. And don't look so jealous, my dear. You've no cause to be jealous of a ghost."

The situation was bizarre, divorced alike from reverence and the true Christmas reaction to the spectre. I felt Chris leaning hard against me as Lou cried out, "Can't you think of her? It's *she* who needs *us*."

I saw James throw her a grateful look. Chris, who has an uncanny way of reading my thoughts, whispered fiercely, "Do you still think it's a trick?"

"Not their trick," I acknowledged. I'd been doing some split-second thinking; you learn that when the lives of a whole crew may depend on your judgment. "Stay here," I said, "try and keep all the rest in the room, and don't let any of them go into the garden." Not that I believed James would let them, anyway.

"If you're going to be in danger I'm coming with you," said Chris.

"You'll do as I say, but keep on the alert. When you hear me call come at once. Tonight we'll solve the mystery of the Green Girl."

In the hall the candles burned like torches; I doubled swiftly up the main staircase, took up my stance by the grim oil painting of the old man who might be held to be responsible for all this supernatural fandango. I now commanded a clear view of the upper landing and the main stairs; if anyone came up the back staircase he must eventually come into my line of vision. I waited, confident whom I should see; and after a moment Joseph appeared. He had no notion I was within earshot, and he began to go quickly through the bedrooms on the upper floor. I had time to reflect on the neatness of the plan. While the Green Girl distracted or appalled all those below, her accomplice ransacked the bedrooms. It's true the big bar winked with jewels, but all the same there'd be handsome pickings, and I didn't suppose the locks on the jewel-cases would present much difficulty to Joseph. I wondered by what name the police knew him. If he went into our room I had him on toast. Most likely, though, he'd realize there was nothing worth taking there. His accomplice would be waiting outside the house, with a car safely hidden. With any luck it would be midnight before the hue and cry was raised, and by that time she'd not only be in London but have disposed of the loot. When a search was made nothing would be found, no one would be missing. James was in it, of course; I'd had my doubts about him from the start.

I was about to shout to Charlie to keep a guard over the back door and all the windows when something happened I hadn't allowed for. The Green Girl actually came up the back stairs and halted in the corridor.

"Joseph!" she called in a low pleading voice that seemed to have no echo. Then he came like a shadow *out of my room*. "Just a minute, Joseph," I said, stepping forward. "What were you doing in there?"

"What's going on?" yelled Charlie from below, and I called back, "Guard all your doors and windows, and you'll soon learn."

The momentary distraction had given Joseph his opportunity; when I looked back he'd vanished. I ran down the servants' passage, but he was in none of those rooms; I tore open the door and met Charlie coming up. Then I noticed the small staircase.

"Where does that lead? He must have gone that way."

"That won't help him much," said Charlie grimly. "It only leads to the attics that are locked, and the central heating apparatus, and a ghost couldn't hide there. And when I lay my hands on him," he added, "he'll wish he was a ghost."

By now turmoil had broken loose downstairs; it was like listening to a gigantic rookery. I went up the stairs, Charlie at my heels, James and Blair and the rest of the party behind us. Charlie flung open the door of the heating cupboard, whirled it shut. He hauled a great bunch of keys from his pocket and opened each attic in turn; a mouse could hardly have been concealed there.

"He was up there, I swear it," I said.

"O.K., Sedley," observed Blair, "you've proved your point. You gave us a ghost, you've caused it to vanish. Now let's go down and have another round and you can tell us how it was done. Mirrors or something, I daresay."

Behind him an unrecognizable voice said, "I know how it was done. My God, so that's the answer."

It was James, and he was standing beside the wall, rapping gently with his knuckles.

"Sedley," he asked, "how long has this paper been up?"

It was heavy red flock paper, not what you'd expect on the attic floor.

"A century for all I know," cried Charlie, recklessly.

"The wall here is hollow," James said. "Well, don't you see what that means? Behind it there is a room, unsuspected, undiscovered…"

"Oh no," cried Chris, "even he couldn't have done that." But I could see she was remembering the unfaithful wives who'd been stoned to death or bound to the stake.

"What am I supposed to do?" demanded Charlie. "Break down the wall?"

"Of course," said Lou. "Have you a knife…?"

We stood like a lot of morons watching James ruthlessly tear the paper away to reveal a frame, then a door… "It's locked," he said. "There's no key."

"There is a key," Lou told him. "Charlie, the key we never used because we didn't know…"

Charlie flipped the keys round on the ring; the key fitted the lock, as we'd all known it would. Only a man of superhuman strength could have turned it after so long, but at last the door was burst open, after 134 years. It revealed a long narrow room with a window shuttered from the inside, the only furniture a chest against the far wall; the floor was thick with dust like pile, like a silvery carpet. But what froze us all was the figure of Joseph standing with his back to us beside the chest.

"How the devil was it done?" Blair demanded. "Well, we'll soon learn." He'd have rushed into the room after the man, but James held him back.

"No," said he, "this is a matter for the police. Murder's murder, even if it is nearly 150 years old. It's no wonder she couldn't rest, the place for a body is hallowed ground. He must have killed her lover—I daresay his bones are in the woods somewhere, there'll be some surprises at the Last Judgment—and prisoned her here, where no one would come, no cry be heard. And all this while—if it's hard for one spirit to return what must it be like for two to synchronize?—there are a number of records of her being seen, but this is the first time for Joseph."

"Joseph!" I cried, and Chris caught my hand.

"That was the name of the groom, did no one tell you?"

"You mean, he too...?" For once Blair was speechless.

"What else?" James asked. "Surely you saw the lady cast no shadow on the snow, and look..." he played his torch over that gleaming empty floor, "there are no footprints in that dust." The words came echoing back in our astonished ears. There—are—no—footprints—in—that—dust.

Downstairs the great bell pealed, voices sounded. The first guests for the fancy dress ball had arrived. Charlie straightened himself and fled like an arrow; I never knew a man with such a power for self-command. The servants, still unaware of what had occurred, were taking wraps.

"So we're the first," boomed a hearty voice, "but the others are on the way. There are lights everywhere, and indeed we passed one couple on the road. Walking on a night like this, if you please, she dressed as the Green Girl and he the Prince of Darkness for all we could tell. We called out to offer them a lift, since they were walking in the wrong direction, but they paid no attention to us, and seemed very well satisfied with their own company."

## AMONG THOSE PRESENT
## WAS SANTA CLAUS

### *Vincent Cornier*

When introducing *The Duel of Shadows: The Extraordinary Cases of Barnabas Hildreth* (2011), the noted anthologist Mike Ashley said: "For over sixty years the work of Vincent Cornier has been something of a secret treasure within the vaults of mystery fiction." This neglect of Cornier (1898–1976), which persists to the present day, is undeserved, since his best work ranks with that of John Dickson Carr and Ellery Queen. High praise, yes, but I'm not alone in my view; indeed the comparison was first made by Otto Penzler and Chris Steinbrunner in *Encyclopedia of Mystery and Detection* back in 1976. Why is Cornier's work not more widely known? Part of the answer may lie in the description of him by another expert on the genre, Francis M. Nevins, as an "unclassifiable maverick". More importantly, he never published a novel, and it is very difficult to establish a significant reputation (let alone make a good living) solely on the strength of short stories.

Cornier's own life story is shrouded in mystery; Ashley's introduction gives the fullest account and explains that the author's actual name was William Vincent Corner. He came from the north east of England and grew up in Middlesbrough. After serving during the First World War, he benefited from an inheritance which enabled him to pursue his literary ambitions. Later in life he worked as Assistant Director of Studies at the London School of Journalism. Many of his finest mysteries were published in *Ellery Queen's Mystery Magazine*, but for this story I am indebted to the expert detective work of Jamie Sturgeon, a book dealer and researcher who found it in a newspaper archive; it was originally published in the *Huddersfield Examiner* on 20 December 1952. As far as I know it hasn't appeared elsewhere—a rare find indeed!

J OHN BURNICLE HALTED A MOMENT ON THE THRESHOLD OF THE
housekeeper's firelit room—and he listened. The whoops and
singing of village children sounded all over the great house. A piano
played "Nuts in May" and hands clapped merrily. Outside, the sleet
and wind of the afternoon made contrast, booming and threshing
at the ivy.

"Well, Mrs. Tateleigh, and how did it go?"

For once Lord Betwode's housekeeper was no longer the Stately
Tateleigh. Her shrewdly handsome Scots face was glowing and she—
actually—extended a welcoming hand.

"Mr. Burnicle," she almost purred, "you was a masterpiece! Oh,
the wee bairnies—didn't they enjoy themselves?"

His cheeks and upper lip still stinging from the spirit gum, the
recent Santa Claus of the Hall children's party rubbed his face ruefully,
and entered the room. Two tall glasses, cold chicken, wine, fruit and
a flaring fire made the sombrely panelled chamber a place of cheer.

"Wicked little devils," Burnicle chuckled. "One potential fire-raiser
was dispossessed of a box of matches and a raid on my whiskers—
otherwise, I agree, they certainly were happy." He still could smell the
fierce breath of a newly cut fir tree set up in the main hall; gleaming
with lights and old German glass toys; laden with presents. "His lordship doesn't do things by halves, does he?"

"A grand old gentleman, Mr. Burnicle. When he goes it'll be a
sore day for this part of the world." She sighed. Then sparkled, as she
indicated the lovely table. "But, come on now, I'm sure you must be
famished."

Burnicle settled down and ate and drank. "All this," he gleefully told himself, "and ten guineas, too"... Yes, old Lord Betwode was one of the best.

"I—I was mortally terrified," Mrs. Tateleigh suddenly and merrily said, as she poured out wine, "when his lordship told me he'd engaged a professional Santa Claus from a big London agency. Ooh!—thought I to myself—losh, he'll be a hairy old nasty, smelling of beer and baccy, and..."

"And I've disappointed you—eh?"

Mrs. Tateleigh found herself blushing. He saw the flush steal up clear-skinned cheeks, accentuating likable Scottish grey eyes and taking years from a woman's age. She saw a neat, iron-grey-haired man in his fifties, as clean and rosy as his lordship, and all as gentlemanly.

"Oh no! For the moment Lord Betwode told me you were an ex-inspector of police, I guessed you—you'd be decent." She handed him chicken and thick ham. "Forbye, and what does a pensioned police officer want, playing Santa at Christmas parties?"

"Loneliness, madam—loneliness." Then, conscious of a stiffness in his attitude, ex-Inspector Burnicle expanded, "I—I was one of a large family, y'see. And, since I'm an old bachelor with too much time on my hands, I took up this annual Santa Claus impersonation job... since it gives me two things, good fellowship and the bubble and squeak of—of kiddies. Frankly, Christmas sets me up, in sheer happiness, I mean, for most of the year."

"I see." Sarah Tateleigh also thought, deeply, craftily, excitedly. "Well, and how do you like our Cotswold countryside?" It seemed an inconsequent question—but she had her own reasons for asking it. "What you've seen of it, of course."

John Burnicle astounded the Hall's housekeeper.

"Why, good lord, I'm a Cotswold man, Mrs. Tateleigh! Did fifteen years o' my service hereabouts. What's more, my old dad was the last Lord Betwode's head gamekeeper..."

Then they were away. The bond was established—Mrs. Tateleigh's last bastions of reserve were down and two cronies sat a-talking. So it came about that Burnicle learned more—much more—than he otherwise would have been told. The housekeeper not only outlined the scope of the after-dinner party at which he was to officiate—she added snippets which, ordinarily, she would have kept to herself.

Sitting back, smoking one of Lord Betwode's cigars, ex-Inspector Burnicle pondered.

His lordship was no fool. He had deliberately singled out "a responsible chap" from the Agency list. When attracted by the name "Burnicle" and found under "Former Occupation"—"Police, attained rank of Inspector, twenty-eight years' service"... the old man went to London to interview his Santa Claus. In the interview Betwode had said searching and uncomfortable things. Now his housekeeper had, in part, confirmed them.

Apparently, more than half a dozen odd incidents of theft had occurred in Betwode Hall during the year. A miniature, a water-colour, a very valuable vase and other odds and ends vanished. Each item was small enough to conceal in anyone's clothing. None was recovered. It seemed that a kleptomaniac, or worse, was at work in the Hall... either one of the family or a servant.

"And since the family consists only of the honourable Agatha and Chloe," Mrs. Tateleigh's eyes twinkled, "and each is a severe and saintly old maid, surely we can rule them out."

"The servants," Burnicle ruminated. "You're sure all are trustworthy?"

"What few of us are left—five in all—have been here for 'teens' of years, Mr. Burnicle. I could vouch for every one. Apart from Hicks, the chauffeur, and he lives outside in the lodge at the gates, none of us is a chicken."

"Hicks? He's young, eh? How long's he been here?"

"Oh, a man in his early forties: a widower—came here in 1945. I believe. He was young Anthony's tank-driver during the war."

("Young Anthony" was the Betwode heir and was in Delhi on the High Commissioner's staff.) "So, I think we can leave him out of it all."

"I learned in police practice never to leave anyone out of anything when mystery was afoot," smiled Burnicle. "But, let's be hearing more about this after-dinner do. Any tips you can give me, Mrs. Tateleigh, I'll be glad to have."

"Inspired" by the year-long problem of the thefts, Lord Betwode had staged a "burglary" for after-dinner entertainment. Burnicle was to play Santa Claus and give each guest his or her present. Then, with lights lowered, one of the younger members of the party had to stage a melodramatic "burglary". The "victims" had to identify the "thief"... If so—Mr. Burglar paid forfeit. If not—if Mr. Burglar got away with it—the "victims" had to pay his car licence for a year and look pleasant about it, too.

"There's Mr. Clavering from Betwode, a nephew—and Sammy Bennet, he's Lord Betwode's steward, and Edward Fortescue," Mrs. Tateleigh explained. "Each is to dress up as a burglar. The guests are to do exactly as they would do in an actual burglary. If any—or all—are identified, they're out of the game... and as a forfeit for a similar business, last year, consisted of no drinks or smokes for a month, you can guess they'll be careful!"

"Oh! So it's been done before—eh?"

"Yes. Every year we have one of these 'murders' or mystery plays.' Young Mr. Anthony began 'em. And," the housekeeper sat up with pride, "they're quite famous, in a way—so cleverly done."

...After a while, since the weather had calmed, ex-Inspector Burnicle muffled up and took a walk through the moonlit gardens of the Hall. He got as far as the gates. He had a talk to Mr. Hicks and, on the way back, fell in with three guests walking over from Betwode village for the night's festivities: Samuel Bennet, Lord Betwode's steward, a slightly tipsy young fellow called Fortescue, an artist and a supercilious type—together with Jack Clavering, Betwode's nephew, a shy, lean fellow.

Among the three—Burnicle recalled something from his official post... which applied to one. Only to one.

His robe stifled him. His beard pricked. He would have given worlds for a glass of water, but wine was all there was to be had, it seemed. But Burnicle had carefully disposed of all his presents and now lurked in the shadows watching the preparations for the play in the great dining-room.

The old Duchess of Malminster—a spry and foxy-faced old thing— sat with a dog-collar of diamonds and a mutation mink cape. "Less to keep her warm," Burnicle mused, "than to make the others envious." The rector wore his purple vest. Sir Gregory Fletcher, financier, affected a magnificent diamond ring and occasionally proffered a platinum cigarette case. "Nice haul, if it were real," thought Burnicle. "But to my mind, that emerald's got 'em all beaten."

The emerald lay, green and deep with beauty, on the breast of Agatha, the elder sister of Lord Betwode. Her ageing skin made a perfect foil for it. A single platinum chain held it, and its historic value—since it belonged to Queen Elizabeth the First—dazzled the mind as much as its green brilliance dazzled eyes.

A hand touched Burnicle's shoulder. Mrs. Tateleigh was there. "Your trunk call is through," she whispered. Burnicle went out silently. He took the call and returned to his place.

When the burglar came, even Burnicle went cold. The others gasped. The Duchess grabbed her collar.

Into the half light had stepped a tall man, in shabby clothes, masked and carrying a cosh.

"Nah then," he growled, "down't tike any liberties. Me pal's outside an' I've gotta gun." Burnicle sank back. Of course—of course this was only a play. But... but, damned realistic: terrifying somehow. "Cough up the rooks." He pointed to the august lady of Malminster. "Kimon, missus, let's be havin' yer necklet."

Amid a babble of voices, the guests began to divest themselves of their jewellery. All except the bright-eyed Agatha. She sat, serenely, eating chocolates and smiling.

The burglar had a pocket full of jewels, when he approached the indifferent lady, his cosh raised.

"Nah, then! Give's that acid drop, or I'll—"

"Ted Fortescue, you're an ass!" Agatha's voice came clearly. "I—er—believe the first forfeit is not too bad... You'll not comb your hair or shave for a week." The burglar groaned and pulled off his mask. "I caught you out simply. Why didn't you think about taking off your ring, Teddy?"

Howls of merriment arose. Poor Fortescue unloaded his loot and the various owners selected their properties. The Duchess glared as she affixed her diamonds. "Missus," she muttered, while Teddy blushed, "missus, indeed!"

"I—I'm sorry, your Grace, but..."

"Shut up, Teddy," the Duchess suddenly roared with laughter. "I thoroughly enjoyed it."

Burnicle relaxed. He found he was sweating. He wished to goodness they would stop their tomfoolery. It—it was too realistic for his liking. Far too realistic.

"Have a drink, Teddy." Lord Betwode was jubilant. Since he had arrayed himself for the occasion with a tinny cigarette case and a cheap wrist watch, he could exult with malicious fervour. "Good show! Pity it came unstuck, but..."

"This won't," said a voice, and the lights snapped out. "This is the real MacKye." Into the firelit hearthside stepped a second "burglar."

Like Fortescue, he had sidled by way of two screens from a conveniently open door. "Shall I show you?" An automatic winked in his fist. "Anyone dare me to shoot at the logs there?"

"Sammy, you ass—that's over the odds." Fortescue sounded nettled. Evidently he felt the newcomer was not playing the game and identified him as Samuel Bennet, the estate steward. "Put that gun away..."

But the burglar just said, "Wrong, old boy. You've wasted your one challenge. I'm not Sam... Tip up, ladies and gentleman."

By the rules of the game, no-one—even though they recognized the roughly clad and masked figure in the semi-darkness—could challenge him again. One by one, and with a curious quietude, as though in creeping fear, they gave the intruder their belongings.

This was too real... it—it was the genuine thing! Burnicle trembled where he sat. He heard a soft breathing near him—an agitated breathing. Mrs. Tateleigh had crept in to watch the play, and she was scared.

Burnicle chanced to touch her hand. It closed strongly on his own.

Backing away, the pistol still levelled, the burglar got to the door. Stupefied and serious tension held the people around the fire. Sir Gregory licked his thick lips and caressed the finger from which his noble diamond had gone. Lord Betwode—despite having been deprived of property worth only two pounds—looked oddly drawn and grey. The Duchess glared, ferociously. Only Agatha was calm. Her square emerald was also gone... but she went on eating chocolates.

Burnicle was getting to his feet. He knew what he had heard on the wire to Scotland Yard, what his trunk call to London had set in motion. He felt, terribly, this was no "play"... as the intruder had mumbled, it was the "real MacKye."

Then, all tension snapped. Suddenly, out of the doorway, the burglar returned. He emptied all his loot on to a table. He pocketed his pistol and laughed.

"There you are," he exulted. "Hat round, please! My car licence for one year." He pulled away his mask and revealed himself as Jack Clavering, Lord Betwode's nephew. "What an actor!"

Amid excited babble the house party regained, each, his or her property. Agatha calmly replaced her emerald and reached out for another chocolate. Clavering had a drink.

Without a sound, two officers of the local police appeared. Lord Betwode shot up in astonishment.

"Metcalfe! And you, Superintendent Cullins! What is all this?"

"Acting on orders received," the Superintendent saluted. He motioned to Sgt. Metcalfe, who moved quietly to the suddenly trembling Clavering's side. "A call from Scotland Yard, m'lord."

Ex-Inspector Burnicle stepped out into the light.

"Lord Betwode," he said—and he looked odd in his robes and whiskers—"I think this ends your trouble. 'Fraid the water-colour can be counted as lost. Mr. Clavering will no doubt restore the miniatures, etcetera, And…"

"Burnicle! Wh-what is this? How dare you?"

"Have a look at that emerald, m'lord. The chain is the same, I'll bet. But the emerald is gone," which sounded silly since Miss Agatha still wore it. "Please take it off and…"

"I'll—I'll go quietly. Here, Aunt Agatha"—and Clavering passed over a great glowing emerald—"this is real; the one you are wearing is paste."

"Been in trouble more'n once," said Burnicle. "Never convicted—but known to us as a master at counterfeiting jewels and the like. Bet he's copied your other stuff to sell the real items and, eventually, restore the counterfeits. He met me in the drive. He didn't recognize me. I recognized him. And, while I sat there as Santa Claus, watching all, he didn't even tumble to my being something more than a bit of furniture, or a hired appurtenance…"

There was no prosecution. Clavering promised to see what Kenya had to offer. And when the police had enjoyed themselves, as police officers at Christmas sometimes do, ex-Inspector John Burnicle sedately kissed Sarah Tateleigh under some mistletoe.

"A Cotswold man," she murmured. "A lonely man… and a gey clever one, too!" Her eyes twinkled in that bright Scottish way. "You wouldna' find it hard to live hereabouts again, would you… John?"

"No, Sarah. In fact, I'm thinking about it seriously." He eyed the mistletoe. "Very," he said.

## GOLD, FRANKINCENSE, AND MURDER

# *Catherine Aird*

Catherine Aird is the pen-name of Kinn Hamilton McIntosh, who was born in 1930; although her birth-place was Huddersfield, she has lived in Sturry in Kent since the late 1940s. Unlike other authors whose work appears in the British Library's Crime Classics series, Catherine Aird is, I am delighted to say, writing detective fiction to this day. Her work is appropriate for inclusion in this anthology because it falls squarely within the finest traditions of well-crafted detective fiction. She is, for instance, an admirer of Josephine Tey, whose *The Daughter of Time* provided a degree of inspiration for Aird's second novel, and only stand-alone, *A Most Contagious Game* (1967).

Aird's other novels form The Calleshire Chronicles, featuring the detectives Sloan and Crosby. The series is set in a fictional county not unlike Kent, and began in 1966 with *The Religious Body*. Elected in 1981 to the prestigious Detection Club (which was founded in the year of her birth), Aird is a former Chair of the Crime Writers' Association and was the first recipient of the "Golden Handcuffs", an award which later became known as the CWA Dagger in the Library, in recognition of the popularity of her books with library readers. In 2015, she received the highest honour in British crime writing, the CWA Diamond Dagger. This story was originally published in 1995 in *A Classic Christmas Crime*, edited by Tim Heald.

"CHRISTMAS!" SAID HENRY TYLER. "BAH!"

"And we're expecting you on Christmas Eve as usual," went on his sister Wendy placidly.

"But…" He was speaking down the telephone from London, "but, Wen…"

"Now it's no use your pretending to be Ebenezer Scrooge in disguise, Henry."

"Humbug," exclaimed Henry more firmly.

"Nonsense," declared his sister, quite unmoved. "You enjoy Christmas just as much as the children. You know you do."

"Ah, but this year I may just have to stay on in London over the holiday…" Henry Tyler spent his working days—and, in these troubled times, quite a lot of his working nights as well—at the Foreign Office in Whitehall.

What he was doing now to his sister would have been immediately recognized in ambassadorial circles as "testing the reaction". In the lower echelons of his department it was known more simply as "flying a kite". Whatever you called it, Henry Tyler was an expert.

"And it's no use your saying there's trouble in the Baltic either," countered Wendy Witherington warmly.

"Actually," said Henry, "it's the Balkans which are giving us a bit of a headache just now."

"The children would never forgive you if you weren't there," said Wendy, playing a trump card; although it wasn't really necessary. She knew that nothing short of an international crisis would keep Henry away from her home in the little market town of Berebury in the heart of rural Calleshire at Christmastime. The trouble was that these days international crises were not nearly so rare as they used to be.

"Ah, the children," said their doting uncle. "And what is it that they want Father Christmas to bring this year?"

"Edward wants a model railway engine for his set."

"Does he indeed?"

"A Hornby LMS red engine called 'Princess Elizabeth'," said Wendy Witherington readily. "It's a 4-6-2."

Henry made a note, marvelling that his sister, who seemed totally unable to differentiate between the Baltic and the Balkans—and quite probably the Balearics as well—had the details of a child's model train absolutely at her fingertips.

"And Jennifer?" he asked.

Wendy sighed. "The Good Ship Lollipop. Oh, and when you come, Henry, you'd better be able to explain to her how it is that while she could see Shirley Temple at the pictures—we took her last week—Shirley Temple couldn't see her."

Henry, who had devoted a great deal of time in the last ten days trying to explain to a Minister in His Majesty's Government exactly what Monsieur Pierre Laval might have in mind for the best future of France, said he would do his best.

"Who else will be staying, Wen?"

"Our old friends Peter and Dora Watkins—you remember them, don't you?"

"He's something in the bank, isn't he?" said Henry.

"Nearly a manager," replied Wendy.

"Then there'll be Tom's old Uncle George."

"I hope," groaned Henry, "that your barometer's up to it. It had a hard time last year." Tom's Uncle George had been a renowned maker of scientific instruments in his day. "He's nearly tapped it to death."

Wendy's mind was still on her house guests. "Oh, and there'll be two refugees."

"Two refugees?" Henry frowned, even though he was alone in his room at the Foreign Office. They were beginning to be very careful about some refugees.

"Yes, the rector has asked us each to invite two refugees from the camp on the Calleford Road to stay for Christmas this year. You remember our Mr. Wallis, don't you, Henry?"

"Long sermons?" hazarded Henry.

"Then you do remember him," said Wendy without irony. "Well, he's arranged it all through some church organization. We've got to be very kind to them because they've lost everything."

"Give them useful presents, you mean," said Henry, decoding this last without difficulty.

"Warm socks and scarves and things," agreed Wendy Witherington vaguely. "And then we've got some people coming to dinner here on Christmas Eve."

"Oh, yes?"

"Our doctor and his wife. Friar's their name. She's a bit heavy in the hand but he's quite good company. And," said Wendy drawing breath, "our new next-door neighbours—they're called Steele—are coming too. He bought the pharmacy in the square last summer. We don't know them very well—I think he married one of his assistants—but it seemed the right thing to invite them at Christmas."

"Quite so," said Henry. "That all?"

"Oh, and little Miss Hooper."

"Sent her measurements, did she?"

"You know what I mean," said his sister, unperturbed. "She always comes then. Besides, I expect she'll know the refugees. She does a lot of church work."

"What sort of refugees are they?" asked Henry cautiously.

But that Wendy did not know.

Henry himself wasn't sure even after he'd first met them, and his brother-in-law was no help.

"Sorry, old man," said that worthy as they foregathered in the drawing-room, awaiting the arrival of the rest of the dinner guests on Christmas Eve. "All I know is that this pair arrived from somewhere in Mitteleuropa last month with only what they stood up in."

"Better out than in," contributed Gordon Friar, the doctor, adding an old medical aphorism, "like laudable pus."

"I understand," said Tom Witherington, "that they only just got out, too. Skin of their teeth and all that."

"As the poet so wisely said," murmured Henry, "'The only certain freedom's in departure'."

"If you ask me," said old Uncle George, a veteran of the Boer War, "they did well to go while the going was good."

"It's the sort of thing you can leave too late," pronounced Dr. Friar weightily. Leaving things too late was every doctor's nightmare.

"I don't envy 'em being where they are now," said Tom. "That camp they're in is pretty bleak, especially in the winter."

This was immediately confirmed by Mrs. Godiesky the moment she entered the room. She regarded the Witheringtons' glowing fire with deep appreciation. "We 'ave been so cooald, so cooaald," she said as she stared hungrily at the logs stacked by the open fireside. "So very cooald…"

Her husband's English was slightly better, although also heavily accented. "If we had not left when we did, then," he opened his hands expressively, "then who knows what would have become of us?"

"Who, indeed?" echoed Henry, who actually had a very much better idea than anyone else present of what might have become of the

Godieskys had they not left their native heath when they did. Reports reaching the Foreign Office were very, very discouraging.

"They closed my university department down overnight," explained Professor Hans Godiesky. "Without any warning at all."

"It was terrrrrible," said Mrs. Godiesky, holding her hands out to the fire as if she could never be warm again.

"What sort of a department was it, sir?" enquired Henry casually of the Professor.

"Chemistry," said the refugee, just as the two Watkins came in and the hanging mistletoe was put to good use. They were followed fairly quickly by Robert and Lorraine Steele from next door. The introductions in their case were more formal. Robert Steele was a good bit older than his wife, who was dressed in a very becoming mixture of red and dark green, though with a skirt that was rather shorter than either Wendy's or Dora's and even more noticeably so than that of Marjorie Friar, who was clearly no dresser.

"We're so glad you could get away in time," exclaimed Wendy, while Tom busied himself with furnishing everyone with sherry. "It must be difficult if there's late dispensing to be done."

"No trouble these days," boomed Robert Steele. "I've got a young assistant now. He's a great help."

Then Miss Hooper, whose skirt was longest of all, was shown in. She was out of breath and full of apology for being so late. "Wendy, dear, I am so very sorry," she fluttered. "I'm afraid the Waits will be here in no time at all…"

"And they won't wait," said Henry guilelessly, "will they?"

"If you ask me," opined Tom Witherington, "they won't get past the 'Royal Oak' in a hurry."

"The children are coming down in their dressing-gowns to listen to the carols," said Wendy, rightly ignoring both remarks. "And I don't mind how tired they get tonight."

"Who's playing Father Christmas?" asked Robert Steele jovially. He was a plump fellow, whose gaze rested fondly on his young wife most of the time.

"Not me," said Tom Witherington.

"I am," declared Henry. "For my sins."

"Then, when I am tackled on the matter," said the children's father piously, "I can put my hand on my heart and swear total innocence."

"And how will you get out of giving an honest answer, Henry?" enquired Dora Watkins playfully.

"I shall hope," replied Henry, "to remain true to the traditions of the Foreign Service and give an answer that is at one and the same time absolutely correct and totally meaningless..."

At which moment the sound of the dinner gong being struck came from the hall and presently the whole party moved through to the dining-room, Uncle George giving the barometer a surreptitious tap on the way.

Henry Tyler studied the members of the party under cover of a certain amount of merry chat. It was part and parcel of his training that he could at one and the same time discuss Christmas festivities in England with poor Mrs. Godiesky while covertly observing the other guests. Lorraine Steele was clearly the apple of her husband's eye, but he wasn't sure that the same could be said for Marjorie Friar, who emerged as a complainer and sounded—and looked—quite aggrieved with life.

Lorraine Steele though, was anything but dowdy. Henry decided her choice of red and green—Christmas colours—was a sign of a new outfit for yuletide.

He was also listening for useful clues about their homeland in the Professor's conversation, while becoming aware that Tom's old Uncle George really was getting quite senile now and learning that the latest of Mrs. Friar's succession of housemaids had given in her notice.

"And at Christmas, too," she complained. "So inconsiderate."

Peter Watkins was displaying a modest pride in his Christmas present to his wife.

"Well," he said in the measured tones of his profession of banking, "personally, I'm sure that refrigerators are going to be the thing of the future."

"There's nothing wrong with a good old-fashioned larder," said Wendy stoutly, like the good wife she was. There was little chance of Tom Witherington being able to afford a refrigerator for a very long time. "Besides, I don't think Cook would want to change her ways now. She's quite set in them, you know."

"But think of the food we'll save," said Dora. "It'll never go bad now."

"'Use it up, wear it out'." Something had stirred in old Uncle George's memory.

"'Make it do, do without or we'll send it to Belgium'."

"And you'll be more likely to avoid food poisoning, too," said Robert Steele earnestly. "Won't they, Dr. Friar?"

"Yes, indeed," the medical man agreed at once. "There's always too much of that about and it can be very dangerous."

The pharmacist looked at both the Watkins and said gallantly, "I can't think of a better present."

"But you did, darling," chipped in Lorraine Steele brightly, "didn't you?"

Henry was aware of an unspoken communication passing between the two Steeles; and then Lorraine Steele allowed her left hand casually to appear above the table. Her fourth finger was adorned with both a broad gold wedding ring and a ring on which was set a beautiful solitaire diamond.

"Robert's present," she said rather complacently, patting her blonde Marcel waved hair and twisting the diamond ring round. "Isn't it lovely?"

"I wanted her to wear it on her right hand," put in Robert Steele, "because she's left-handed, but she won't hear of it."

"I should think not," said Dora Watkins at once. "The gold wedding ring sets it off so nicely."

"That's what I say, too," said Mrs. Steele prettily, lowering her be-ringed hand out of sight again.

"Listen!" cried Wendy suddenly. "It's the Waits. I can hear them now. Come along, everyone… it's mince pies and coffee all round in the hall afterwards."

The Berebury carol-singers parked their lanterns outside the front door and crowded round the Christmas tree in the Witheringtons' entrance hall, their sheets of music held at the ready.

"Right," called out their leader, a young man with a rather prominent Adam's apple. He began waving a little baton. "All together now…"

The familiar words of "Once in Royal David's City" soon rang out through the house, filling it with joyous sound. Henry caught a glimpse of a tear in Mrs. Godiesky's eye; and noted a look of great nostalgia in little Miss Hooper's earnest expression. There must have been ghosts of Christmases Past in the scene for her, too.

Afterwards, when it became important to recreate the scene in his mind for the police, Henry could only place the Steeles at the back of the entrance hall with Dr. Friar and Uncle George beside them. Peter and Dora Watkins had opted to stand a few steps up the stairs to the first-floor landing, slightly out of the press of people but giving them a good view. Mrs. Friar was standing awkwardly in front of the leader of the choir. Of Professor Hans Godiesky there was no sign whatsoever while the carols were being sung.

Henry remembered noticing suppressed excitement in the faces of his niece and nephew perched at the top of the stairs and hoping it was the music that they had found entrancing and not the piles of mince pies awaiting them among the decorative smilax on the credenza at the back of the hall.

They—and everyone else—fell upon them nonetheless as soon as the last carol had been sung. There was a hot punch, too, carefully mulled to just the right temperature by Tom Witherington, for those old enough to partake of it, and home-made lemonade for the young.

Almost before the last choirboy had scoffed the last mince pie the party at the Witheringtons' broke up.

The pharmacist and his wife were the first to leave. They shook hands all round.

"I know it's early," said Lorraine Steele apologetically, "but I'm afraid Robert's poor old tummy's been playing him up again." Henry, who had been expecting a rather limp paw, was surprised to find how firm her handshake was.

"If you'll forgive us," said Lorraine's husband to Wendy, "I think we'd better be on our way now." Robert Steele essayed a glassy, strained smile, but to Henry's eye he looked more than a little white at the gills. Perhaps he, too, had spotted that the ring that was his Christmas present to his wife had got a nasty stain on the inner side of it.

The pair hurried off together in a flurry of farewells. Then the wispy Miss Hooper declared the evening a great success but said she wanted to check everything at St. Faith's before the midnight service, and she, too, slipped away.

"What I want to know," said Dora Watkins provocatively when the rest of the guests had reassembled in the drawing-room and Edward and Jennifer had been sent back—very unwillingly—to bed, "is whether it's better to be an old man's darling or a young man's slave?"

A frown crossed Wendy's face. "I'm not sure," she said seriously.

"I reckon our Mrs. Steele's got her husband where she wants him, all right," said Peter Watkins, "don't you?"

"Come back, William Wilberforce, there's more work on slavery still to be done," said Tom Witherington lightly. "What about a night-cap, anyone?"

But there were no takers, and in a few moments the Friars, too, had left.

Wendy suddenly said she had decided against going to the Midnight Service after all and would see everyone in the morning. The rest of the household also opted for an early night and in the event Henry Tyler was the only one of the party to attend the Midnight Service at St. Faith's church that night.

The words of the last carol, "We Three Kings of Orient Are..." were still ringing in his ears as he crossed the Market Square to the church. Henry wished that the Foreign Office had only kings to deal with: life would be simpler then. Dictators and Presidents—particularly one President not so very many miles from "perfidious Albion"—were much more unpredictable.

He hummed the words of the last verse of the carol as he climbed the church steps:

> Myrrh is mine; it's bitter perfume
> Breathes a life of gathering gloom;
> Sorrowing, sighing, bleeding, dying,
> Sealed in the stone-cold tomb.

Perhaps, he thought, as he sought a back pew and his nostrils caught the inimical odour of a mixture of burning candles and church flow-ers, he should have been thinking of frankincense or even—when he saw the burnished candlesticks and altar cross—Melchior's gold...

His private orisons were interrupted a few minutes later by a sudden flurry of activity near the front of the church, and he looked up in time to see little Miss Hooper being helped out by the two churchwardens.

"If I might just have a drink of water," he heard her say before she was borne off to the vestry. "I'll be all right in a minute. So sorry to make a fuss. So very sorry…"

The rector's sermon was its usual interminable length and he was able to wish his congregation a happy Christmas as they left the church. As Henry walked back across the square he met Dr. Friar coming out of the Steeles' house.

"Chap's collapsed," he murmured. "Severe epigastric pain and vomiting. Mrs. Steele came round to ask me if I would go and see him. There was blood in the vomit and that frightened her."

"It would," said Henry. "He's pretty ill," said the doctor.

"I'm getting him into hospital as soon as possible."

"Could it have been something he ate here?" said Henry, telling him about little Miss Hooper.

"Too soon to tell but quite possible," said the doctor gruffly. "You'd better check how the others are when you get in. I rather think Wendy might be ill, too, from the look of her when we left, and I must say my wife wasn't feeling too grand when I went out. Ring me if you need me."

Henry came back to a very disturbed house indeed, with several bedroom lights on. No one was very ill but Wendy and Mrs. Godiesky were distinctly unwell. Dora Watkins was perfectly all right and was busy ministering to those that weren't.

Happily, there was no sound from the children's room and he crept in there to place a full stocking beside each of their beds. As he came back downstairs to the hall, he thought he heard an ambulance bell next door.

"The position will be clearer in the morning," he said to himself, a Foreign Office man to the end of his fingertips.

It was.

Half the Witherington household had had a severe gastro-intestinal upset during the night, and Robert Steele had died in the Berebury Royal Infirmary at about two o'clock in the morning.

When Henry met his sister on Christmas morning she had a very wan face indeed.

"Oh, Henry," she cried, "isn't it terrible about Robert Steele? And the rector says half the young Waits were ill in the night, too, and poor little Miss Hooper as well!"

"That lets the punch out, doesn't it?" said Henry thoughtfully, "seeing as the youngsters weren't supposed to have any."

"Cook says…"

"Is she all right?" enquired Henry curiously.

"She hasn't been ill, if that's what you mean, but she's very upset." Wendy sounded quite nervous. "Cook says nothing like this has ever happened to her before."

"It hasn't happened to her now," pointed out Henry unkindly but Wendy wasn't listening.

"And Edward and Jennifer are all right, thank goodness," said Wendy a little tearfully. "Tom's beginning to feel better but I hear Mrs. Friar's pretty ill still and poor Mrs. Godiesky is feeling terrible. And as for Robert Steele… I just don't know what to think. Oh, Henry, I feel it's all my fault."

"Well, it wasn't the lemonade," deduced Henry. "Both children had lots. I saw them drinking it."

"They had a mince pie each, too," said their mother. "I noticed. But some people who had them have been very ill since…"

"Exactly, my dear. Some, but not all."

"But what could it have been, then?" quavered Wendy. "Cook is quite sure she only used the best of everything. And it stands to reason it was something that they ate here." She struggled to put her fears into words. "Here was the only place they all were."

"It stands to reason that it was something they were given here," agreed Henry, whom more than one ambassador had accused of pedantry, "which is not quite the same thing."

She stared at him. "Henry, what do you mean?"

Inspector Milsom knew what he meant.

It was the evening of Boxing Day when he and Constable Bewman came to the Witheringtons' house.

"A number of people would appear to have suffered from the effects of ingesting a small quantity of a dangerous substance at this address," Milsom announced to the company assembled at his behest. "One with fatal results."

Mrs. Godiesky shuddered. "Me, I suffer a lot."

"Me, too," Peter Watkins chimed in.

"But not, I think, sir, your wife?" Inspector Milsom looked interrogatively at Dora Watkins.

"No, Inspector," said Dora. "I was quite all right."

"Just as well," said Tom Witherington. He still looked pale. "We needed her to look after us."

"Quite so," said the Inspector.

"It wasn't food poisoning, then?" said Wendy eagerly. "Cook will be very pleased…"

"It would be more accurate, madam," said Inspector Milsom, who didn't have a cook to be in awe of, "to say that there was poison in the food."

Wendy paled. "Oh…"

"This dangerous substance of which you speak," enquired Professor Godiesky with interest, "is its nature known?"

"In England," said the Inspector, "we call it corrosive sublimate…"

"Mercury? Ah," the refugee nodded sagely, "that would explain everything."

"Not quite everything, sir," said the Inspector mildly. "Now, if we might see you one at a time, please."

"This poison, Inspector," said Henry after he had given his account of the carol-singing to the two policemen, "I take it that it is not easily available?"

"That is correct, sir. But specific groups of people can obtain it."

"Doctors and pharmacists?" hazarded Henry.

"And certain manufacturers…"

"Certain… Oh, Uncle George?" said Henry. "Of course. There's plenty of mercury in thermometers."

"The old gentleman is definitely a little confused, sir."

"And Professors of Chemistry?" said Henry.

"In his position," said the Inspector judiciously, "I should myself have considered having something with me just in case."

"There being a fate worse than death," agreed Henry swiftly, "such as life in some places in Europe today. Inspector, might I ask what form this poison takes?"

"It's a white crystalline substance."

"Easily confused with sugar?"

"It would seem easily enough," said the policeman drily.

"And what you don't know, Inspector," deduced Henry intelligently, "is whether it was scattered on the mince pies… I take it it was on the mince pies?"

"They were the most likely vehicle," conceded the policeman.

"By accident or whether it was meant to make a number of people slightly ill or…"

"Or," put in Detective Constable Bewman keenly, "one person very ill indeed?"

"Or," persisted Henry quietly, "both."

"That is so." He gave a dry cough. "As it happens it did both make several people ill and one fatally so."

"Which also might have been intended?" Nobody had ever called Henry slow.

"From all accounts," said Milsom obliquely, "Mr. Steele had a weak tummy before he ingested the corrosive sublimate of mercury."

"Uncle George wasn't ill, was he?"

"No, sir, nor Dr. Friar." He gave his dry cough. "I am told that Dr. Friar never partakes of pastry."

"Mrs. Steele?"

"Slightly ill. She says she just had one mince pie. Mrs. Watkins didn't have any. Nor did the Professor."

"The one without the parsley," quoted Henry, "is the one without the poison."

"Just so, sir. It would appear at first sight from our immediate calculations quite possible that…"

"Inspector, if you can hedge your bets as well as that before you say anything, we could find you a job in the Foreign Office."

"Thank you, sir. As I was saying, sir, it is possible that the poison was only in the mince pies furthest from the staircase. Bewman here has done a chart of where the victims took their pies from."

"Which would explain why some people were unaffected," said Henry.

"Which might explain it, sir." The Inspector clearly rivalled Henry in his precision. "The Professor just wasn't there to take one at all. He says he went to his room to finish his wife's Christmas present. He was carving something for her out of a piece of old wood."

"Needs must when the devil drives," responded Henry absently. He was still thinking. "It's a pretty little problem, as they say."

"Means and opportunity would seem to be present," murmured Milsom.

"That leaves motive, doesn't it?" said Henry.

"The old gentleman mightn't have had one, seeing he's as he is, sir, if you take my meaning and of course we don't know anything about the Professor and his wife, do we, sir? Not yet."

"Not a thing."

"That leaves the doctor…"

"I'd've murdered Mrs. Friar years ago," announced Henry cheerfully, "if she had been my wife."

"And Mrs. Steele." There was a little pause and then Inspector Milsom said, "I understand the new young assistant at the pharmacy is more what you might call a contemporary of Mrs. Steele."

"Ah, so that's the way the wind's blowing, is it?"

"And then, sir," said the policeman, "after motive there's still what we always call down at the station the fourth dimension of crime…"

"And what might that be, Inspector?"

"Proof." He got up to go. "Thank you for your help, sir."

Henry sat quite still after the two policemen had gone, his memory teasing him. Someone he knew had been poisoned with corrosive sublimate of mercury, served to him in tarts. By a tart, too, if history was to be believed.

No, not someone he knew.

Someone he knew of.

Someone they knew about at the Foreign Office because it had been a political murder, a famous political murder set round an eternal triangle…

Henry Tyler sought out Professor Godiesky and explained.

"It was recorded by contemporary authors," Henry said, "that when the tarts poisoned with mercury were delivered to the Tower of London for Sir Thomas Overbury, the fingernail of the woman delivering them had accidentally been poked through the pastry…"

The professor nodded sapiently. "And it was stained black?"

"That's right," said Henry. History did have some lessons to teach, in spite of what Henry Ford had said. "But it would wash off?"

"Yes," said Hans Godiesky simply.

"So I'm afraid that doesn't get us anywhere, does it?"

The academic leaned forward slightly, as if addressing a tutorial. "There is, however, one substance on which mercury always leaves its mark."

"There is?" said Henry.

"Its—how do you say it in English?—its ineradicable mark."

"That's how we say it," said Henry slowly. "And which substance, sir, would that be?"

"Gold, Mr. Tyler. Mercury stains gold."

"For ever?"

"For ever." He waved a hand. "An amalgam is created."

"And I," Henry gave a faint smile, "I was foolish enough to think it was diamonds that were for ever."

"Pardon?"

"Nothing, Professor. Nothing at all. Forgive me, but I think I may be able to catch the Inspector and tell him to look to the lady. And her gold wedding ring."

"Look to the lady?" The refugee was now totally bewildered. "I do not understand…"

"It's a quotation."

"Ach, sir, I fear I am only a scientist."

"There's a better quotation," said Henry, "about looking to science for the righting of wrongs. I rather think Mrs. Steele may have looked to science, too, to—er—improve her lot. And if she carefully scattered the corrosive sublimate over some mince pieces and not others it would have been with her left hand…"

"Because she was left-handed," said the Professor immediately. "That I remember. And you think one mince pie would have had—I know the English think this important—more than its fair share?"

"I do. Then all she had to do was to give her husband that one and Bob's your uncle. Clever of her to do it in someone else's house."

Hans Godiesky looked totally mystified. "And who was Bob?"

"Don't worry about Bob," said Henry from the door. "Think about Melchior and his gold instead."

# SECRETS IN THE SNOW

## J. Jefferson Farjeon

Joseph Jefferson Farjeon (1883–1955), generally known as Joe, was the son of Benjamin Farjeon, a prolific and successful novelist whose output included crime novels such as *Great Porter Square: a mystery* and *The Mystery of M. Felix*. Early in his career, while living in New Zealand, Farjeon senior published a novel called *Shadows on the Snow: a Christmas story*, which he dedicated to Charles Dickens, hoping (in vain) that Dickens would publish a serialized version in his periodical *All the Year Round*.

His father's influence is evident in Joe Farjeon's choice of name for the merchant-sailor-turned-tramp who became his most famous character. "Ben" first appeared in a stage play, *No. 17*, in 1925. The following year, Joe turned the story into a novel, commenting in a preface that the success of the play "has formed one of the happiest and most important milestones of my career". In 1932 the story was filmed by Alfred Hitchcock. There were also German and Swedish film versions. This success prompted Joe to write seven more books featuring Ben, the last of which appeared in 1952. Three of his stand-alone novels have been published as Crime Classics, and *Mystery in White* enjoyed particular success. The set-up of this story owes something to that book; it previously appeared in *Best Stories of the Underworld* in 1942.

T HE CHRISTMAS EVE MOTOR-COACH STOPPED IN THE MIDDLE OF nowhere. Rubbing the steam from her window, Janet looked out into a whirling white wilderness. She could not see any sign of town or village, and nobody got in and nobody got out saving the conductor, who had vanished the moment the coach had come to a halt.

"Is anything wrong?" she asked the untalkative man next to her.

For two hours this man had taken no advantage of the fact that, at a season of easy comradeship, he had been sitting beside an exceptionally pretty girl.

"Don't know, can't say," he answered, shortly.

"*I'm* betting it's a jolly old snowdrift!" exclaimed the more loquacious young man in the seat behind. He had been doing his best to cheer a woman with a toothache, and had failed signally. "Any takers?"

The bet was not accepted, which was a misfortune for him since his guess proved accurate. In a short while the conductor returned with a gloomy face to report that the road was blocked. "There's snowdrifts as big as St. Paul's," he added. "We've got to go back for help."

The untalkative man jumped up. "That doesn't suit me!" he grunted. "I was getting out at the next stop, anyway."

"So was I," said Janet. "You're not going to West Mallerton, by any chance?"

He hesitated, then murmured, "That direction," and the next moment was outside.

"Whoa, wait a minute!" exclaimed Janet, seizing her suit-case. "That's my direction, too!"

To her surprise, the loquacious passenger interposed.

"I say! I wouldn't, really!" he urged, thrusting out his foot.

"Why not?" she demanded, frowning at him.

"Why not? Well—just look at the weather!" he replied. "You'd better wait here. You'd never do it."

"Thanks, but I've got a house-party on," she retorted, "and I *mean* to do it! Do you mind moving your foot, or I'll lose my guide!"

She stepped over the impeding boot, and a couple of seconds later was out in the blinding snow.

For an instant, as the cold caught her and the flakes flung themselves into her face, she wondered whether the loquacious young man's advice had not been sound. Still, sound or not, she was not going back, and she plunged forward after a dim figure that was rapidly becoming obliterated. The figure moved as quickly as she, and it was not until she had increased her pace that she caught it up in a narrow lane.

"You *are* in a hurry!" she cried, breathlessly.

The pursued one turned, and his expression, a mixture of surprise and annoyance, was not complimentary.

"You said you were going to West Mallerton," Janet explained, "so I thought we might walk together. I don't know the way."

"I said I was going in that direction," the man corrected her.

"But you didn't mention that you loathed company!" she shot back, incensed by his rudeness. "Don't worry—I'll keep behind!"

He regarded her fixedly for a few seconds, as though sizing her up. Then he said, in a slightly changed tone.

"Let me advise you, young lady, to keep well behind—otherwise you may walk into more trouble than you've just come from."

"Really?"

"Really."

"What sort of trouble?"

"Curiosity killed a cat."

"Only I don't happen to be one."

He smiled rather grimly, and responded after a moment's consideration.

"Very well. I'm on a Scotland Yard job—and there *may* be some rough stuff coming along."

He patted a side-pocket suggestively.

The weather chose this moment to create a diversion. A sudden wind drove a flurry of snow viciously into her eyes, and her suit-case slipped from her cold fingers. She stopped to regain it, stumbled, and took a soft fall. When she had picked herself up, she found herself alone.

"And policemen are supposed to be polite!" she thought. "Well, if I've lost my guide, I've still got his footprints!"

They ran down the virgin carpet of the lane till they were lost in the white kaleidoscopic mist. She began to follow them, but stopped almost at once.

"That's funny!" she murmured. "*Two* sets of prints! Whose are the others?"

Both sets of prints were very recent; of that there was no doubt. With fresh snow falling all the while, old marks soon ceased to be, and new marks had but a short life. Moreover, before she had overtaken the Scotland Yard man, she had been following only one set... Yes, but if that were so...?

She gave it up, and hastened down the lane.

The lane turned and twisted. The footprints became less and less distinct. That meant that those ahead of her were outpacing her, and that the length of time between the reaching and the making of the marks was increasing. "They must be in a hurry!" she reflected, as she accelerated.

Presently, near a snow-covered barn, one set faded out completely. She had met nobody and there were no sign-posts, so all she could do was to follow the remaining set and hope Heaven would be kind to her. The joy of Christmas was fast oozing away, and she was wet and shivery. Already she regretted that she had not taken the advice of the idiotic young man.

Yes, he *had* been idiotic. The scraps of conversation she had overheard behind her in the coach had, in Shakespearean terms, written him down an ass. Yet, as he had tried to dissuade her, and had impudently stuck out his boot, there had been something not unpleasant in his ingenuous blue eyes. Perhaps, if a man were born a fool, he could not help it!

She found herself walking mechanically. She had a sensation that if she stopped she would stop for good. She was growing colder and colder, her feet had become two lumps of squelching numbness, and tiny streams of chilly moisture were running down her neck. Then the worst happened. The last footprints faded out, and she reached a fork where the lane divided into two.

"*Now* what?" she asked herself.

She tossed up in her mind. Heads right, tails left, The imaginary coin came down heads, and she took the right-hand fork.

Walking became increasingly difficult. The lane narrowed to a snow-clothed track. Once, avoiding a big white mound, she trod deeply and sprawled into a ditch. She rose spluttering, rescued her suit-case, and wondered whether to turn back.

But now the blessed miracle for which she had prayed occurred. A little way ahead, its roof just visible behind a high hedge, was a cottage. She staggered towards it, as a spent man staggers towards the oasis in the desert.

The small gate in the hedge was closed, but the door of the house was open. Without hesitation, when her knock failed to produce any response, she walked in.

The sight that met her gaze was as welcome as it was unexpected. On a small table by a smaller fire was a pot of tea. A saucerless cup was half-filled with milk-less fluid. A chair near the table was at an untidy angle, and on the floor was a large spade, its metal moist; but if the last items were less welcome than the first, in that quick initial glance the tea towered above everything.

But for these frugal signs of a meal, and the open front-door, the house seemed unoccupied. It had a musty, closed-in smell, and dust was everywhere.

"Anybody at home?" she called.

Only her echo answered her.

She walked to the table. The tea in the cup was still hot. The spade on the floor was still wet. She glanced towards a door at the back of the room. It was ajar.

About to call again, she paused. Her ears, grown acute through tension, had caught a sound on the other side of the door. At first she could not decipher it; then, as it was repeated with a sort of jerky regularity, she guessed what it was. It resembled the breathing of a short-winded ghost, but she did not believe in ghosts.

"Are you coming in, or shall I come out?" she asked, adopting bold tactics.

In a moment or two the door moved, and a head peered in cautiously.

It was not a prepossessing head. Small, pale, with straw-coloured hair, a flat nose, and eyes that did not agree, it came round the door like a bad joke. For a few seconds, beauty and ugliness stared at each other. Then the head inquired, in a husky voice,

"'Oo are you?"

"My name won't interest you," answered Janet, "but my condition may—if you've a heart. I'm cold and sopping, and I've lost my way."

"Oh! 'Ave yer," blinked the head. "Yus, I've got a 'eart, but it ain't a strong 'un. Yer give me a proper scare."

"I'm sorry. May I know who you are?"

"Me? Oh, Caretaker!" Now he entered completely. From the look of his shabby suit, he did not earn a high salary for his job. "I was just 'avin' a cup o' tea." His eyes fixed themselves on the spade. "Arter doin' a bit o' snow-shovellin'. Mikes yer 'ot. See, I dropped the spade when I 'eard yer comin'."

"Did you think I was a ghost?"

He smiled queerly. He was a horrid little fellow, but Janet found herself feeling rather sorry for him.

"Tha's right, miss. Bein' alone in a hempy 'ouse gives yer the creeps, speshully at Chrismus, tha's right, ain't it?" He looked at her earnestly. "This 'ouse is 'aunted. I wouldn't reckermend nobody ter stay 'ere!"

"At the present moment, I'm not in a mood to be particular," she pointed out.

"Oh, I see. Where yer tryin' ter git ter?"

"West Mallerton."

"Never 'eard of it." He saw the astonishment in her eyes, and added hastily, "See, I on'y bin caretaker 'ere cupple o' days. Yer better arsk some'un helse."

"Thank you! Who?" He scratched his head. "Listen," she went on to her unsatisfactory host, "I don't want to trouble you, but I'm really in a frightful mess. If I can sit by your fire and dry myself for ten minutes, and if you could let me have just one cup of tea from that pot, I'll give you a jolly good Christmas present."

She produced from her sopping bag a dry ten shilling note, and the caretaker's eyes gleamed.

"And if you could add a towel," she said, with sudden inspiration, "and could give me those ten minutes to myself, I might turn this note into a pound one!"

"It's a go!" exclaimed the caretaker, and dived back to the kitchen.

In a few moments he reappeared with an empty cup and a roller-towel.

"I fahnd this 'angin' up, I 'ope it'll do," he said hoarsely. "The cup's clean, any'ow."

"Any chance of a drop of milk?" she asked.

He shook his head.

"Sugar?"

"Sorry, miss. See, I ain't started orderin' things proper yet," he explained, "and the bloke wot engaged me didn't leave no stores, on'y the tea. But there's plenty o' that in the pot, so 'elp yerself, miss—and yer can 'ave 'arf-a-hour, if yer like, while I goes on with me diggin'."

He seized the spade and ran out of the room again. She heard his hurried footsteps fading away across a floor. She gazed after him with a little frown, trying to quell disturbing thoughts.

"Of course, it hasn't really been shopping weather lately," she reflected, "but if you've been here for two days, Mr. Caretaker, have you been living *entirely* on tea-leaves? And whose ghost did you expect to walk in on you?"

Well, these things were nothing to do with her. Her own concern was to make good use of this half-hour, and she proceeded to do so very thoroughly.

Her first action was to lock the doors of the parlour, to ensure privacy. Then she drew a blue check curtain across the window. The pale, subdued light gave her a comforting sense of peace, and the little fire, coming into its own, added to her pleasure. Secure against interruption, she took off her wet coat and slipped out of her dress, almost purring with pleasure as the warmth of the fire caressed her bare arms.

"This is the moment for that tea!" she thought.

She filled the empty cup, then sipped gingerly. Minus milk, the tea was still too hot to gulp. Somewhere outside she believed she heard the sound of shovelling, but she could not be sure. Where was he? At the back or front? Drawn by idle curiosity she began to move towards the window, but retreated quickly as her shadow fell upon the blue check curtain. She heard soft steps outside. He was in the front.

"Well, I hope he's enjoying himself," she murmured, "but it isn't *my* idea of fun!"

In her retreat she had nearly stumbled over her suit-case on the floor, and the incident gave her a new idea, or elaborated a previous one. She opened the case and, after removing a top layer of gifts destined for sundry folk at West Mallerton, if she ever reached them, she unpacked a complete change of lingerie. Then she stripped, life growing better and better as she shed each damp garment.

Naked, she laughed. The outrageous absurdity of her position swept over her, and she wondered what the absent house-owner would have thought had he known of the use that was being made of his parlour! Would he have been amused or indignant? Pleased or annoyed? Well, he would never know, so why worry? She laughed again. Then, suddenly, stood rigid.

A sound she could not—or would not—interpret had broken the velvet silence outside, and frozen her laughter. She remained motionless, waiting for its repetition. When it was not repeated, and the only sound she could hear was the beating of her heart, she began diving into her clothes with desperate speed, striving to comfort herself as she dressed.

"Of *course* it wasn't!" she thought. "It was an owl hooting! Or some animal or other. Or—yes—the whistle of a distant train! That silly idiot talking about his precious ghost—he's given me the jim-jams!"

Redressed, she unlocked the back door with definite distaste, and called into the dim kitchen.

"Are you in there?"

As once before, her echo answered her, but this time it was a particularly unpleasant echo, repeating her question with ironic derision.

Then she unlocked the front door, and looked out into the gloaming. Dusk had come abruptly. It was a dusk choked with thick flakes. For a short space she could see nothing but the snow, falling as relentlessly as ever, and drowning the world, beneath its dull white monotone. But presently, as she stared, shapes and outlines grew, and she made out the laden trees, the muffled bushes, and the boundary hedge.

What she did not see was the little, flat-nosed, pale-faced caretaker.

Her mind fretted nervily, swinging inconsistently from one decision to another.

"I must find him," it ran; then recanted. "Why should I find him? I can just go. I expect I'll come across somebody somewhere who'll direct me. And of *course* it was an owl! No, Janet, you don't think that! Stop playing tricks with yourself! You know you can't go yet. Why, you haven't even paid him... I could leave the note on the table, couldn't I? Yes, why not?... You know very well why not!"

She had just decided to brave the elements, this time not on her own behalf, when a figure came round the angle of the wall. At first she thought it was the caretaker, and she breathed a sigh of relief, but then she realized that even the illusions of the snow could not have increased him to this size, and as the newcomer stopped abruptly and stared at her, she stared back in equal astonishment. It was the Scotland Yard detective.

"Get back!" he ordered, sharply.

To ensure her obedience, he advanced and thrust her back unceremoniously into the room. Then he entered after her, glanced quickly around, and closed the door behind him.

"How did *you* get here?" he demanded.

Her nerves on edge, she was not in a mood for cross-examination and she retorted,

"How did *you*?"

"You seem to be a very disobedient young lady," he frowned. "I think I advised you not to follow me?"

"Since I seem to have got here first," she returned, "I suppose you're quite sure you haven't followed me? And what right have you to call me disobedient? I'm not under your orders!"

He apologized impatiently.

"Forgive me, but you'll recall I told you I was on a job, and—"

"Perhaps, if you're more polite, I can help you with the job!"

"I beg your pardon?"

"You heard me. Let's start fresh. A few minutes ago somebody gave a cry out there."

"Are you sure?" he asked.

"Sufficiently. Didn't you hear it?"

"We'll have your story first, if you don't mind. When did you hear the cry?"

"Four or five minutes ago. I can't say exactly."

"But you didn't go out?"

She flushed slightly as she recalled the reason, but she did not give the reason. She answered simply, "No".

"Are you alone in here?"

"Don't you think", she suggested, "it would be quicker if I told you my story in my own words? Unless it would be an even better idea to go out first and look for the trouble? There was a caretaker here when I arrived. He went out while I was trying to get dry. He hasn't come back."

The detective hesitated, then nodded.

"You're right. Will you wait here?"

"If you don't want me to come with you."

"It wouldn't help, and there's no need to put you into unnecessary danger. Where did the cry seem to come from? Which direction?"

"The back."

"Thank you. Stay in this parlour. Don't move out of it." He added, with a faint smile, "You don't mind being obedient this time?"

"I don't mind being sensible," she replied. "I don't call that obedience."

He turned to the door, but paused with his hand on the knob.

"For a couple of hours, you and I sat side by side without saying a word," he remarked. "Since then, we've got to know each other quite well!"

Then he left her.

She returned to the fire and finished her tea, but the comfort had gone out of it, and she found herself starting at shadows and eyeing the doors apprehensively. It would have helped if the detective had had a more appealing personality. She wanted the fiction brand. Apparently there was nothing appealing in the real thing. Romance, sentiment, even common politeness, were lacking. She almost preferred the quaint little horror who had gone out into the snow with his spade and not come back again!

The minutes dragged by. A grandfather clock on the wall should have ticked them away, but it had stopped. Like everything else but the snow. She had stopped herself. She ought to be travelling to West Mallerton, or moving about the gay and bustling house there—unpacking, chatting, laughing, or drinking tea, with milk and sugar in it, out of a delicate, expensive cup!

Instead... She glanced round the musty, dusty parlour, now transferred from a sanctuary to a sort of prison.

"I've had enough of this!" she exclaimed, jumping up suddenly. "I'm going to have a look for myself!"

The front-door opened, and the detective returned.

"Still here?" he observed, superfluously.

"Just," she answered. "Did you find anything?"

He shook his head.

"Then what's your solution?" she asked.

"Quite a simple one, I imagine," he said, "but let me have the rest of your story."

She gave it to him briefly. He listened without interruption. When she had finished, she recalled one point she had forgotten to mention.

"Oh, there's just one more thing," she added, "if it's important. You remember, you left me rather hurriedly after I'd caught you up from the motor-coach?"

"I recall it," he admitted.

"After you left me, I found two sets of footprints. I'm practically sure that, before then, there had only been one set. Your own."

"What about yours?"

"Excluding mine, of course."

He stared at the fire for a few moments, then said,

"Yes, you're right. And the whole thing fits. So here is my side of the story. I told you I was on a job. Your so-called caretaker was the job. I came to this neighbourhood to track him—he broke prison a few days ago, and had been reported in this locality. Just as you and I were talking in that lane, I spotted the fellow dashing by. In effect, I've been chasing him ever since."

"You mean—he came here?" she exclaimed.

"Obviously. Thinking himself safe, he lit a fire and made himself some tea. Then you came in, and gave him the shock of his life. Probably he thought you were me. He posed as a caretaker, played his cards carefully, and as soon as he got a chance, hopped it. Naturally, he extended those ten minutes to half-an-hour! It gave him longer for his getaway."

"I—see," replied Janet, slowly. "Yes, of course. Only—"

"What?"

"That cry?"

"He probably tripped and banged his nose."

"You don't bang your nose in soft snow. I've tried it myself."

"You may bang it against something else, or imagine you're going to."

"And—if he was making his getaway, why didn't he do it at once?"

"I've told you. He had to pose as the caretaker first and make quite sure you weren't suspicious. He didn't want you following him."

"You haven't got me," she corrected him. "What I meant was, why didn't he make his getaway as soon as he left me the last time?"

"How do you know he didn't?"

"Because that cry didn't come till quite a while afterwards. I'd—begun to get dry—had some tea—gone to the front door to listen to those steps outside—returned—unpacked some things from my case—I'm sure it was quite seven or eight minutes."

"I see your point," answered the detective. "It's a good one."

"Then how do you get over it?"

"He may have been delayed through some cause unknown to us, or—the cry may not have come from him at all."

"Who from, then?"

"An owl."

"I thought of that."

"Well, think of it again."

"Yes, but now I'm thinking of something else," she said.

"For a modern young lady," smiled the detective, "you seem to do an unusual amount of thinking. What is your thought this time."

"His spade."

"What about the spade?"

"If he'd just dived in here to get away from you—if he wasn't a caretaker—why was he digging the snow away?"

"Perhaps he was trying to make a funk-hole."

"Did you find the spade?"

"Not a sign of it. And the next?"

She stared at the tip of her toe before putting her last question.

"Can you tell me the way to West Mallerton?"

He laughed. "This time our thoughts match," he said, "for I was just about to suggest myself that you continued your journey. I'm afraid I have a little disappointment for you, though."

"What is it?"

"The direction of West Mallerton. A detective on the job doesn't care to give his own direction away in public, so—when you made your enquiry in the coach, I implied I was going towards West Mallerton when actually I was going precisely the opposite way. You'll remember, I tried to dissuade you from following me, but you were somewhat pig-headed. Return to the high-road, and take the lane on the other side."

"Thank you for not very much," she answered. "What will you do?"

"Light a pipe, take five minutes off by this fire, and then catch my man. Good afternoon."

He opened the front door and gave a stiff little bow.

She took up her suit-case, but paused in the doorway.

"He looked a misery," she said. "What had he done?"

"Eighteen months for housebreaking," replied the detective, "and he has another eighteen to come."

Then she passed out into the snow, and heard the front door close behind her.

She walked towards the gate, slowly and dissatisfied. Before she reached it, something caught her eye. It was a long object on the ground on her right. The falling flakes had almost covered it.

Quickly she glanced back at the cottage. The blue curtain glowed faintly in the firelight behind it. It was in position, and if the detective had drawn it aside to watch her go, he had replaced it. Darting to the object, she bent and examined it. It was a spade.

The detective had said that, for a modern girl, Janet did an unusual amount of thinking. In the next few seconds she justified the assertion, and she acted while she thought. She was back at the gate in a flash. In another she had opened and closed it with a loud click, though whether the click was heard inside the parlour she had no means of knowing. In another, she had slipped behind the cold, snow-laden foliage of a big clump of bushes.

A second assertion of the detective's proved less accurate. He had promised himself five minutes respite in the parlour. He came out in less than two. From her white bower she watched him emerge; watched the smudge of his form, a grim blot in the gloaming, pause in a listening attitude, move swiftly to the gate, peer over, and then slip in front of the bushes towards the spade. He had said he had not found the spade, but he knew where it was! A third assertion tested; and, like the second, disproved.

Risking whatever might be coming to her, Janet crept from her concealment, and was just in time to see the detective pick up the spade and make for the back of the cottage.

She left her suit-case under the bushes and followed him. He walked slowly and cautiously, and once he stopped dead and looked round. If she had not anticipated the movement and dodged behind a large water-butt he would have seen her, with what results she could not guess. Proceeding, the stalker and the stalked reached a back-yard, and what seemed, as far as Janet could make but from the irregular white surface, an untidy kitchen garden or neglected, half-worked field beyond. Here the man suddenly stopped.

He stared at the ground. From where she stood she could not see what he was staring at, but it appeared to be a small mound of snow. She waited breathlessly. Would he never move again? But presently he stopped staring, and began shovelling. He was shovelling snow on to the mound with the spade. After working for three minutes or thereabouts, he ceased the shovelling and again stared at the mound. Then he moved on again.

But Janet did not move. She dreaded to. Through the blinding snow she could just discern the shape of the mound, and it terrified her; yet, mixed with the terror was a queer, compelling anger.

It was not until she feared his slowly-moving form would fade out beyond the mound that she advanced. As she neared the spot the man stopped once more, and began digging in the snow ten yards away. Reaching the mound, she bent over it, and failed to stifle her exclamation at what she saw. The man turned swiftly. The next moment he was confronting her.

"What the hell are you doing here!"

His expression was livid.

"What are *you* doing here?" she answered, astonished at the steadiness of her voice. "And how do you explain—that?"

She did not have to point to the snow-covered shape on the ground. His gaze followed hers.

"I didn't tell you—I didn't want to frighten you," he rasped. "He was digging, and he fell on his spade, cracking his skull."

"And why are *you* digging?"

"To find out why he was! What silly ideas have you got into your head?"

She faced his challenging eyes.

"Shall I tell you?"

"Do you dare?"

He seized her wrist and held it cruelly.

"I suppose you're trying to impress me with your strength," she said, with scorn in her voice, "but isn't that a bit superfluous? You've got a heavy spade—and evidently know how to use it!"

She regretted her remark immediately afterwards, for in a sudden mad frenzy he raised the spade, and she knew it was not the first time he had raised it so that afternoon. But the next moment the implement dropped harmlessly to the ground, and the man himself dropped, too, with a shout of pain.

"Put your hands up, Benson," said a quiet voice behind them, "or the next one won't be in your foot."

Janet turned, weakly. It was the loquacious young man from the coach.

The man on the ground glared helplessly, then obeyed the order as the newcomer advanced. A pair of handcuffs clicked. After that the young man stooped to the mound, brushed aside some of the snow, and stared for a long while at what lay beneath.

"I see—you got Smith," he murmured.

"The damned double-crosser!" muttered Benson.

"You talked too much, eh, before he was let out?"

"Smart, aren't you?"

"And so you broke prison to try and race him to the spot."

"And you were the also ran!" sneered Benson.

"Who nevertheless appears to have won the race," the young man pointed out. "Well, Benson, let's have it. Which of you dug up the necklace you buried before you were caught for the West Mallerton robbery? You or Smith?"

Benson moistened his dry lips.

"I didn't talk then," he growled, "and I'm not talking now!"

"No? Well, I don't expect it matters. The reason I didn't settle you in the coach was because I wanted you first to lead me all the way—and the only mistake I made," he added, turning to Janet for a moment, "was to show myself too soon in that lane when *you* were talking to him. You'll remember, I tried to dissuade you from following him, didn't I?"

"You did," she answered. "I suppose it was you who caused him to vanish so suddenly—and who made that second set of footprints."

"Yes—when I vanished after him," smiled the young man. "But he was too quick for me that time—I lost him for half-an-hour." Addressing Benson again, now without the smile, he went on, "Come along. I gather you've been busy a little way off. Let's see what you've been up to—or got down to!"

Picking up the spade, he forced the unwilling Benson to the spot where he had been digging. Janet followed them slowly, reaching them just as the young man gave an exclamation. He stooped, and picked a long string of pearls from the snow-cleared earth.

"May I have it, please?" she asked.

The young man turned and stared at her. Even the handcuffed thief forgot for a moment the injured foot he was nursing.

"I'm spending Christmas at the house where that robbery occurred," she explained, "and I'd rather like to give my hostess her necklace as a present!"

But the young man, after looking at her oddly, shook his head, and became unprofessionally human.

"For two hours", he said, "I have had the tantalizing experience of sitting behind the back of your head. If you don't mind, I think I'll give your hostess her necklace myself tomorrow morning—using it as a means to a frontal introduction!" The unprofessional moment passed. He added, gravely, "Meanwhile, since the snow is stopping, perhaps you'd better continue with your pleasure—while I continue with my business?"

As Janet resumed her way, this time in the right direction, by all the laws of logic she should have been thinking of an extremely interesting young man with whom, on the morrow, she was to renew her acquaintance. Instead she found herself dwelling on a mound of snow, and a miserable, pathetic little fellow with a squint, for whom no morrow would dawn.

# WHO KILLED FATHER CHRISTMAS?

## Patricia Moyes

Patricia Pakenham-Walsh (known to her friends as Penny) was born in Dublin in 1923. She joined the WAAF in 1939 (adding a year to her age, so the story goes, in order to be accepted) and after the war she worked as Peter Ustinov's assistant for eight years. During that time she married a photographer, John Moyes and her first novel, *Dead Men Don't Ski*, was published by Collins Crime Club in 1959 as by Patricia Moyes. She was an enthusiastic skier and wrote the book while recovering from a serious accident on the slopes; other detective novelists who started writing during a lengthy period of recuperation from illness or injury include Freeman Wills Crofts and G. D. H. Cole.

At around this time, her marriage ended in divorce. Her second husband shared her love of international travel and after he was recruited by the International Monetary Fund, they moved to Washington D.C. Following his retirement they settled in Virgin Gorda in the British Virgin Islands, where she died in 2000, the year after receiving a lifetime achievement award at the Malice Domestic convention, which is held annually in Washington D.C. and where she was for many years a popular figure. In all, she published nineteen novels, all of them featuring the Scotland Yard man Henry Tibbett, whose wife Emmy appears on the first page of the first novel and continues to play a major part throughout the series. This story first appeared in *Whodunnit?* in 1980 and gave its name to a collection of her short fiction published by Crippen & Landru in 1996. It's such a good title that I'm delighted that Doug Greene and Jeffrey Marks of Crippen & Landru were more than happy for me to use it for this book as well.

"GOOD MORNING, MR. BORROWDALE. NIPPY OUT, ISN'T IT? You're in early, I see." Little Miss MacArthur spoke with her usual brisk brightness, which failed to conceal both envy and dislike. She was unpacking a consignment of stout Teddy bears in the stockroom behind the toy department at Barnum and Thrums, the London store. "Smart as ever, Mr. Borrowdale," she added, jealously.

I laid down my curly-brimmed bowler hat and cane and took off my British warm overcoat. I don't mind admitting that I do take pains to dress as well as I can, and for some reason it seems to infuriate the Miss MacArthurs of the world.

She prattled on, "Nice looking, these Teddies, don't you think? Very reasonable, too. Made in Hong Kong, that'll be why. I think I'll take one for my sister's youngest."

The toy department at Barnum's has little to recommend it to anyone over the age of twelve, and normally it is tranquil and little populated. However, at Christmastime it briefly becomes the bustling heart of the great shop, and also provides useful vacation jobs for chaps like me who wish to earn some money during the weeks before the university term begins in January. Gone, I fear, are the days when undergraduates were the gilded youth of England. We all have to work our passages these days, and sometimes it means selling toys.

One advantage of the job is that employees—even temporaries like me—are allowed to buy goods at a considerable discount, which helps with the Christmas gift problem. As a matter of fact, I had already decided to buy a Teddy bear for one of my nephews, and I mentioned as much.

"Well, you'd better take it right away," remarked Miss MacArthur, "because I heard Mr. Harrington say he was taking two, and I think Disaster has her eye on one." Disaster was the unfortunate but inevitable nickname of Miss Aster, who had been with the store for thirty-one years but still made mistakes with her stockbook. I felt sorry for the old girl. I had overheard a conversation between Mr. Harrington, the department manager, and Mr. Andrews, the deputy store manager, and so I knew—but Disaster didn't—that she would be getting the sack as soon as the Christmas rush was over.

Meanwhile, Miss MacArthur was arranging the bears on a shelf. They sat there in grinning rows, brown and woolly, with boot-button eyes and red ribbons round their necks.

It was then that Father Christmas came in. He'd been in the cloakroom changing into his costume—white beard, red nose, and all. His name was Bert Denman. He was a cheery soul who got on well with the kids, and he'd had the Father Christmas job at Barnum's each of the three years I'd been selling there. Now he was carrying his sack, which he filled every morning from the cheap items in the stockroom. A visit to Father Christmas cost 50 pence, so naturally the gift that was fished out of the sack couldn't be worth more than 20 pence. However, to my surprise, he went straight over to the row of Teddy bears and picked one off the shelf. For some reason, he chose the only one with a blue instead of a red ribbon.

Miss MacArthur was on to him in an instant. "What d'you think you're doing, Mr. Denman? Those Teddies aren't in your line at all— much too dear. One pound ninety, they are."

Father Christmas did not answer, and suddenly I realized that it was not Bert Denman under the red robe. "Wait a minute," I said. "Who are you? You're not our Father Christmas."

He turned to face me, the Teddy bear in his hand. "That's all right," he said. "Charlie Burrows is my name. I live in the same lodging house with Bert Denman. He was taken poorly last night, and I'm standing in for him."

"Well," said Miss MacArthur. "How very odd. Does Mr. Harrington know?"

"Of course he does," said Father Christmas.

As if on cue, Mr. Harrington himself came hurrying into the stockroom. He always hurried everywhere, preceded by his small black moustache. He said, "Ah, there you are, Burrows. Fill up your sack, and I'll explain the job to you. Denman told you about the Teddy bear, did he?"

"Yes, Mr. Harrington."

"Father Christmas can't give away an expensive bear like that, Mr. Harrington," Miss MacArthur objected.

"Now, now, Miss MacArthur, it's all arranged," said Harrington fussily. "A customer came in yesterday and made a special request that Father Christmas should give his small daughter a Teddy bear this morning. I knew this consignment was due on the shelves, so I promised him one. It's been paid for. The important thing, Burrows, is to remember the child's name. It's... er... I have it written down somewhere."

"Annabel Whitworth," said Father Christmas. "Four years old, fair hair, will be brought in by her mother."

"I see that Denman briefed you well," said Mr. Harrington, with an icy smile. "Well, now, I'll collect two bears for myself—one for my son and one for my neighbour's boy—and then I'll show you the booth."

Miss Aster arrived just then. She and Miss MacArthur finished uncrating the bears and took one out to put on display next to a female doll that, among other endearing traits, actually wet its diaper. Mr. Harrington led our surrogate Father Christmas to his small canvas booth, and the rest of us busied and braced ourselves for the moment when the great glass doors opened and the floodtide was let in.

The toy department of a big store on December 23 is no place for weaklings.

It is curious that even such an apparently random stream of humanity as Christmas shoppers displays a pattern of behaviour. The earliest arrivals in the toy department are office workers on their way to their jobs. The actual toddlers, bent on an interview with Father Christmas, do not appear until their mothers have had time to wash up breakfast, have a bit of a go around the house, and catch the bus from Kensington or the tube from Uxbridge.

On that particular morning it was just twenty-eight minutes past ten when I saw Disaster, who was sitting in a decorated cash desk labelled "The Elfin Grove," take 50 pence from the first parent to usher her child into Santa's booth. For about two minutes the mother waited, chatting quietly with Disaster. Then a loudly wailing infant emerged from the booth.

The mother snatched her up, and—with that sixth sense that mothers everywhere seem to develop—interpreted the incoherent screams. "She says that Father Christmas won't talk to her. She says he's asleep."

It was clearly an emergency, even if a minor one, and Disaster was already showing signs of panic. I excused myself from my customer—a middle-aged gentleman who was playing with an electric train set—and went over to see what I could do. By then, the mother was indignant.

"Fifty pence and the old man sound asleep and drunk as like as not, and at half-past ten in the morning. Disgraceful, I call it. And here's poor little Poppy what had been looking forward to—"

I rushed into Father Christmas's booth. The man who called himself Charlie Burrows was slumped forward in his chair, looking for all the world as if he were asleep; but when I shook him, his head lolled horribly, and it was obvious that he was more than sleeping. The red robe concealed the blood until it made my hand sticky. Father Christmas had been stabbed in the back, and he was certainly dead.

I acted as fast as I could. First of all, I told Disaster to put up the *CLOSED* sign outside Santa's booth. Then I smoothed down Poppy's mother by leading her to a counter where I told her she could select any toy up to one pound and have it free. Under pretext of keeping records, I got her name and address. Finally I cornered Mr. Harrington in his office and told him the news.

I thought he was going to faint. "Dead? Murdered? Are you sure, Mr. Borrowdale?"

"Quite sure, I'm afraid. You'd better telephone the police, Mr. Harrington."

"The police! In Barnum's! What a terrible thing! I'll telephone the deputy store manager first and *then* the police."

As a matter of fact, the police were surprisingly quick and discreet. A plainclothes detective superintendent and his sergeant, a photographer, and the police doctor arrived, not in a posse, but as individuals, unnoticed among the crowd. They assembled in the booth, where the deputy manager—Mr. Andrews—and Mr. Harrington and I were waiting for them.

The superintendent introduced himself—his name was Armitage—and inspected the body with an expression of cold fury on his face that I couldn't quite understand, although the reason became clear later. He said very little. After some tedious formalities Armitage indicated that the body might be removed.

"What's the least conspicuous way to do it?" he asked.

"You can take him out through the back of the booth," I said. "The canvas overlaps right behind Santa's chair. The door to the staff quarters and the stockroom is just opposite, and from there you can take the service lift to the goods entrance in the mews."

The doctor and the photographer between them carried off their grim burden on a collapsible stretcher, and Superintendent Armitage began asking questions about the arrangements in the Father Christmas booth. I did the explaining, since Mr. Harrington seemed to be verging on hysteria.

Customers paid their 50 pence to Disaster in the Elfin Grove, and then the child—usually alone—was propelled through the door of the booth and into the presence of Father Christmas, who sat in his canvas-backed director's chair on a small dais facing the entrance, with his sack of toys beside him. The child climbed onto his knee, whispered its Christmas washes, and was rewarded with a few friendly words and a small gift from Santa's sack.

What was not obvious to the clientele was the back entrance to the booth, which enabled Father Christmas to slip in and out unobserved. He usually had his coffee break at about 11:15, unless there was a very heavy rush of business. Disaster would pick a moment when custom seemed slow, put up the *CLOSED* notice, and inform Bert that he could take a few minutes off. When he returned, he pressed a button by his chair that rang a buzzer in the cashier's booth. Down would come the notice, and Santa was in business again.

Before Superintendent Armitage could comment on my remarks, Mr. Harrington broke into a sort of despairing wail. "It must have been one of the customers!" he cried.

"I don't think so, sir," said Armitage. "This is an inside job. He was stabbed in the back with a long thin blade of some sort. The murderer must have opened the back flap and stabbed him clean through the canvas back of his chair. That must have been someone who knew the exact arrangements. The murderer then used the back way to enter the booth—"

"I don't see how you can say that!" Harrington's voice was rising dangerously. "If the man was stabbed from outside, what makes you think anybody came into the booth?"

"I'll explain that in a minute, sir."

Ignoring Armitage, Harrington went on. "In any case, he wasn't our regular Father Christmas! None of us had ever seen him before. Why on earth would anybody kill a man that nobody knew?"

Armitage and the deputy manager exchanged glances. Then Armitage said, "I knew him, sir. Very well. Charlie Burrows was one of our finest plainclothes narcotics officers."

Mr. Harrington had gone green. "You mean he was a policeman?"

"Exactly, sir. I'd better explain. A little time ago we got a tipoff from an informer that an important consignment of high-grade heroin was to be smuggled in from Hong Kong in a consignment of Christmas toys. Teddy bears, in fact. The drug was to be in the Barnum and Thrums carton, hidden inside a particular Teddy bear, which would be distinguished by having a blue ribbon around its neck instead of a red one."

"Surely," I said, "you couldn't get what you call an important consignment inside one Teddy bear, even a big one."

Armitage sighed. "Shows you aren't familiar with the drug scene, sir," he said, "Why, half a pound of pure high-grade heroin is worth a fortune on the streets."

With a show of bluster Harrington said, "If you knew this, Superintendent, why didn't you simply intercept the consignment and confiscate the drug? Look at the trouble that's been—"

Armitage interrupted him. "If you'd just hear me out, sir. What I've told you was the sum total of our information. We didn't know who in Barnum's was going to pick up the heroin, or how or where it was to be disposed of. We're more interested in getting the people— the pushers—than confiscating the cargo. So I had a word with Mr. Andrews here, and he kindly agreed to let Charlie take on the Father Christmas job. And Charlie set a little trap. Unfortunately, he paid for it with his life." There was an awkward silence.

He went on. "Mr. Andrews told us that the consignment had arrived and was to be unpacked today. We know that staff get first pick, as it were, at new stock, and we were naturally interested to see who would select the bear with the blue ribbon. It was Charlie's own idea to concoct a story about a special present for a little girl—"

"You mean, that wasn't true?" Harrington was outraged. "But I spoke to the customer myself!"

"Yes, sir. That's to say, you spoke to another of our people, who was posing as the little girl's father."

"You're very thorough," Harrington said.

"Yes, sir. Thank you, sir. Well, as I was saying, Charlie made a point of selecting the bear with the blue ribbon and taking it off in his sack. He knew that whoever was picking up the drop would have to come and get it—or try to. You see, if we'd just allowed one of the staff to select it, that person could simply have said that it was pure coincidence—blue was such a pretty colour. Difficult to prove criminal knowledge. You understand?"

Nobody said anything. With quite a sense of dramatic effect Armitage reached down into Santa's sack and pulled out a Teddy bear. It had a blue ribbon round its neck.

In a voice tense with strain Mr. Andrews said, "So the murderer didn't get away with the heroin. I thought you said—"

Superintendent Armitage produced a knife from his pocket. "We'll see," he said. "With your permission, I'm going to open this bear."

"Of course."

The knife ripped through the nobbly brown fabric, and a lot of stuffing fell out. Nothing else. Armitage made a good job of it. By the time he had finished, the bear was in shreds: and nothing had emerged from its interior except kapok.

Armitage surveyed the wreckage with a sort of bleak satisfaction. Suddenly brisk, he said, "Now. Which staff members took bears from the stockroom this morning?"

"I did," I said at once.

"Anybody else?"

There was a silence. I said, "I believe you took two, didn't you, Mr. Harrington?"

"I... em... yes, now that you mention it."

"Miss MacArthur took one," I said. "It was she who unpacked the carton. She said that Dis—Miss Aster—was going to take one."

"I see." Armitage was making notes. "I presume you each signed for your purchases, and that the bears are now with your things in the staff cloakroom." Without waiting for an answer he turned to me. "How many of these people saw Burrows select the bear with the blue ribbon?"

"All of us," I said. "Isn't that so, Mr. Harrington?"

Harrington just nodded. He looked sick.

"Well, then," said Armitage, "I shall have to inspect all the bears that you people removed from the stockroom."

There was an element of black humour in the parade of the Teddies, with their inane grins and knowing, beady eyes: but as one after the other was dismembered, nothing more sensational was revealed than a growing pile of kapok. The next step was to check the stockbook numbers—and sure enough, one bear was missing.

It was actually Armitage's sergeant who found it. It had been ripped open and shoved behind a pile of boxes in the stockroom in a hasty attempt at concealment. There was no ribbon round its neck, and it was constructed very differently from the others. The kapok merely served as a thin layer of stuffing between the fabric skin and a spherical womb of pink plastic in the toy's centre. This plastic had been cut open and was empty. It was abundantly clear what it must have contained.

"Well," said the Superintendent, "it's obvious what happened. The murderer stabbed Burrows, slipped into the booth, and substituted an innocent Teddy bear for the loaded one, at the same time changing the neck ribbon. But he—or she—didn't dare try walking out of the store with the bear, not after a murder. So, before Charlie's body was found, the murderer dismembered the bear, took out the heroin, and hid it." He sighed again. "I'm afraid this means a body search. I'll call the Yard for a police matron for the ladies."

It was all highly undignified and tedious, and poor old Disaster nearly had a seizure, despite the fact that the police matron seemed a thoroughly nice and kind woman. When it was all over, however, and our persons and clothing had been practically turned inside out, still nothing had been found. The four of us were required to wait in the staff restroom while exhaustive searches were made for both the heroin and the weapon.

Disaster was in tears, Miss MacArthur was loudly indignant and threatened to sue the police for false arrest, and Mr. Harrington developed what he called a nervous stomach, on account, he said, of the way the toy department was being left understaffed and unsupervised on one of the busiest days of the year.

At long last Superintendent Armitage came in. He said, "Nothing. Abso-bloody-lutely nothing. Well, I can't keep you people here indefinitely. I suggest you all go out and get yourselves some lunch." He sounded very tired and cross and almost human.

With considerable relief we prepared to leave the staffroom. Only Mr. Harrington announced that he felt too ill to eat anything, and that he would remain in the department. The Misses MacArthur and Aster left together. I put on my coat and took the escalator down to the ground floor, among the burdened, chattering crowd.

I was out in the brisk air of the street when I heard Armitage's voice behind me.

"Just one moment, if you please, Mr. Borrowdale."

I turned. "Yes, Superintendent. Can I help you?"

"You're up at the university, aren't you, sir? Just taken a temporary job at Barnum's for the vacation?"

"That's right."

"Do quite a bit of fencing, don't you?"

He had my cane out of my hand before I knew what was happening. The sergeant, an extraordinarily tough and unattractive character, showed surprising dexterity and speed in getting an arm grip on me. Armitage had unscrewed the top of the cane, and was whistling in a quiet, appreciative manner. "Very nice. Very nice little sword stick. Something like a stiletto. I don't suppose Charlie felt a thing."

"Now, look here," I said. "You can't make insinuations like that. Just because I'm known as a bit of dandy, and carry a sword stick, that's no reason—"

"A dandy, eh?" said Armitage thoughtfully. He looked me up and down in a curious manner, as if he thought something was missing.

It was at that moment that Miss MacArthur suddenly appeared round the corner of the building.

"Oh, Mr. Borrowdale, look what I found! Lying down in the mews by the goods entrance! It must have fallen out of the staffroom window! Lucky I've got sharp eyes—it was behind a rubbish bin, I might easily have missed it!" And she handed me my bowler hat.

That is to say, she would have done if Armitage hadn't intercepted it. It didn't take him more than five seconds to find the packages of white powder hidden between the hard shell of the hat and the oiled-silk lining.

Armitage said, "So you were going to peddle this stuff to young men and women at the university, were you? Charming, I must say. Now you can come back to the Yard and tell us all about your employers—if you want a chance at saving your own neck, that is."

Miss MacArthur was goggling at me. "Oh, Mr. Borrowdale!" she squeaked. "Have I gone and done something wrong?"

I never did like Miss MacArthur.

## DEATH AT CHRISTMAS

# Glyn Daniel

Glyn Daniel (1914–86) was a Welsh archaeologist, scientist, and academic. Born in Lampeter Velfrey, he went up to St. John's College, Cambridge in 1932 and after graduating with a First, he remained at the college for the rest of his career. Among those he taught was Jessica Mann, who later became a successful crime writer and critic; she contributed an article about crime fiction by or concerning dons to a book of essays compiled in Daniel's honour. He wrote two detective novels. *The Cambridge Murders* was published in 1945 under the pen-name Dilwyn Rees. In 1954, *Welcome Death* appeared under his own name. Both books feature the archaeologist Sir Richard Cherrington, a character inspired by Sir Mortimer Wheeler, who—like Daniel—became a well-known TV personality, noted for popularizing archaeology in the 1950s. Unfortunately, Daniel felt dissatisfied with *Welcome Death* and moved away from the genre.

Or so I thought until I discovered this enjoyable story. I was pleasantly surprised, when researching potential material for the British Library Crime Classics anthology *Crimes of Cymru*, to find "Death at Christmas" tucked away in the anthology *Welsh Short Stories*, edited by George Ewart Evans and published in 1959. There is no record of the story in the usual sources of information about short mysteries; my guess is that Evans encouraged Daniel to contribute to his collection, and this story was the result.

I SUPPOSE I SHOULD BEGIN BY EXPLAINING WHO I AM. YOU WILL then be better able to understand the curious events that occurred last Christmas. I've said *understand* and *curious*—but perhaps these are not very happily chosen words. Curious is certainly an understatement—a pleasant way of saying that I can really offer no explanation of what happened on Christmas Night last year, a way of reassuring myself—for if I am to keep my peace of mind I must resolutely refuse to believe what seemed to be the truth. There are times, it seems to me, when the truth is too horrible to contemplate. It must be concealed. You think this is cowardly? Wait a minute. Let me tell you what happened. You may not understand, you may not wish to understand; but at least you will sympathize with me. And it will help me to tell you. I have kept silent for too long. Now that I am telling my story, I might as well tell as many people as possible—might as well broadcast those terrifying moments in that cold Christmas night of last winter.

My name is Dilwyn Rees. What? That's my name as far as you are concerned. You will see as I go on that I can't really reveal my identity. I don't think it would be wise. I'm a don, and there again I don't think it would be helpful if I told you whether I am at Oxford or Cambridge. I'm a bachelor and I live in college. Some colleges close down at Christmas. We don't, and last Christmas night a small group of us—six in fact, the Master and five Fellows—dined together in the Parlour. It was a good dinner—the food was traditional turkey and plum pudding—but we drank some of our very best pre-war wines: champagne and port. Everyone was in good form and in very high spirits—everyone that is, except Dickson. Peter Dickson. Dickson was—I wish I could say *is*, how I wish I could say that!—he was our Fellow in Engineering and our Third Bursar. He was an extremely good teacher and a very efficient bursar. I hadn't known him much before the war—he was married and lived in the country. But soon after I came back to the college after the war—it would be somewhere early in 1947—his wife died. A car accident late at night: she was killed but he escaped uninjured. After that I saw a lot of him. He kept on his house, living in it at weekends and in vacation, but sleeping in his college rooms in term-time.

I was sorry for him—so I think were we all. His rooms were on the next staircase to mine. We slipped into the habit of looking in on each other late at night for a cup of tea or a glass of whisky. I got to know Peter well. We talked of many things—he was a man of wide interests—but never his wife. He never mentioned her and naturally I didn't bring up the subject. His silence didn't strike me as odd at the time. I thought he was deliberately keeping his emotions under control. And so he was. The point is what were those emotions? But I'm getting too far ahead in my story.

I was telling you about the dinner. We sat drinking port round the fire after the tables had been cleared. Then after a while the Master suggested a rubber of bridge. I don't play, and Peter Dickson didn't like the game. The other four played. I suggested to Peter that he should come to my rooms. We left the Parlour and walked across the court. You'll remember it was a bitterly cold night—it had been a fresh sunny cold day but from tea-time onwards it had been getting steadily colder. "It feels like snow," I said to Peter—or something like that. I can't remember my exact words. I do remember pulling my overcoat around me, and Peter saying: "I hope it doesn't snow. I don't want to drive home in a snowstorm."

"But surely you're staying in College tonight?" I said.

"No; I've got to go home." His voice was firm and I didn't mention the subject again until we were up in my rooms. I threw some logs and some pine-cones on the fire. We soon had a bright blaze. I poured out some generous helpings in whisky. "This'll keep the cold out," I said. "Here's to your good health." We chinked our glasses. I little thought at that moment I should never drink with him again.

We sat by the fire in silence. Then I tried to persuade him not to drive back to his house that night. The village in which he lived was nearly ten miles from the college gates; his house was on top of a steep hill outside the village—a lonely spot on a dark cold night. For a moment he said nothing. Then he turned to me. "Dilwyn," he said, "I could give you a host of reasons why I should go home tonight and you'd believe them. I suppose I know you well enough for me not to give you any reason at all. But I'll tell you the truth. I think I know you as well as that. And I want to tell someone."

And then in a flash I knew what was coming. How I knew it's quite impossible to tell, but I did know. At that moment I knew he was going to talk to me about his wife. And I was embarrassed. I felt a slight shiver go down my back. I felt afraid, and was glad that I did not have to look into his face, glad that I had only turned on the reading lamps. I have often wondered—looking back on that evening as God knows, I have done many times—why I felt fear at that moment. Had my intuition reached some fact which even now my reason denies? Perhaps you can answer that question, better than I can.

I looked across at Peter Dickson. His face was in shadow and he spoke slowly. "It's this way," he began; "I must go home. Tonight is an anniversary of mine. A special anniversary. You might almost say a very special anniversary. You see it was two years ago tonight that Anna, my wife, was killed. You'd never met Anna had you? Well, we'd been dining in the town and been on to a party. It was late—the roads were frozen—it was snowing. Anna was driving. You know that my house is on top of the hill outside the village. The road to it curves round the edge of a chalk pit; it's the only way to the house. Anna was driving fast: we'd had rather a lot to drink at the party, though of course we weren't drunk. The car skidded and struck a tree and fell over the edge of the pit. I must have been thrown out when the car struck the tree. When I came to I was lying on the bank, bruised and dazed. We found Anna—still in the car—in the bottom of the pit. She was dead, of course."

He stopped speaking. I was silent for a while then I said: "What a terrible story! I am sorry. You see I never heard. It all happened while I was still away."

I marvelled at his self-control. His voice had not betrayed any emotion as he told me in those few brief sentences of the death of his wife. He had not as much as shaded his eyes from the visual picture which might have formed in the flames of the fire. It was as though he had been reciting some story he had learnt by heart—a story that concerned not himself, but other people.

"Every year of our married life", he went on, paying no attention to what I had said, "we had brewed ourselves at midnight on Christmas night a special bowl of hot punch. It was a custom with us. The first time we did it—we were very young then, young, imaginative and a bit sentimental perhaps—we pledged ourselves that if anything should happen to one of us, the other would go on brewing and drinking the punch on Christmas night. We even said—it was a silly thing to have said—that at such occasions we would be reunited again in the spirit."

I was not reassured by what he said. I began to think that my instinctive fear was justified. But my curiosity got the better of my fears. "And last Christmas?" I asked.

"I was coming to that," he went on. "Last Christmas was the first anniversary of my wife's death. I dined in College just like tonight and I drove home alone. A most extraordinary thing happened to me as I was nearly home. I wasn't tight or tired or anything like that. But as I drove up the hill from the village and passed the place where we had our accident, I had an almost irresistible impulse to swing the wheel round and to drive over the edge into the chalk pit. I know it sounds stupid here by the fire in your warm hospitable rooms; but, believe me, it was different out there in the cold and dark on that lonely narrow road. It seemed as though another hand was tugging at the steering wheel. Yet there was no one there. I had to grit my teeth and grip the wheel as tightly as I could with both hands. It seemed to be turning against my wishes. I shouted and wrenched at the wheel. The moment passed. I got home safely. But my hands were shaking and I was white with fright. I looked at myself in the mirror in the hall; I was like a ghost—or like a man who has met a ghost."

He paused. A log on the fire turned over and spluttered.

"And that wasn't the end," he said. "I had put all the ingredients for the punch in the study. I hastily brewed it, adding an extra ration of rum to steady my nerves. I reckoned that I needed it. As I sat by the fire, sipping the punch, I began to get warm again. I persuaded myself that my nerves were in a thoroughly bad condition, that I needed a holiday. And then, an even more frightening thing happened. Very slowly, as I sat looking in the fire, I became aware that I was not alone. There was someone else in the room. This may sound foolish to you but it's true; I knew that I was no longer alone. It was as though my heart had stopped beating. A shiver ran down my back; my flesh began to creep. I have lived alone since Anna died, except for a woman in the village who comes to char for me in the mornings. I knew that she had a key but I also knew that I had locked the front door when I came in—locked it and bolted it securely on the inside. The house was empty; there couldn't be anyone else in the room. Leastways, not another human being. In a flash I remembered the pact I had made with my wife and was frightened as I have never been before. For a while I dared not turn round. The something in the room—the presence, whatever it was—seemed to come nearer and nearer. I could bear it no longer. By a great effort of will I jumped up from my chair and turned round: 'Anna,' I shouted, 'Anna...'

"But there was nothing there. The room was empty. I shaded my eyes and peered around. I searched the dark corners of the room. Nothing. I mopped my face, telling myself that it was all nerves. And then, in the distance, I heard the front door shut with a bang. I hurried down the passage into the hall and pulled at the door. It was as I had left it—locked on the inside and fastened with a chain. It could not have been opened. I unlocked it and looked outside. It had stopped snowing. A carpet of snow covered the garden and the path. Nowhere were there the marks of any footsteps."

His voice stopped. I poured out some more whisky. I noticed my own hands were shaking. Dickson helped himself to soda. His hands were steady. He seemed unaffected and I marvelled again at his composure. He drank his whisky quickly and got up. "So you see why I must go home," he said. "I must go and keep a date with my wife." There was a false note in his voice. "You're not serious, surely?" I said. He was putting on his coat. "Serious?" he said, and his voice for the first time that night had an intensity that alarmed me. "I wish I knew, Dilwyn, I wish I knew. Maybe it was only nerves."

I saw that his mind was made up and I said no more. I went down with him to his car and saw him out of the college grounds. It was still bitterly cold, but so far no snow had fallen. "Good night," I said to him; "Good night, Peter, and a Happy Christmas." Of course the moment I said this, I knew it was a silly thing to say; but I couldn't have prevented myself. He didn't smile. "Good night, old boy," he said, and drove off. I heard his car stop at the traffic lights, and then drive away across the town. The night was still. I shivered as I walked back to my rooms. The bridge party was over: there were no lights in the

Parlour. I would dearly have loved some company at that moment; but there was a light on only in the Master's study and I did not feel like disturbing him.

I went back to my rooms and locked my outer door securely. I didn't go to bed at once. I felt wide awake. At first I thought over Peter Dickson's extraordinary story. I didn't know what to make of it. I picked up a book—several books—and tried to read; but with very little success. I couldn't keep my mind on what I was reading. My thoughts kept coming back to Dickson, and I felt apprehensive. Tonight, I thought, he might in the same way, have a fit of nerves as he drives up the hill past the chalk pit, and plunge headlong over the cliff-edge. For of course it was, I told myself, all nerves.

Impulsively I took up the telephone and dialled Dickson's number. It was over half an hour from the time I had seen him off; long enough, I calculated for him to drive home. He drove fast and there would be little traffic. That is, if he had got home. The telephone went on ringing. I had a sudden vision of it ringing on and on in the empty house. Then it stopped and I heard a voice—Dickson's voice—say: "Hello."

"Thank God you're safe!" I said.

"Hello? Who's that?" he asked.

I explained it was me and that I had only rung up to see if he was safe. I laughed with nervous relief. "Your story frightened me so," I said, "that I had a picture of you tonight driving over the edge of the chalk pit."

"Not on your life!" His voice was cheery: "I came quickly home without a care in the world. We raced up the hill. Don't pay any attention to what I said. It was all nerves. I really shouldn't have bothered you with my story."

I told him I had appreciated his confidences. "Ah well," he said, "nice of you to ring up. I must go back into my study by the fire and brew myself some punch." And he rang off.

I put the receiver down. Somehow I should have been more relieved if he hadn't mentioned the punch. It brought back his story too vividly to me. I went to bed. It took me a long time to get to sleep, and when I did, I slept fitfully. Once I woke out of a nightmare, a horrible nightmare in which I was a prisoner in a room that was locked from the inside; I heard steps approaching the door, and slowly, the locked door began to open. I woke with a start just as the door was about to open, wide enough for me to see who was the other side. My forehead and hands were clammy with sweat.

It was a fresh crisp morning on Boxing Day. The snow had been slight. I ate my breakfast, got out the car and drove to the Boxing Day meet. I do not often ride to hounds—somehow I don't seem to be able to manage to make the time—but I try not to miss the Boxing Day meet, if the weather is good. I had a good day's hunting and I must say that I never gave Peter Dickson a thought the whole day long, until I drove the car back in the dark and put it away in the college garage. I wondered how he would meet me at dinner that night after his unusual confidences. When I got to my rooms I found a note from the Master. This is what it said: "Will you please come and see me in the Lodge as soon as you return? This is very urgent."

I went across to the Lodge at once. The Master was in his study. He greeted me abruptly.

"You haven't heard?" he said.

"I've heard nothing," I said. "I've been in the country since breakfast-time. Anything serious?"

"Yes. Peter Dickson is dead."

"How did he die?" I asked quickly. At once I was convinced that he had crashed in his car into the chalk pit. But how was it that I had talked to him. Had I talked to a ghost?

"It was an accident," the Master said. "He seems to have gone home from College late last night and was brewing himself some punch in his study. Apparently he slipped on the hearthrug, and fell into the fireplace. Poor fellow!"

I said nothing and the Master went on: "I sent for you because you were his friend, and because I want you to take over his work as Third Bursar."

"I see," I said. I was dazed. "Of course, anything I can do to help you for the time being."

The Master poured me out a glass of sherry. Then he turned to me. "Why", he asked, "did you say, 'How did he die?' just now? Wasn't that a curious first question?" I told him then what Dickson had told me the previous night: the car accident, the anniversary punch-drinking, his experiences on the previous Christmas night. The Master listened to me carefully. His face was grave. When I had finished there was a pause and then he spoke.

"There are two things I want to say here and now, Dilwyn," he said, "and afterwards I do not wish you to raise these topics with me. Now, first of all, I think you should know that in my mind there's no doubt that Dickson murdered his wife."

I started as though to say something, but he lifted up his hand and went on: "First hear what I have to say. You were away during the war and for over a year afterwards," he said. "You don't know what went on. I think Dickson and his wife had realized they were badly matched even before the war came. They had no children. During the war Anna Dickson stayed here—he was off in the Navy. She did some secretarial work at the aerodrome and had a very good time—that's a useful phrase. That she was unfaithful to Dickson on many occasions I have no doubt. That after the war when he came back, he knew this, I also have no doubt. She wouldn't divorce him, nor provide the evidence for him to divorce her. *De mortuis* and all that; and I know Dickson was a colleague of ours—but I believe he took a dangerous way out of what was to him an intolerable situation."

"But how could he have done it? How could he have faked the accident, if that's what you mean?" I asked.

"Apparently these things are not too difficult. Anna Dickson certainly died from a blow on the top of her head; but whether it was given before the car left the road or when it crashed into the bottom of the chalk pit, the doctors of course couldn't say. She was too badly damaged for the doctors really to make much of her, you know. But there were two curious things which were noted at the time. Dickson says that Anna was driving the car at the time of the accident, but when they left the party, *he* was driving the car. Actually someone thought they saw the car go through the village with Dickson driving; but they couldn't be sure about it. Now why should they have changed drivers so near home—that is if they did change? The second thing the police were worried about: the marks on the tree were there all right, but they didn't seem such as would have been made by a car travelling at great speed. Unfortunately—or fortunately for Dickson—it was snowing heavily and the skid marks, if they ever existed, were covered by snow. It's my view that Dickson stopped the car, killed his wife, crashed the car into the tree, then put her in the driving seat, put the car in top gear, and pushed it over the edge. But of course these things can never be proved. The police knew they hadn't the shadow of a case against Dickson. Those of us who suspected his story soon forgot our suspicions; but in view of what you have told me I think I should tell you what I think."

He paused. I gazed at him not knowing what to think. I was still grasping my empty sherry glass in my hand. "The other thing I wanted to say was this." He spoke deliberately. "Dickson died last night of heart failure. Heart failure was the cause of death. He was dead when he fell backwards into the fireplace. His burns were after death—not the cause of death. That's what the doctors told me. Now, of course," he went on, "heart failure may occur to anyone."

"But there was nothing the matter with Dickson's heart!"

"As far as I know, no; but then very few of us—thank God—really know our own medical histories."

"You say he fell backwards into the fire," I persisted.

"Yes."

I paused and then I said—I couldn't prevent myself saying it: "Heart failure may occur due to sudden shock, mayn't it?"

"Yes."

"You say his wife's body was very badly mutilated by the accident?"

"What are you driving at?"

"I was just thinking," I said slowly. "Let us suppose that some of what Peter Dickson told me last night was true. Can't you see him sitting by the fire alone in the house? The house is locked from inside—he is quite alone; and then suddenly the front door flies open—the front door which he has just padlocked. He starts up and listens as very slowly footsteps, dragging footsteps, come along the passage towards the study door. They get nearer and nearer and there is nothing he can do about it. They stop outside the door and then slowly, very slowly, the door begins to open. He looks across the lighted room to the darkened passage, and what he sees standing in the doorway causes his heart to stop beating with mortal fright."

I had put into words my thoughts and I stopped speaking. There was quiet in the room except for the ticking of the clock on the mantel-piece. "Imagination," said the Master after a while, "imagination. You must not let your imagination run away with you. Dickson suffered from hallucinations, that's clear. One might even say that he went out of his way to encourage them. Maybe his conscience gave him no peace. I shouldn't be surprised if that was so. But that's no reason why you should deliberately foster hallucinations yourself. The sort of things you are imagining, don't happen you know." But the tone of his voice had less confidence than his words.

I found that Dickson had made me sole executor of his estate. I have had to go all through his papers in the last few months; but I have found nothing that would throw the slightest light on the mysterious circumstances of his wife's death or of his own. As far as I know most people have now forgotten about them both by now—except me. I sometimes have that terrible nightmare that I first had last Christmas night: I hear footsteps, dragging footsteps, coming slowly towards me along a passage—I am in a small room and I have securely locked the door—then slowly the locked door begins to open. I awake in a sweat. Once I screamed out aloud in the night. The Master said it is all hallucinations and of course he is right. He is a much wiser man than I am. Dickson said it was nerves. Nerves. But then Dickson is dead.

I have had to visit the Dickson house frequently while settling up the estate. But I always leave before it gets dark. And nothing would induce me to stay there. Nothing I say. Nothing. You do understand, don't you? One mustn't encourage one's hallucinations. What I say is: let the dead rest—if only they will.

# SCOTLAND YARD'S CHRISTMAS

## *John Dickson Carr*

John Dickson Carr (1906–1977) was one of the major writers of "the Golden Age of Murder" between the world wars, and a brilliant exponent of the locked room mystery. His first four novels featuring Henri Bencolin have been republished in the Crime Classics series, as have notable books such as *The Black Spectacles*, *He Who Whispers* and *The Seat of the Scornful*.

This particular story earns its place here in part because it is a literary curiosity. It was first published in *Weekend*, December 25–29 1957, as "Detective's Day Off", but we are using Carr's original title. The story features an intriguing impossible vanishing trick in duplicate. As Carr's biographer Douglas G. Greene has said, the story does "have a number of distinctively Carrian touches, including an attempt to solve a puzzle propounded to him years earlier by [fellow crime writer and amateur magician] Clayton Rawson—how can a person disappear from a telephone booth that is constantly under observation? I suspect that the publishers cut Carr's typescript drastically; especially the solution, which (most unlike Carr's work) is short and unclear." Greene has explained that the story had only been reprinted twice since its first appearance—by Jack Adrian in *Crime at Christmas* and by Greene himself in *Merrivale, March, and Murder*. Intriguingly, both editors felt it necessary to add paragraphs to the original printed story to clear up the solution. I'm grateful to Doug Greene, unquestionably the world's leading expert on Carr, for permission to use *his* version of the story's ending.

W ITH CHRISTMAS ONLY THREE DAYS AWAY, MEN AND WOMEN throughout London were celebrating the season of joy and goodwill by elbowing and pushing each other ferociously through every shop and department store.

And at Omnium's, the giant store in Oxford Street, it was worse than anywhere.

Outside, past lanes of lighted windows, festive snowflakes sifted from a darkening sky. A loudspeaker van blared "Hark the Herald Angels Sing" to crowds struggling in slush.

Inside, frantic shoppers assailed the gift counters, and assaulted each other in the process.

Their noise was a shuffle and roar. Their aroma was a steam of wet overcoats.

And at the entrance to Toyland on the fifth floor stood a pretty, fair-haired girl. Her loving glance at the tall, handsome man beside her was clouded with annoyance. The little boy, clutching his hand, jumped up and down in a desperate attempt to break his far-away look of intense preoccupation.

The girl said: "For heaven's sake, Bob, what is the matter with you?"

Detective Superintendent Robert Pollard for a moment did not reply. Officially off duty, he was still thinking hard about the case he had left for others to solve at New Scotland Yard—so that he could take his fiancée, Elsa Rawson, shopping at Omnium's, and her six-year-old nephew, Tommy, to the toyfair.

"Bob," said the girl again, in exasperation, "do look as though you're enjoying yourself."

"I've just thought," said Bob, returning once again to the shopping battle. "When I left the office, I didn't ring the Duty Room to say where I was going."

"And that's all?" asked the astonished Elsa. "That's all you're worried about?"

"Elsa, everybody has to phone the Duty Room when he leaves Scotland Yard…"

Young Tommy, saucer-eyed, leaped high in the air.

"Scotland Yard!" he cried in ecstasy. "Scotland Yard… Yeepee!"

"Tommy, please do be quiet," said Elsa, "or Uncle Bob won't take you to see Father Christmas." Tommy writhed. Privately, he thought this Father Christmas business all a gag. But you couldn't be sure, and it was too close to Christmas to take any risks.

"Anyway, Bob, is it all that important?" she asked, searching his face closely for an endearing look.

From the moment they left for their shopping expedition, Elsa's suspicion grew—Bob did not have his mind on her. She wondered if perhaps Tommy's presence had annoyed him. Was he really more concerned about his precious crime work than pleasing her?

She couldn't restrain a petulant note when she asked:

"And how are all the little coppers at Scotland Yard? Are they having a happy Christmas?"

To Det. Supt. Pollard this was the last straw. He raised his powerful voice above a din which included the whiz of toy trains and a radio loudly blaring "Hark the Herald Angels Sing".

"If anybody at the Yard started singing about herald angels," Pollard said. "I hate to think what would happen to him. Anyway, they've got something else to think about right now, Elsa. It's a really big case. And we're all in a flap about it."

"Is it a murder, Uncle Bob?" screamed Tommy.

"No, old chap, it's not a murder. And yet, in way, it's worse."

"Crumbs," said Tommy, and jumped so high that he seemed to be levitated from Pollard's hand.

"Bob, stop it!" snapped Elsa. "You mustn't tease the child."

"I am not teasing. This case isn't a teasing matter. It's not every day that we hear about two people, at exactly the same moment, but in completely different parts of London, both disappearing like soap-bubbles before the eyes of police witnesses."

"Tommy, don't listen! He's joking!"

"Elsa, I'm not. A crook known as 'The Colonel', and another crook known as 'Shorty', both vanished off the face of the earth. Twenty thousand pounds' worth of uncut diamonds went with them. The point is *how did they vanish?*"

"Tommy, don't believe a word of this," cried Elsa, gripping Tommy's other hand so that he was tugged between them. "Uncle Bob never talks about police work. I can't make him talk about it!"

In fact, having just reached the howling centre of Toyland, Bob couldn't make himself heard.

Tommy was yanked away between his captors to a place of comparative quiet. There, behind his counter, the conjuror was exhibiting a large skull which first made whistling noises and then talked like Marshal Wyatt Earp.

Elsa was shivering with excitement.

"Why do they call him The Colonel?"

"Because he looks like a colonel in a comic paper. Middle-aged; military bearing; usually wears an eyeglass. Even when he doesn't wear an eyeglass, he has a gesture he can't help making. He keeps dragging down the side of his left eye. Like this!"

"Darling, for heaven's sake, don't leer. You look horrible."

"Well, so does The Colonel. But you can spot that gesture a mile away, and you can spot him. As a rule, he's a confidence man."

"A confidence man? You mean he swindled somebody out of £20,000 worth of uncut diamonds?"

"No!" Pollard snapped. "It's worse. For the first time in his life, the fool used violence."

"Did he murder somebody?" shouted Elsa. "Cut some poor man's throat?"

Tommy, who had been trying vainly to scream gave it up and writhed in an agony of fascination. But Pollard only shook his head.

"Elsa, don't be so infernally bloodthirsty! No."

"Then what was it?"

"In Sykes Street, a little turning off Upper Regent Street, there's a diamond-merchant named Van Bele. For years, Van Bele's been carrying regularly a fortune in uncut stones in a little wash-leather bag in his pocket. Up to now he's got away with it; nobody's bothered him."

"And now?"

"On Tuesday, about 10.15 a.m., Van Bele had a phone-call asking him to visit some clients. It was a fake call; The Colonel sent it. Van Bele walked downstairs from his office. The Colonel, in his best Savile Row suit and overcoat, was waiting in the entry. He just walloped Van Bele on the jaw, knocked him out, took the little leather bag, and ran for it."

Elsa spluttered.

"But—my dear Bob! Wouldn't they have caught him straight away?"

"No. With all this Christmas rush, he could have got clean away. But he had bad luck. Two constables were coming along Sykes Street opposite the Regent Street end. They saw our friend grab the bag and run.

"The Colonel jumped aboard a bus crossing Oxford Circus and went along Oxford Street. One of the constables followed; the other phoned the Yard.

"Within a few minutes they had the whole area covered in a net. In just two minutes, one of the Sweeneys—sorry, I mean a Flying

Squad car—pulled up beside the bus in Oxford Street. The Colonel was standing on the platform.

"He jumped down, and dodged across the street. Two of our men followed, keeping him in sight. The Colonel, believe it or not, ran into Omnium's. Our men still had him in sight when he ducked into a telephone box in the basement. And that's all."

"All? What do you mean?"

"The Colonel just vanished."

"In the telephone box?"

"Apparently, yes."

"But he can't have done!"

"I know it's impossible. But it happened."

Behind them, at the magician's counter, the talking skull left off gibbering and now loudly sang "Silent Night" in competition to the radio's version of "Silent Night". But Elsa, Tommy, and Pollard himself had forgotten the pandemonium of Toyland.

"Remember," Pollard insisted, "that these diamonds were uncut. That's to say: they were only greyish lumps, like pebbles, and of no use to The Colonel until they were cut and polished.

"What's the first thing he would do? He'd get in touch with his diamond-cutter, of course. Naturally, Criminal Records knew who it was."

"And this diamond-cutter was the other man you mentioned… Shorty?"

"Yes. Except that Shorty is a woman."

"A woman?" said Elsa, yanking Tommy forward.

"Yes; why not?" retorted Pollard, yanking Tommy back. "She's The Colonel's girlfriend. They live not far apart.

"After the first phone-call to the Yard, the division had orders to put a tail on Shorty. Not to arrest her—"

"Why ever not?"

"Dammit, Elsa, Shorty hadn't done anything—yet.

"But where was The Colonel meeting her to give her the diamonds? And how was he going to give her the diamonds? And when? That's what they had to know."

"So…?"

"Two policewomen, in plain clothes, picked up Shorty outside her lodgings. Shorty was carrying a large parcel. She knew she was being followed. You'll have guessed she and The Colonel planned this before-hand, in case they were followed. Shorty's quite an attractive trick, by the way: brunette, smooth skin, in her early twenties. She walked faster. So did the policewomen. Shorty hurried into Ilkley's—that big women's dress shop not far from here. So did the policewomen. And in the shop, Shorty dodged into a telephone box…"

Here Pollard had to stop.

"You're not going to tell me," said Elsa, who still thought that her beloved was spinning a fairy story, "that *she* disappeared out of a 'phone box?"

"Apparently, yes. Parcel and all."

Elsa's pretty face coloured pink with anger. She turned away abruptly.

"I don't believe it," she said, violently jerking Tommy's left arm. "It's silly! Look at the crowd here now. Just look!"

"Very well," said Pollard, jerking Tommy's right arm. "I'm look-ing. What about it?"

"Crowds and crowds and crowds," said Elsa, "all moving. Could you be certain somebody's disappeared out of a 'phone box, even if you were only ten feet away?"

"You could be pretty certain that two different people couldn't vanish out of two different shops under the conditions the police estab-lished. As soon as The Colonel entered Omnium's, and Shorty entered Ilkley's, both places were surrounded. Every possible entrance or exit was guarded. Every nook and cranny was searched. Every customer was stopped and questioned…"

"Wait! What about all the sales staff?"

"They were the first to be questioned. Both Omnium's and Ilkley's open at nine o'clock. The managers could tell from their time-sheets that every person was at his or her proper place. No employee could have been larking about with a pocket full of diamonds, or could have changed places afterwards with somebody who had. Face it, my dear! Shorty and The Colonel didn't leave the shops. And yet they weren't in the buildings either. They'd simply vanished."

Elsa marched forward, dragging the others like a string of sausages.

"Come along, Tommy," she said in exasperation.

"It's not very nice of Uncle Bob to enrage you like this. He's insufferable, and I'll never speak to him again."

"Now wait a bit, Elsa!"

"This way, Tommy; mind where you're going. We'll take you to see Father Christmas."

They had pushed through to a long grotto, a kind of mysterious and softly lighted cavern, where even in Toyland voices were hushed.

Here children walked slowly.

At the grotto pay box, over which large red letters said that Father Christmas would be in attendance from 11 a.m. to 6 p.m., Pollard bought three tickets.

The grotto was murmurous with "Oh's!" and "Ah's!" Brightly painted in cardboard or plaster, figures and backgrounds showed fairy stories. They were well along in the cavern when Pollard stopped. His mouth fell open. He stood rigid, staring straight ahead.

At the end of the cavern, on a platform festooned in holly where children could mount the two steps and whisper their wishes, sat Father Christmas himself.

At Father Christmas's right hand was a table piled with small gift-boxes wrapped in bright paper.

Even as Pollard stared, a little girl of possibly twelve years walked up the steps.

She was very dainty in white fur jacket and white cap. Her long yellow curls fell forward as she bent to whisper.

Father Christmas chuckled. He nodded. Selecting a gift-box from the table, he turned back in one vast beam to give this present to his small friend. And, as he did so, Father Christmas's large left eyebrow closed down as though he leered or held an eyeglass.

"Uncle Bob!" screamed Tommy. "Did you see it? The funny eyes. You remember. You said The Colonel..."

Detective Superintendent Pollard, Criminal Investigation Department, quickly turned to the boy and hushed him.

Then, in a flash, he charged.

He was a big man. He avoided the children, but parents scattered before him like skittles. There was a crash as he jumped up on the platform.

I don't think you'd like that one, my dear," he said pleasantly to the little girl, and nodded towards the box held out in Father Christmas's hand.

In a low voice he added: "Better give me the diamonds, Colonel. As for you, Shorty..."

The little girl lifted sweet and innocent eyes.

"Coppers!" she whispered, showing her teeth. "He's a copper, Colonel; that's what the so-and-so is."

"When a man is called Shorty," said Pollard in the same low tone, "it may not mean much. But when a woman is called that, as we ought to have realized, she must be almost a dwarf. I suppose your little-girl clothes, and the blonde wig, were in that parcel? And you changed in the dress-shop? Nobody would notice a twelve-year-old; the police weren't to blame for that mistake.

"But we were to be blamed about you, Colonel," he added, "Omnium's opens at nine; we thought everybody had to be on duty then. And yet, as you can see by a sign over the pay-box back there, this grotto doesn't open until eleven. You could slosh Van Bele and get back on time. [Both you and Shorty vanished by becoming someone else, someone whom the police would not suspect. The parcel Shorty was carrying contained her wig and clothes which made her look twelve years old, and when she ducked into a 'phone box she quickly changed clothes. You did something similar. I don't know whether you had the Father Christmas costume hidden in the 'phone box and were willing to take a chance that the box would be unoccupied when you needed it, or whether you were wearing it under your overcoat and Savile Row suit, but when you stepped out you were Father Christmas, not The Colonel. The police, trying to keep you in sight in the hordes of Christmas shoppers, did not suspect Father Christmas, whom they thought had been at work when the crime was committed."]

In that paralysed scene, the bright-coloured box was still held out in Father Christmas's hand. "Cut and run for it, Shorty!" he chuckled. "I hate to spoil the kids' Christmas, but I'll get this copper before they get me."

"Think so?" smiled Pollard. "You haven't a chance against me and you know it. I can't help you. But it's Christmas—and I can help Shorty get away. Fair?"

"Turn it up, copper!" sneered the sweet-faced girl—and yet an edge of hope appeared in her face.

"Give me the box," Pollard said. "If the diamonds are inside, she hasn't officially received them. She can go now and take her chance of being picked up later. Fair?"

Father Christmas looked warily at Pollard before exchanging a knowing glance with the girl.

Then, without a word, he handed over the box to Pollard.

As he did so, he noticeably sagged with relief behind his beard.

Then his rich, soothing, cultured voice rang out.

"Ladies and gentlemen!" carolled Father Christmas. "This gentleman is particularly anxious to have this box. I hope he finds in it what he's looking for.

"Personally, I'd rather give the little girl another box. Here it is. Now hurry down the steps, and out of this store. Others are waiting."

At the sight of a monocled Father Christmas, a ripple of laughter spread out over the grotto, carrying with it the spirit of Christmas as children crowded forward.

Tommy, pushing forward, hardly noticed that Elsa was no longer watching Father Christmas.

She was looking at Pollard—and in her eyes shone admiration—and unconcealed adoration!

# THE BIRD OF DAWNING

## Michael Gilbert

Michael Gilbert (1912–2006) was, quite simply, one of the finest male British crime writers of the second half of the twentieth century. He was also astonishingly versatile, combing a full-time career as a partner in a prominent firm of solicitors with the authorship of novels, short stories, and plays for television, radio, and the stage. His praiseworthy determination to keep trying something new meant that he created many appealing lead characters—policemen, spies, and solicitors were specialities—but never allowed the stories in which they appeared to become repetitive or formulaic.

His most famous novel, *Smallbone Deceased* (1950), which has been republished with great success as a Crime Classic, introduced the young lawyer Henry Montacute Bohun, who works in tandem with Gilbert's earliest series detective, Chief Inspector Hazlerigg. Bohun is one of Gilbert's most likeable protagonists, yet he never appeared in another novel. Gilbert did, however, include him in a number of short stories, mainly written for *John Bull* and *Argosy*. This story was first published in the *National and English Review* in 1956. When it was reprinted under the title "The Craven Case" in *The Man Who Hated Banks and other mysteries* in 1997, Gilbert said in an introduction to the book that: "people were not slow to suggest that Bohun was me in disguise. This is not correct. I sleep excellently at night and have never felt any desire to dabble in real life crime. My criminals all come from my pen." Of course, as a good solicitor, he would say that, wouldn't he?

"SPEAKING AS YOUR SOLICITOR," SAID BOHUN, "IT SOUNDS AN impossible assignment. But speaking as a man, it needs no argument to get me down to Vambrill Court for Christmas. Sir Hubert's reputation as a host has reached even my ears. Wasn't he the man who said, 'Turkeys are old-fashioned, but there's nothing wrong with a well-boiled peacock'?"

"That's just newspaper talk," said John Craven. "But why do you call it an impossible assignment?" He leant forward to say, through the communicating panel, "Better stick to the Great North Road, Peters. The A.A. say there's snow north of Hitchin." Then he shut the panel carefully.

"Well," said Bohun, "admitted that Captain Miller will be a member of the Christmas party. And therefore, in a sense, under our observation. I shouldn't have thought that a social weekend was the time or place to investigate financial dishonesty. Alleged financial dishonesty," he added, carefully, being himself a solicitor.

"Maybe not." Craven sat back and pulled the rug over both of them. "I'd like you to meet him, all the same. He's an odd mixture. When I took up this politics game, I thought it was a fairly straightforward sort of business. Once you were lucky enough to get elected. You sat up at Westminster, and spoke when you could, and voted the right way—."

Bohun grinned. "It's no use your coming the simple soldier man with me, John," he said. "I've checked up on you. If you don't look out you're going to get a job when they have their semi-annual stocktaking in the new year."

"A Parliamentary Secretaryship, maybe," said Craven. But he couldn't quite conceal his satisfaction. For a man who had been in Parliament only five years he had undoubtedly done well.

A first-class war record had helped. Perhaps an inherited income had helped even more. But undoubtedly there was ability under that thatch of smooth light hair. The ability to plan and to persevere. Possibly even to accomplish. Time would show.

"What I hadn't visualized," he said, "is the constituency end of it. Hamboro West is a good constituency, I think. For me, certainly. It's full of ex-Army types ruining themselves on farms and that sort of thing and I get on with 'em. But you can't let up. You've got to think about them the whole time. Every time you open your blessed mouth there are all those thousands of householders sitting in judgment and all of 'em ready to take offence."

"I quite see why it's important to have a good agent," said Bohun, thoughtfully.

"He's not just got to be good. He's got to be a miracle of tact and ability and organization and probity. And the Constituency Association pay him—what? £500 a year, if he's lucky. A bit more in the big constituencies. But not much. You can't buy miracles today for £500 a year."

"I take it," said Bohun, "that that's why you so often get a man who's retired from some other job with a pension. Like Miller."

"Miller seemed all right. A nice little man. Obviously as tough as nails. The M.C. he got in Holland wasn't something that came up with the rations. I took the trouble to read the citation. And that was the piece of the war I was in—hard, cold, dirty, damp fighting."

He seemed to be looking out again across the steel grey dykes, their surface whipped alternately by hail and bullets.

"You were saying," said Bohun, "that he seemed all right."

John Craven gave an involuntary shiver, and pulled himself back into the comfortable warmth of the car. "You can imagine," he said, "that I was prepared to give a man like that every latitude. Anyway, I was in the constituency so little that I wasn't in a position to notice things. But a week ago Priday—Alan Priday, he's Chairman of the Constituency Association—came to see me. Alan's a very able man. If he says something, you listen to it. And when he said he wasn't quite happy about the finances of our organization, I sat up."

Bohun said, "Priday? What is he besides being your Chairman?"

"He was an accountant of some sort. Now he gives his whole time to politics. You'll meet him tonight. He's a bachelor, like me. And Sir Hubert always asks us both down for Christmas. It gives us a real opportunity to talk. Also I think he hopes one of us will marry his daughter, Vanessa."

"Miller," said Bohun, firmly.

"Yes," said Craven. "Well Priday told me that he'd been looking into the Association accounts—we're not a business, you understand that. But we handle quite a lot of money and have to keep things pretty straight. The first thing that struck Priday was that Miller seemed to pay almost all his bills in cash. Even things you'd always expect to pay by cheque, like the rent of the headquarters office."

"I know people like that," said Bohun. "It's a form of phobia."

"All right. Suppose it was just a habit he'd got into. It meant that he was constantly drawing large cheques to 'Self' or 'Cash.' Nothing actually wrong with that. But he seemed a bit vague when Priday questioned him about where it had all gone."

"Did he like Priday questioning him?"

"Not a bit. He's got a temper like a Mills bomb."

"Then his evasiveness might have been annoyance more than guilt."

"It could have been. Yes." Craven was obviously trying hard to be fair. "There was one other thing. It was Sir Hubert who pointed it out to me last time I was down there—quite innocently. He said, 'Miller seems to be smartening up a bit.' Got himself a nice new car, and stopped dressing like a tramp.' It was true, too. During the last two years he's been showing distinct signs of prosperity."

"Which wouldn't be accounted for by an agent's salary."

"We pay him as well as most. But I don't think he could do it on his salary. Might have come into money, but I never heard of it. These things usually get out."

"Yes," said Bohun. "I think you've made out a *prima facie* case. The real proof will be in Miller's bank account. If that has got a lot of fairly large, fairly regular unexplained payments in of cash, I'd say that would clinch it."

"Can one look at his bank account?"

"With a judge's order," said Bohun. "Which you won't get without something a lot more definite than what you've told me. However, I'll keep my eyes open."

Sir Hubert Vambrill was an excellent host. A very tall, very thin, outwardly serious man, who had started life as an office boy in Liverpool and made a fortune in cotton before he was forty. He had, for the past twenty-five years, been living the life of a country gentleman and fighting to preserve what he had won.

The success of his fight was evidenced by the fact that he was still able to maintain a large house and an adequate staff of servants.

Clare, Lady Vambrill, a square, leathery woman, had hunted until she was fifty and then relapsed into almost complete insensibility. The daughter of this curious couple, Vanessa, was a strikingly pretty girl with characteristics derived, in unexpected proportions, from both sides of the family.

"What does it mean," she said confidingly to John Craven, at dinner that Christmas Eve, "when it says that outside calling was normal, but the clearing banks were active as buyers of bills?"

"Well, it's a bit difficult to explain."

"I read that in the *Financial Times* this morning. Daddy couldn't explain it either."

"I dare say I understood it once," said Sir Hubert. "Curious girl. Only papers she ever reads are the *Financial Times* and *Horse and Hounds*."

"The other papers are so impossible," said Vanessa. "*The Times* is so stodgy you can't even light the fire with it—or that's what Jane says. The others are just impertinent. Why should they always be trying to run people's lives for them?"

Craven thought rapidly of those organs of the Press which his calling forced him to read every morning, and was inclined to agree with her. He was not certain whether he disliked more the papers which normally supported his party or those which openly attacked it.

"Did you have a good run today?"

"Not bad," said Vanessa. "Two-mile point. The ground's still a bit soggy."

"It's freezing now," said Priday.

"It's going to be a real old-fashioned Christmas Eve," said Sir Hubert. "At least, I hope it is, because I've got a surprise for you all."

"Daddy. Not carols."

"Wait and see," said Sir Hubert.

"At the fourth tee," said Captain Miller to Lady Vambrill, "I hit a humdinger. Right down the middle."

"I hope you didn't hurt him," said Lady Vambrill.

Bohun on her right, choked on a walnut, and said, "Do you play golf, Lady Vambrill?"

"Waste of time," said her ladyship, briefly. "Come, Vanessa."

The departure of the only two ladies left the five men to their devices. Sir Hubert tipped the remains of the port into his own glass, fetched a full decanter from the sideboard and circulated it to Captain Miller, who filled his glass gratefully. His chances of drinking a 1924 vintage port were few and far between, and the fact that he was adding it to the Burgundy drunk at dinner and the gin drunk before dinner seemed to cause his seasoned stomach no qualms. In fact, however, he was getting very slightly drunk.

Craven filled his own glass. Priday said "no," Bohun topped his own up.

"Another Christmas," said Craven. "A barbaric and outdated ceremony, but useful as a sort of milestone."

"That's the trouble with milestones," said Sir Hubert. "At the start of your journey they show you how far you have gone. After a certain point they get turned round and only show you how far you have to go."

"In my opinion," said Priday precisely, "the traditions of Christmas are mainly kept up by shopkeepers for the good of their profit and loss accounts. It carries them nicely over the dead season at the end of autumn, and anything that's over can be 'marked down' for the January sales."

"Thank God we're not all accountants," said Miller.

Priday said acidly, "A little accountancy isn't out of place sometimes." And Bohun looked at him sharply.

Captain Miller seemed to be debating whether to accept the challenge. His face was normally the colour of a south wall, so it was difficult to see whether he was flushing. Before he could reply—

"I sincerely hope," said Sir Hubert mildly, "that none of you are actively opposed to a little entertainment at Christmas."

"You mustn't take any notice of them," said Craven, "they're just trying to shock you."

"I must admit," said Bohun, "that I rarely let Christmas go past without casting my eye back to other Christmasses. Last year I spent it in Germany. Never again. The Germans may have invented Christmas, but they've forgotten the secret."

"Past Christmasses," said Sir Hubert, with a sigh.

He walked across to the window and pulled back the heavy, swinging curtain. Outside the moon was riding in glory. The snow had stopped falling and the frost had laid its iron fingers on the world.

"When I was a boy," he said, "I could remember each Christmas on its own. Each one was distinct and separate and each had its own glories. Now, I'm afraid they seem to blur and run together. I wonder if I shall remember this one."

Three of the others had joined him at the window as he was speaking and stood, looking out at the glittering snowscape. The silence was broken by an almost hysterical laugh. It came from Captain Miller, seated alone at the table. He had recharged his glass and was gazing into the red heart of the thirty-two-year-old wine.

"There's one Christmas," he said, "that *I'm* not going to forget in a hurry."

"And which was that?" enquired Sir Hubert, politely.

"Just a war-time reminiscence," said Miller. "I won't bore you with it now."

Bohun was not unduly sensitive but he could feel, almost as if it was something physical, the shock waves of emotion loosed by that innocent remark. Priday was staring fixedly into his empty glass. Craven had his back turned and was looking out of the window.

"In that case," said Sir Hubert, "I suggest we join the ladies."

One of the delights of Sir Hubert's hospitality was its unexpectedness. Vanessa's "Daddy, not carols" was based on experience. Sir Hubert was capable of asking his guests not only to listen to carols, but to sing them too.

This time the ordeal in front of them was of a milder nature. Just after eleven o'clock he looked over his glasses. Bohun was doing his best with Lady Vambrill. Craven and Priday were deep in political shop. Captain Miller was gazing lovingly with one eye into a full glass of whisky and with the other at Vanessa. He seemed to be telling her a story.

"Now," said Sir Hubert. "I don't want to disturb any of you—"

"A sinister gambit," observed Vanessa.

"But if you'd like to come along with my wife and me, we're just going down to the stables. You'll need coats."

"A midnight steeplechase," said Captain Miller. "I remember once in Ireland—"

Sir Hubert cut him short with a charm and a ruthlessness which he must have learned from Balfour (who was, indeed, his ideal statesman). "Another time, Captain. We mustn't keep our mummers waiting."

In the stables which were large, well appointed and, fortunately, adequately heated, they found the servants and quite a number of friends and neighbours. And there the mummers (whom Bohun found fascinating) performed their age-old ritual to the snorts of the horses, the lowing of the cattle and, more distantly, the outraged clucking of the hens.

Bohun, finding himself next to Sir Hubert in an interval when the Dragon was removing his head in order to become St. George's old mother in the final scene said, "I think I've guessed your secret, sir."

"Indeed," said Sir Hubert, "then tell it to me."

"Isn't there a tradition that on Christmas Eve the cattle all talk together in the stable? I believe you're doing this to give them something to talk about."

Sir Hubert laughed immoderately; but Bohun saw him making a mental note and realized that he might have let some future house party in for a truly terrifying ordeal.

Half an hour after midnight he was standing at the open window of his bedroom, drinking in the sharp air. Outside the white countryside was asleep. His bed looked most inviting. He hopped into it and turned out the lights.

At first sleep seemed just round the corner, but the harder he wooed it the more firmly did it retreat. Something was worrying him. Some remark which had been made. The curious strain he had sensed earlier in the evening. After what Craven had told him, he had indeed expected a strain, but this, surely, had been of the wrong sort?

One o'clock struck from the clock over the stable, and, as if echoing the note, a cock crowed, once, twice, three times, angrily. Later Bohun woke again. He was far from certain what had disturbed him. He looked at his watch. It was a minute after two. Then he heard it again, sharp and clear. The crowing of the cock.

Into his sleep-drugged mind crept a line or two of Shakespeare, long known and loved.

> Some say that ever 'gainst that season comes
> Wherein our Saviour's birth is celebrated,
> The bird of dawning singeth all night long,
> And then they say—

Sleep was crowding out thought.

> And then they say, no spirit dare stir abroad.

No spirit. No angry spirit. None of the evil dangerous spirits released by the drunken Captain.

He woke to broad daylight and someone shaking his arm. It was Priday, and he was white as paper.

"Come quickly, Bohun," he said. "Sir Hubert wants you. Better get some clothes on."

"If this is one of his bright ideas—"

"It's not a joke," said Priday. "They've just found Miller. Hanging in the stable. He's been dead for hours."

One of the things which normal people faced with murder tended to do, Bohun reflected, was to behave as if they were characters in a book. Reasonably so, since very few people had any real life experience to guide them. Bohun himself, fortuitously, had been concerned in more than one such episode, and Superintendent Monks soon realized that he had found in him an admirable, disinterested and observant witness. He therefore questioned him twice. Once at the beginning, and once at the end.

It was at this second interrogation that Bohun was able to make a helpful suggestion.

"I gather," said Monks, in his slow, Midland voice, "from what you've told me and what Mr. Craven says, that you were brought down here with an object, as it were."

"I hope they welcomed me for my company too," said Bohun. "But yes. There was the idea of keeping an eye on Miller."

"The idea being that he was playing fast and loose with the constituency funds."

It was clearly no time for reticence, and Bohun repeated all that Craven had said to him in the car on the way down.

"Yes," said Monks. "You see, it makes a sort of motive, if it's true."

"Then you do think it was suicide?"

"It's possible. In fact, I'd say it's very possible. Putting all the stories together, it's clear that no one saw Captain Miller come back to the house at all. And he'd been drinking. If you add up all the drinks everyone said they saw him drinking it comes to quite a lot."

"You think he subsided gently into one of the mangers to sleep it off. Got overlooked, woke in that terrible, thin, time between midnight and dawn, when nothing looks worth it any more. Realized he was in an inescapable spot and hanged himself."

"Something like that," said Monks. "It was a bit of rope out of the stable," he added. "No doubt about that."

"There *was* one thing—it might have precipitated it—at dinner that night, Miller said something rather rude about accountants to Priday.

And before Priday could stop himself he cracked back at him. To the effect that accountants had their uses. If Miller had a guilty conscience, don't you see, that would be a pretty plain hint."

"Yes," said Monks. "Well, we'll know more when we get the pathologist's report. I gather you're all staying on over Boxing Day."

"That's right," said Bohun. "You'll be able to keep all your suspects together quite painlessly."

By common consent the festivities of Christmas Day were abandoned. Sir Hubert retired to his study, and left his enforced guests to themselves. Lady Vambrill remained doggedly in the drawing-room. She was unable to understand the fuss. Captain Miller was a tiresome little man, tolerated at Vambrill Court only on account of the office he held. She could not see that his taking his own life (a typical lower middle-class piece of self-importance) should have caused such an upset.

Bohun wandered down to the stables. A constable forbade him entrance sourly, but he was allowed to prowl around the outside. It was a well-thought-out, composite block, with a range of stables and stalls all open to a first-storey hay loft, which, in its turn, gave on to a run of chicken houses at the back; and enabled one man to feed, water and look after all the livestock.

As Bohun examined it, a first, uncomfortable, premonition formed at the back of his mind.

It was late that afternoon that Priday sought him out. He was not a man who gave his confidence easily, and Bohun could see that he was making a considerable effort.

"You've had experience of these—these sort of things," he said. "So I wanted to ask you a question. If you knew something—or had done something—nothing to do with the 'crime' itself—only it might lead to questions being asked—would you tell anyone about it, or would you keep quiet?"

"There are rather a lot of if's about that," said Bohun, "but I know enough about criminal investigation to have learned the First Rule. And that is, not to try and keep things back from the police. Unless you're the murderer, of course. Then, I suppose you've got to do your best."

"This isn't a joke," said Priday, stiffly.

"No, of course not," said Bohun. "I'm sorry. What was it you wanted to tell me?"

Priday said, slowly, "I went down to the stables last night at about two o'clock. And I found Miller. He was quite dead. There was nothing I could do."

"Good God," said Bohun, really startled and upset. "Do you mean you just left him?"

"There was nothing I could do," said Priday miserably.

"How could you be sure—good heavens man—artificial respiration—"

"There was no question of that. He was cold. I can see now that it was silly. But I was sure it was suicide. And really, in a way, it seemed the best way out. Miller was facing a criminal prosecution. And there was the scandal—"

Typical accountant's outlook, thought Bohun. Balance against each other one political scandal, one criminal prosecution and one human life. And draw a firm red line.

"Why did you go down?" he asked.

"I noticed he hadn't come back," said Priday. "I think I was the only person who did notice. I thought he was drunk and a night in the hay wouldn't do him any harm. Then I couldn't get to sleep myself and started worrying. I mean, if he'd fallen down outside he might have died of cold—"

Bohun remembered the strange, hard white world he had seen from his window and nodded. "Well," he said, "it was a Christian act. But I think, all the same, I should have cut him down and called for help. I don't know. It's easy to be wise after the event. One thing's plain. You'll have to tell the Superintendent all about this."

"I was just wondering," said Priday, "whether you'd handle it for me. You're a lawyer and used to telling stories."

"That might, perhaps, have been better put," said Bohun. "But all right. He's coming up after dinner this evening."

Monks took the story calmly. He almost looked as if he might have been expecting it. At the end he said, "I've got two new facts you might like to hear, sir. The first is that I've got the autopsy report. Miller died by hanging all right. No doubt of it. But the pathologist found enough sodium pentothal in the stomach to have put three men to sleep."

"Enough to kill?"

"No. But enough to make Miller unconscious. Particularly on top of the alcohol he'd had already."

"And your idea from that," said Bohun, "is that someone offered the Captain a nip—say from a flask—of brandy and pentothal, and then waited to see if anyone was going to notice his absence. If they did, no harm done. Captain Miller drunk again. But if they *didn't*—how easy to slip down later and fake a hanging."

"Not easy," said Monks. "Damned difficult to do. But possible, if the man was bigger than Miller."

"That hardly narrows the field," said Bohun. "Priday, Craven, Sir Hubert and I are all tall men, and Miller was jockey-size."

"Agreed," said Monks. "But only one of you left finger-prints all over the stall where he was hanging."

"And that, no doubt, was Priday, when he made his two o'clock visit."

"No doubt," said Monks drily.

"You don't believe him then?"

"I haven't got as far as believing or disbelieving. I'll just say I'm not very happy about it."

"Time of death?"

"You know what doctors are like," said Monks. "Any time between midnight and three."

"Motive?"

"That's where I was hoping you could help me, sir."

"I'm not sure," said Bohun. "I was brought down here on the assumption that Miller was the villain of the piece. That he was embezzling money. Now that he's turned out to be the victim, I've had to re-orientate my ideas. I think I see how it might work. But it's only supposition. And I'm not sure how far it's a breach of confidence. Would you mind if we had Craven in on it?"

The Superintendent tilted his head on one side, and considered the idea. Then he said, "If you like, sir."

When he had been brought up to date, John Craven said, "The whole idea is mad. Mad and bad. Of course it was suicide. Why should Priday do such a thing?"

Bohun said, so slowly that he might have been measuring and weighing each word, "You told me that Miller had been showing signs of affluence. I suggested that we should try somehow to get a sight of his bank passbook. And that if we found frequent credits to cash it would be proof that he had been fiddling the funds. *But it could prove something different.* Suppose Miller was blackmailing someone. Someone connected with the Constituency Association. Someone who knew of his unbusinesslike habit of drawing frequent large cheques to cash. And suppose that someone said to Miller, 'All right. I'll pay you,' and took the precaution of paying the hush money in cash, each time at a different branch, into Miller's account. Do you see?"

Neither man said anything.

Bohun went on. "It would be perfect cover, wouldn't it. A fake suicide. That leads to an examination of Miller's own bank book. We find all these sums being paid in all over the place. Clearly Miller's a crook. He's faced with exposure. He takes his own life."

Craven's face took on an obstinate look that Bohun recognized of old.

"Can you prove this?" he said.

"I should think so," said Bohun. "Bank clerks are trained observers. If I'm right, and the money was paid in in this way, and the police go round the various branches with a photograph, someone will be bound to pick Priday out."

Craven looked at the Superintendent, who nodded his head. "I'd say it was likely," he agreed.

"There is one other thing," said Bohun. "It's only a trifle, but if I can borrow a torch and get down to the stable I can probably prove it."

"Prove it and be damned," said Craven, and slammed out of the room.

Bohun sought out Lady Vambrill. She evinced no interest in his request but said she thought there was a torch in the cupboard in the gun room. There was; a large, nickel-plated affair. Bohun armed himself with it and he and the Superintendent stepped down the path towards the dark stable block. In the frosty distance church bells were ringing out a Christmas night peal.

"I don't know what you want the torch for," said the Superintendent. "There's electric light in all the outbuildings."

"The murderer wouldn't turn the lights on," said Bohun.

After that no more was said. The police guard had gone, and they opened the big end door with difficulty. In the warm, hay-smelling interior, the animals snuffled and snorted and stamped. The two men made their way between the stalls to a ladder at the end, and Bohun motioned the Superintendent to climb first. A few minutes later they were kneeling in the darkness, a few feet from the beam from which Captain Miller had swung and jerked.

"I think," said Bohun, quietly, "that the murderer would have to use his torch a little for this bit."

"Bound to," grunted the Superintendent.

Bohun pressed the switch and a white swathe of light cut the darkness. It revealed nothing but the dancing dust motes. The Superintendent was about to speak when Bohun laid his hand on his arm.

Beyond the open-topped partition they heard a rustling. Then a muted clucking. Then suddenly, so loud that Bohun almost dropped the torch, the strident crowing of a cock. Once, twice, three times. Then almost as if it had been an echo, from the direction of the house, came the crack of a gun.

"What the devil's that?" said Monks, jumping to his feet.

"I think," said Bohun, steadily, "that the murderer has taken a very plain hint which I just gave him."

"Do you mean to say," said Vanessa, very much later that night, "that John Craven was a murderer. And took his own life? I, for one, refuse to believe it."

"I'm passing no judgments," said Bohun. "In fact, I'm sorry for him. But you can't avoid the facts."

He was sitting in the library with Sir Hubert and his wife and daughter.

"What facts?" said Sir Hubert. "Why should he do such a thing?"

"I'm not sure," said Bohun. "I know exactly what sort of motive it was, but I don't know the details yet. Craven was a politician. And a part of his reputation was his war record. I'm as certain as I can be that Miller—they'd soldiered together remember—knew of some disgraceful secret—it may only have been a ludicrous secret. Some time when Craven, for once, didn't behave quite as a soldier should."

"Then I'd guess," said Sir Hubert, "that it was something that happened on a Christmas Day. Christmas 1944, I suppose, in Holland. That would account for his extraordinary remark at dinner last night."

"I think you're right," said Bohun. "Craven had been paying blackmail for two years. Ever since Miller demanded, as part of the price of his silence, the vacant job of agent. Craven had also made up his mind, in a general way, to kill him. As I explained to the Superintendent. But what he did was, I think, largely impromptu. I mean, the actual timing and staging of it. Possibly Miller's drunken remark finally convinced him that he couldn't afford to let him stay alive."

"Look here," said Vanessa. "You're saying all this just as if you were certain of it. Priday says he went down to the stable at two o'clock. He admits it. He left finger-prints. How do you *know* that any one else was there at all?"

"I heard it happening," said Bohun. "I heard the cock crowing. On two occasions. First at one o'clock when the murder was committed. Again at two o'clock when Priday went down. At the time I vaguely assumed that the chiming of the stable clock had woken up the cock and made him crow. But that was nonsense, of course. He heard the chimes every night. He wouldn't take any notice of them. There was one thing, and one thing only that would make him open his beak. He saw the glow of the torch over the partition and sang out the news to the sleepy world that the sun was getting up once more in the east."

Lady Vambrill said suddenly and decisively, "Fiddlesticks!"

"What is fiddlesticks, my dear?" said Sir Hubert. "It sounds unhappily convincing to me."

"I don't believe what this young man said. That Craven did it on the spur of the moment. It's plain to me that he'd been planning it for at least six months."

"How can you possibly know that, my dear?"

"Didn't he vote for the Abolition of the Death Penalty?" said Lady Vambrill. "Don't tell me he hadn't got some good reason for that."

## THE CHRISTMAS TRAIN

# *Will Scott*

William Matthew Scott (1893–1964), generally known as Will Scott was, like Vincent Cornier, born in Yorkshire and the first twenty years of his life were spent in Leeds. He studied art and frail health meant that he was rejected for active service in the First World War. He moved first to London and then, to benefit from the sea air, to Herne Bay, publishing his first short story in 1920. He became a prolific contributor to magazines and wrote a good deal of journalism as well as novels, stage plays, and film scripts. In his early days, his specialism was humorous writing, and after the Second World War, he became noted as a children's author.

During the course of a highly prolific career, Scott dabbled in crime and detective fiction. He wrote three novels about the corpulent and conceited (but talented) detective Theodore Disher, who features in his 1930 play *The Limping Man*. The play enjoyed considerable success and was twice filmed. Like J. Jefferson Farjeon, Scott created a character who was a tramp, known as "Giglamps" who appears in a collection of short stories which takes its title from his nickname; Giglamps sometimes acts as detective but occasionally ventures towards the windy side of the law. Another recurrent character was Jeremiah Jones, also known as "The Laughing Crook" and presented rather in the tradition of A. J. Raffles and Simon Templar. Jones features in this story, which first appeared in *Passing Show* on 23 December 1933.

"You're sure of your facts, Maxwell?" Mr. Jeremiah Jones inquired.

"Positive, sir," replied the sober Maxwell. "Mr. Hadlow Cribb landed this morning at Southampton. He has the jewels with him. Forty thousand pounds' worth. The trouble is, you can't get that lot through the Customs without somebody getting to know. And I got to know. It cost a bit!"

"Luxuries," reflected Mr. Jones, with a grin, "are always expensive. But go on."

"Mr. Hadlow Cribb leaves Liverpool Street tonight for his country home at Friars Topliss where he intends to spend Christmas," Maxwell proceeded. "The jewels, of course, go with him. The train is due out at fourteen minutes past six."

"Four hours," murmured Mr. Jones, with a glance at his watch. "Busy train. It won't be too easy. Still, nothing ventured, nothing gained. I wish I'd had a little experience of this kind of work."

"I ought to add," Maxwell resumed, "that Mr. Hadlow Cribb was accompanied up from Southampton by Marks."

"Marks?" Mr. Jeremiah Jones' eyebrows lifted quickly. "The new fellow in Beecham's office?"

"Exactly," said Maxwell with a sigh.

"Scotland Yard protection! No, it isn't going to be too easy," Mr. Jones repeated. "Can you get word to Dawlish," he added as he reached for the telephone.

"Dawlish?"

Mr. Jones nodded.

"You mean—as it were—put him wise?"

"Very wise, in a tactful way."

"I might," said Maxwell doubtfully.

"Aren't you sure?"

"I'm positive," said Maxwell.

"Right. Then go and do it. Meet me here at five-thirty. Have everything ready—most important—mind you've got a bag that's as near as blow it to the one Mr. Hadlow Cribb will carry his jewels in."

"It shall be done," Maxwell promised. And away he went.

Mr. Jones unhooked the receiver.

"That Scotland Yard?" he was saying presently. "Inspector Beecham? Say Mr. Jones—an old friend!"

A minute passed and then a sly smile spread across Mr. Jones' cheerful face.

"That you, Beecham? How are you? Merry Christmas! Well, why not? Peace on earth, goodwill to all men, and that kind of thing.

"Listen, Beecham, my own—I've a Christmas box for you. You remember I promised you, if I could get it, the—er—inside dope, as it's called—crude expression, I know, but it *is* called that, isn't it? I thought you'd know... My dear fellow, I *am* getting on with it; do let me finish...

"About that hold-up at Clapham the other week, when the girl was knocked out. You know how I hate brutality. I mean, he could have drugged her quite as easily, couldn't he?... But I'm telling you! I've got your man, address and everything.

"Listen, I shall be in the Baltic at four... No, no, Beecham, dear, I'd much rather see you personally... It's your face. It brightens my day. Baltic at four. Better write it down. You're *so* forgetful!"

After which Mr. Jones, with a happy chuckle, hooked the receiver, went to Liverpool Street, bought a couple of first-class train tickets, and proceeded to his accustomed corner in the dim saloon of the Baltic Hotel, off Piccadilly.

Promptly at four o'clock the stolid face of Detective-Inspector Beecham of Scotland Yard appeared in sight, and the Scotland Yard man took a seat beside Mr. Jones without a word.

"Compliments of the season!" said the latter brightly.

Beecham grunted.

"Cheer up!" Mr. Jones beamed.

"You owe me some information," Beecham reminded him.

"I have it here," said Mr. Jones, producing a pocket-book, which he placed on the table.

"When I say *owe* I mean owe," Beecham added. "Don't imagine you're paying off a debt. You're merely paying off arrears. You've slipped through my fingers so often that I take this without hesitation. I've a right to it. But it wipes nothing off. If I can get you tomorrow, I'll get you!"

"Why not tonight?" Mr. Jones smiled.

"The first chance I get," Beecham growled.

Mr. Jones pulled a slip of paper from his pocket-book and began to unfold it. If he heard the suppressed gasp at his side he took no notice of it. He proceeded to unfold the little slip. But it wasn't the slip that had caused the Scotland Yard man to gasp. It was the sight of the two railway tickets. First class. To Friars Topliss.

"Here's the address," said Mr. Jones, passing the slip to the detective. "You'll find your man there. You'll find the evidence too. And he richly deserves what's coming to him. You can tell him I said so, if you like, when you explain I obtained the information against him and so did your job for you."

"Anything else?" asked Beecham.

"Nothing," said Mr. Jones, "unless you'll let me call the waiter again, so that we can toast each other in the true festive—"

"I'll be going," said Beecham curtly as he rose.

"You have a heart of stone, dear Beecham," sighed Mr. Jones. "And yet, on Christmas Eve, when you see your stocking and the chimney shaft—who knows?"

But Detective-Inspector Beecham was already on his way to the door—and Scotland Yard.

Back in his office the big man rang a bell and summoned his new assistant Marks to his side.

"Ah, Marks," he said crisply. "About Mr. Hadlow Cribb. He's being accompanied tonight on the train?"

"I'm going myself, sir," said Marks.

"You needn't trouble," Beecham grunted.

"Not trouble, sir?"

"*I'm* going, myself!"

And as Beecham pecked the end off a big cigar he almost smiled his self-satisfaction.


The six-fourteen out of Liverpool Street faced the snow before it started. The snow blew in through the open end of the great building, covering the front of the engine and the sides of the passengers and the friends who were seeing them off. It was agreed by the majority that the weather was seasonable, but the vote was unanimous that the journey was certain to be long and uncomfortable.

In the laughing, grumbling, cheerful and anxious holiday crowds a small greyish man passed unnoticed. The cheerful ones were too cheerful to take the slightest interest in a figure so small and grey; the anxious ones too anxious. He passed through to the train as though he and the inconspicuous black bag he carried did not in fact exist, and when he sank wheezily into the corner of a first-class compartment that compartment still seemed empty.

Whereas everybody, cheerful or anxious, had at least one glance to spare for the tall and handsome Mr. Jeremiah Jones, who, with the grave and dignified Maxwell at his heels, strode along the platform with an assurance which implied that if he had not bought the station at least he had a ten-day option upon it.

But since nobody had noticed the first greyish man, nobody noticed now that the inconspicuous black bag which Maxwell carried in the wake of Mr. Jones was the very twin brother of the inconspicuous black bag which the greyish man had carried a few moments before.

Except, that is, just one eager watcher with a black half-moon moustache, who now moved out of the obscurity of a dark corner and passed through the barrier not twenty feet behind Mr. Jones and Maxwell.

Mr. Jones and Maxwell passed the first-class compartment in which the greyish Mr. Hadlow Cribb sat with his forty thousand pounds' worth of jewels, walked on until they were beyond the dining car and then selected a first-class compartment of their own.

But the eagerly watchful Detective-Inspector Beecham had a few quiet words with the guard at the other end of the train and sank back into obscurity once more, this time in the shadows of the guard's van.

The train moved out of the station and Detective-Inspector Beecham moved out of the guard's van together. The train moved out into the unfriendliness of the winter night, but Beecham moved out into the comparative cosiness of the corridor. This he traversed as far as the second coach where, having satisfied himself that Mr. Hadlow Cribb was still alone and his shabby case unmolested, he took up his stand round the angle of the passage at the end of the coach and watched.

Mile succeeded mile, minute succeeded minute. Detective-Inspector Beecham began to grow restless. The corridor windows were coated with snow. There was nothing to see and as little to do. Cheerful Christmasy shouts reached his ears from the ends of the train. He began to feel out of it. He began to feel bored. He shook himself and set out to walk the length of the train.

He passed through the dining car. He passed through two coaches beyond the dining car—satisfied that neither Mr. Jones nor Maxwell had seen him do so—before he pulled up, again round the angle of a passage at the end of a coach.

Again he had perforce to play a waiting game. Again he began to feel out of it and bored. But at last, about an hour out of Liverpool Street he was pleased to hear a door slide down the corridor and thrilled to see that the two men who came out of the first-class compartment and made off in the direction of the rear of the train were Mr. Jones and Maxwell. And Maxwell carried the second shabby little bag.

"Ah!" said Beecham softly to himself.

He let them get round the angle at the end of the coach; then he followed. He followed them through the next coach. He gave them three-quarters of a minute, then he plunged into the dining car prepared for the interesting bit in the rear section of the train.

But there he stopped.

And there Mr. Jones stopped, too. Stopped ordering turkey and Christmas pudding to stare up at Detective-Inspector Beecham and exclaim:

"Why, look who's here! Who could have thought it? Maxwell—wish the gentleman a Merry Christmas!"

"A Merry Christmas to you, sir," said Maxwell, with a respectful dip of the head to the detective.

"Sit down and join us," Mr. Jones invited. "After all, it only comes once a year and you can mutter 'Without prejudice' under your breath as you drink my beer. Or shall it be port?"

Beecham sank wearily into the comfortable chair opposite the pair of them.

"I—" he stopped.

"Yes, dear fellow?" Mr. Jones prompted.

"Nothing," the detective mumbled.

"Don't tell me you're going away for Christmas," said Mr. Jones. "I understand you don't believe in such tosh. Or am I wrong? Does that hard face of yours hide a heart that weeps after three glasses of rum punch and the sight of a holly berry?"

"The point is where are *you* going?" Beecham demanded.

"I don't see that's the point at all," Mr. Jones smiled. "Waiter—or should it be steward? I travel so little—bring my friend Detective-Inspector Beecham, of Scotland Yard, turkey and plum pudding and all things seasonable to eat and drink. Beecham, I don't think you know the steward, do you? The steward—Detective-Inspector Beecham. Of Scotland Yard, you know. My very good friend."

The attendant departed smiling, while the detective, with a neck going steadily pinker, attempted the futility of looking out of the window.

"When I want to advertise…" he said fiercely.

"You never will," Mr. Jones assured him. "Too well known to need it. Too deeply established in the affections of the multitude to require such a cheap device. Advertise? You? When you have to civilization will have perished. What about the skating prospects for the holidays? I'd like your opinion."

"What I'm never sure about," said Beecham, turning a fierce glare on Mr. Jones, "is whether you're a crafty fool or just a fool."

"Shall we say a lucky fool?" suggested Mr. Jones.

"Luck, yes!" snapped Beecham.

"That shows," said Mr. Jones, "how little you know me. You must get to know me better. Call round some time. Second Thursdays, you know. Tea. *And* cakes."

To give the grim old man of Scotland Yard his due he almost enjoyed the turkey and plum pudding and the port that followed.

Despite his company he would have enjoyed the unusual even entirely had it not been for the business which found him there. As it was he said little. Nor did he do more than listen occasionally to the ceaseless flow of light-hearted chatter which poured from the lips of Mr. Jones.

He gave himself up to a waiting game and tried to calculate the number of miles that had pounded themselves out under the wheels of the train.

Mr. Jones glanced at his watch.

"Eight o'clock? The snow's keeping us back. We were due in at Friars Topliss at five minutes to, surely?"

Beecham looked up at the mention of Friars Topliss, but still he said nothing. Mr. Jones offered a cigar, which was refused, and then lit one himself.

Ten minutes later the train began to slow down.

"Now where are we?" said Mr. Jones.

All down the dining car there was much rubbing of steamed windows, which answered no questions. An attendant, laden with Christmas fare on a tray passed quickly.

"Tell me, steward, where are we?" Mr. Jones inquired.

"Running into Etching Vale, sir," replied the attendant. "Friars Topliss in twenty-five minutes."

"Thank you," said Mr. Jones, and turned to Maxwell.

"This is where we get off," he said. "Got everything, Maxwell?"

"Everything, sir," Maxwell answered.

"Don't forget the bag."

Maxwell stopped and picked up the shabby bag.

"Here it is, sir."

Mr. Jones rose. Maxwell rose too. Beecham stared, dissatisfied with he knew not what.

Maxwell helped Mr. Jones into his big overcoat, pulled on his own and waited. Mr. Jones pulled his hat down over his ears and turned up the collar of his coat.

The train stopped.

"Well, good-bye, Beecham, dear fellow," Mr. Jones said breezily. "And, if I don't see you before, a Happy New Year."

And out to the snow-covered platform he went, with Maxwell and the shabby little bag after him.

Beecham blinked. That little bag... Was it possible? Even before Hadlow Cribb reached the train? Or, by some trick, while he, Beecham, had been waiting his chance in the guard's van?

"Crafty, but I wonder if he's *really* a fool?" he thought solemnly.

The driving wind covered Mr. Jones and the faithful Maxwell with snow in the twinkling of an eye. They dashed across the bleak platform of Etching Vale to the shelter of the station wall. And under this shelter they hurried to the barriers. Here Mr. Jones offered two tickets.

The collector peered at the tickets in the doubtful lamplight.

"Pardon, sir," he said, "but this is Etching Vale."

"Remarkable how you can tell, with all this snow on it," remarked Mr. Jones.

"These tickets are for Friars Topliss, sir," said the collector.

"I know," said Mr. Jones, "but I've changed my mind. I thought I'd get off here. It sort of called to me."

"Not allowed to break the journey, sir," the collector reminded him. "I'm afraid you'll have to pay again."

Mr. Jones thrust a note into the collector's hand.

"Take it out of that," he said, "and buy your wife something for Christmas out of the balance."

"No wife, sir," the collector grinned.

"Soon will have," Mr. Jones assured him, "with such charm as yours."

He passed out into the snow-covered station square of Little Etching Vale, the soft footfalls of Maxwell on his left and, as he soon realized, other soft footfalls on his right. He turned and there once more was the stolid figure of Detective-Inspector Beecham.

"Not again!" he exclaimed. "But, my dear Beecham, I thought you were going on?"

"I thought you might be, too," said Beecham.

"I changed my mind," Mr. Jones informed him.

"I changed my mind," retorted Beecham.

"A costly process, I found it," said Mr. Jones.

"I didn't!" said Beecham.

"Oh, well, of course, you're known to the police," said Mr. Jones, "which makes a difference!"

He smiled and waited, but Beecham waited too.

"Where now?" he asked.

"Where would you like to go?" said Beecham.

"You don't mean, do you, that the drinks are now on you?" said Mr. Jones. "But Beecham, my own, this is too touching! Very well—there's a decent-looking, old fashioned hostel over there. Shall we?"

"Anywhere," growled Beecham.

They crossed the square to the old-fashioned hostel where, to Mr. Jones' surprise, the Scotland Yard man immediately booked a private room and ordered the drinks to be sent up there.

"If you'll join me," he said to Mr. Jones.

"Delighted," Mr. Jones agreed. "Does Maxwell remain in the weather and hold the horses' heads?"

"There'll be room for the three of us upstairs," said Beecham.

"What could be better?" said Mr. Jones.

And upstairs they went, with a waiter and tray to follow them.

"Cosy," remarked Mr. Jones, when the waiter had left them and closed the door. "Shall you be staying here long?"

"About as long as it will take me to go through that little bag of yours," Beecham answered.

"Beecham!" Mr. Jones gasped. "I don't understand you."

"You will," said Beecham. "I always thought you'd be too clever. You let me see your train tickets this afternoon. After that, I just had to take this trip with you. Hand over the bag."

"You know, Beecham, my sweet," said Mr. Jones, "really I don't think you have the right."

"I can soon get that," said Beecham. "Please yourself, if you want to waste time. You'll waste it in my presence, that's all."

Mr. Jones sighed.

"Maxwell," he said, "nobody trusts us. It's a suspicious world. Pass the little bag to the gentleman."

Maxwell passed the little bag to the gentleman, and the gentleman, frowning, promptly dragged it open. Out fell pyjamas, combs, and toothbrushes. Nothing else. Beecham clicked his teeth and looked up.

"Pockets, probably?" he said.

"No friendliness at all," observed Mr. Jones with a fresh sigh. "Your pockets, Maxwell."

Maxwell emptied his pockets. Mr. Jones emptied his. The detective's complexion darkened. He turned once more to the little bag, fumbled inside it, threw it on the floor. His hands passed swiftly, but certainly, down the attire of the other two men; then, with a muttered exclamation, he picked up a telephone that stood on a corner table.

"Friars Topliss police, quick!" he shouted.

"You might tell me, sweet Beecham," Mr. Jones put in, "what *is* on your mind."

But Beecham didn't. He sat glaring at the instrument in front of his nose until there was a faint tinkle.

"Yes?" he roared. "This is Detective-Inspector Beecham of Scotland Yard. Is the six-fourteen from Liverpool Street—what? Good Lord! Battered up? But I saw him—the jewels? Gone! I'll come along!"

He dropped the receiver and spun round.

"Without having the faintest idea as to what is on your mind," said Mr. Jones, "I think you must admit that I never batter them up. I may have many failings, but *never* that."

"I don't exactly know where you come into this," snapped Beecham, "but bear this in mind. I'll land you."

"I doubt it," Mr. Jones smiled. "You'd like to, I fear, but it's such a disappointing world."

Beecham strode to the door.

"Say good-bye to the gentleman, Maxwell," said Mr. Jones.

And Maxwell said good-bye to the gentleman.


"Dapper" Dawlish, expert but unlikeable, let himself into his Baker Street flat and snapped on the lights. He was satisfied with himself and the world in general. Or, at least, he was until he snapped on the lights.

Then he found himself looking down the barrel of an automatic, and he changed his opinion of the world at once.

"Good evening," said Mr. Jones. "Or morning. Or what is it? Travelling about the world in a snowstorm makes one lose one's sense of time."

"Who are you?" snarled Dawlish.

"Doesn't matter in the least," said Mr. Jones.

"What do you want?"

"The jewels you stole from Mr. Hadlow Cribb on the Friars Topliss train," said Mr. Jones. "And I want them now. I've been waiting two hours without a fire. I'm depressed. And when I'm depressed I'm nasty. That bulge in your right pocket, I believe. Come on! One—two—"

Which was where "Dapper" Dawlish threw in.

"I'm hanged if I see how you knew," he grumbled.

"But, of course, I knew," said Mr. Jones. "It was I who had you put wise this afternoon that the stuff would be on the train."

"You?"

"Mind, you wouldn't have stood an earthly if I hadn't been on the train to take their attention away," Mr. Jones added. "They watched dear old Cribb and you'd never have got near him. Brains, my lad. That's what gets you to the top.

"Mind, I *couldn't* have got the things. I'm too popular with the C.I.D. They won't let me out of their sight. Which is why I sometimes have to leave the labouring to others. Which reminds me."

He opened the parcel of gems, separated one from the rest, and tossed it on the table.

"The labourer is worthy of his hire," he said, with a smile. "You'd have got two—or even three—if you hadn't battered him up. Battering-up is a thing I detest. Or, at least, I've always thought so. I may change my mind one day. Even this day. Try following me and see! Good-bye, Mr—Dawlish the name is, I believe. Charmed to have met you. And a Merry Christmas."

# THE GREY MONK

## Gerald Verner

Gerald Verner pursued twin careers in writing and pyrotechnics which inspired the neat title of *Plots and Gunpowder*, a biography written by his son Chris Verner and published in 2022. Verner's name at birth was John Robert Stuart Pringle, but (to cut a long story short) family complications led to his changing his name to one inspired by the stage identity of his actress mother, Geraldine Verner. He wrote prolifically and under several names, notably Donald Stuart, Derwent Steele, and Nigel Vane. Like Frank Howel Evans, he was one of the many authors who produced stories about the exploits of Sexton Blake. Chris Verner sums up his credo thus: "My father didn't want his readers to stop and think about his characters too much. He was far more interested in the puzzle of an impossible murder, or the identity of a master criminal, and didn't want character studies to hold up the action."

Among Gerald Verner's more noteworthy projects was a theatrical adaptation of an excellent if often under-rated novel by Agatha Christie, *Towards Zero*. His son's book gives an interesting account of a troubled venture. However, *Meet Mr. Callaghan*, Verner's adaptation of Peter Cheyney's novel *The Urgent Hangman* achieved greater commercial success. Over the years, Verner created a number of series characters, including Simon Gale and Felix Heron, but the most significant were the shrewd but down-to-earth and apparently ponderous policeman Robert Budd and his lugubrious sidekick Sergeant Leek. The duo appear in this story, which was first published in *The Leader* on 17 December 1934.

"YOU CAN CANCEL THAT TURKEY YOU'VE ORDERED," SAID MR. Budd, removing the evil-smelling cigar he was smoking from his lips, and eyeing the thin and melancholy Sergeant Leek, who had just entered his office. "An' you can put all ideas of puddin' an' mince pies, an' all the things your carnal soul craves for, out of your mind. The flesh pots of Egypt aren't for you this Christmas."

The Sergeant blinked at his superior, his weak eyes bewildered.

"I don't understand," he said.

Mr. Budd shook his large head sadly.

"You've never understood anythin', have you?" he remarked. "An' you never will. You haven't got an understandin' nature!"

"I haven't ordered any of the things you've mentioned," said the aggrieved Leek, "I always go to my aunt's for Christmas."

The "Rose-bud" groaned.

"You would," he answered disparagingly. "You're just that sort of feller. I'll bet you have a hectic time!"

"We play a hand or so of snap," said the Sergeant brightening, "and there's always some very good red currant wine—"

"Snap and red currant wine!" broke in Mr. Budd, screwing up his face in disgust. "Well, you won't have any of those sinful luxuries this Christmas. We're goin' on a job."

Sergeant Leek's long face became even longer.

"Oh!" he said disappointedly. "Where are we going?"

"We're goin' to chase ghosts," said the "Rose-bud" calmly. "Which is a better occupation on a Christmas Day than playin' snap, anyway. You ever heard of Sir Isaac Lewin?"

Leek frowned and shook his head.

"Well, if you haven't, say so, don't make faces!" said Mr. Budd irritably. "He's a very rich man."

"Is 'e?" said the Sergeant.

"Don't call him Izzy," admonished the "Rose-bud" severely. "It isn't respectful!"

"I wasn't," protested Leek. "I meant, is 'e rich?"

"He's so rich," said Mr. Budd impressively, "that 'e gives money to anybody who asks for it—on note of hand alone!"

"Oh, a moneylender," grunted the Sergeant, and the big Superintendent looked shocked.

"A financier," he corrected in a hushed voice. "Never call a financier a moneylender, Leek. It's like a red rag to a bull!"

"What's all this got to do with ghosts?" asked Leek, not unreasonably.

Mr. Budd took a long pull at his cigar and blew a cloud of rank smoke towards the ceiling.

"Everythin'," he murmured lazily. "This feller Lewin has just bought Monk's Abbey, an old house in Berkshire that belonged to Lord Ruce, and was once a monastery, and he's been seein' things."

"Ghosts?" asked the Sergeant interestedly.

"So 'e says," answered Mr. Budd sceptically. "Though I've yet to meet the ghost that uses a .32 calibre automatic!"

"Automatic?" repeated the puzzled Sergeant. "What do you mean?"

"It was a bullet from a .32 automatic pistol that killed Lewin's butler at half-past two this mornin'," said Mr. Budd, glancing sideways at a note pad on his desk, "an' if that's the kind of weapon ghosts are usin' these days it's time that spook was put where he can't do any further harm!"

Monk's Abbey had pretensions to beauty even when seen under the leaden sky of a winter's afternoon. Built of grey stone it stood and had stood for centuries in two hundred acres of heavily wooded ground, its rugged line softened by the trees that clustered round it. A hundred yards from the main entrance the ruins of the original building were visible—the hint of a broken wall, the remains of an arch like a gigantic question mark...

Mr. Budd eyed these relics with sleepy interest as he climbed with difficulty out of the police car that had brought him from London.

"Take a look at those," he said to the weary and shivering Sergeant Leek. "That's where the ghost comes from."

Sir Isaac Lewin, a round, flabby man with a bald head and a large nose received them in the library, a sombre room with many books and pictures, and which Mr. Budd thought rather out of place as a background for its present owner. There were two other people with Sir Isaac when the "Rose-bud" and Sergeant Leek were shown in, a thick-set, ruddy-faced man, whose uniform proclaimed him to be the local Inspector of police, and a tall, distinguished-looking man whom Sir Isaac introduced as "My friend, Lord Ruce."

"This is a terrible affair, Superintendent," said the bald-headed man with a gesture of his ring-laden hands. "I saw the 'ole thing."

"So I understand, sir," said Mr. Budd heavily, suppressing a yawn. "Inspector Winscon told us briefly what had happened when he 'phoned the Yard. I should like to hear the account, though, from your own lips, if you don't mind."

Far from minding, Sir Isaac was apparently only too eager. Straddle-legged in front of the blazing log fire he told his story with a great deal of gesticulation.

"It is my 'abit," he began, "to work late. I 'ave quite a lot of business to attend to and I find the quietest time is at night after the 'ousehold 'as retired. I 'ave quite a lot of people staying for Christmas, including 'is lordship—" He waved a fat hand in the direction of the silver-haired old man who had not as yet spoken—"and I 'ave to entertain my guests most of the day. Last night I worked in 'ere till a quarter-past two. Usually before going to bed I take a breather round the 'ouse, but last night it was very cold and I was too tired. I switched out the lights and was going upstairs when I met Hewitt, my butler, coming down. He said he had seen somebody lurking about in the ruins—his window faces that way—and was going out to discover who it was. He was only clad in shirt and trousers, so I made 'im put on a 'eavy coat of mine that was 'anging in the 'all.

"He opened the front door and was crossing towards the ruins when a figure glided out of the shadows of that broken arch, there was a loud report and Hewitt stumbled and fell. I immediately woke the footman, but when we reached poor Hewitt he was dead. Shot through the 'ead.'"

Sir Isaac stopped, shivered and mopped his damp forehead with a large silk handkerchief.

"This figure that came out of the arch," said Mr. Budd gently, rubbing each of his chins in turn, "what was it like?"

Sir Isaac glanced at Lord Ruce uneasily and then back again.

"It was a monk," he answered, dropping his voice. "A monk in a grey cowl and habit."

The "Rose-bud" closed his eyes completely.

"There was some mention in the report passed on to me by the Assistant Commissioner," he murmured wearily, "of a ghost—" Inspector Winscon's ruddy face went a deeper hue. "—Am I to understand that you believe this figure you saw wasn't human?"

"I don't know what it was," declared Sir Isaac.

"There is a legend connected with this house," Lord Ruce spoke hesitantly and in a voice that was curiously gentle. "It was built on the site of a monastery; the ruins are actually part of the old building. The head of the monastery was murdered one Christmas by one of the monks who went mad and his ghost is supposed, at this season of the year, to haunt the scene of his death. Many of my family say they have seen it."

Mr. Budd opened his eyes suddenly very wide.

"Have *you* ever seen it, sir?" he asked.

The silver head shook slowly from side to side.

"What happened to the monk after he shot your butler?" went on the "Rose-bud," turning his sleepy eyes towards Sir Isaac.

"He seemed to melt away," answered the flabby man. "One minute he was there the next there was—nothing."

"Did you find any traces?" the big Superintendent addressed Inspector Winscon.

"There were no footprints," replied the Inspector. "It was freezing and the ground was too hard to take any impressions."

"Ghosts don't leave any," murmured Mr. Budd, and smoothed his hair gently. "I think I'll see the body now."

It lay under a sheet in the butler's room. He gazed at it dispassionately, noting the tiny reddish rimmed hole in the centre of the forehead. The Inspector produced the bullet, which the doctor had extracted, and the "Rose-bud" examined this with more interest.

"It's not easy to hit a moving target in the moonlight," he remarked presently. "Your ghost was a pretty good shot." He twisted the bullet about between his fat thumb and finger, and then gave it back to the Inspector. "H'm," he said. "I think I'll take my Sergeant and show him round the neighbourhood. Walkin' is the only thing that prevents him fallin' asleep!"

It was quite late in the evening when Mr. Budd and the tired Sergeant returned, and for so lazy a man the big Superintendent had been very energetic indeed. He had called at the vicarage and chatted to the vicar, dropped in and consumed beer at the local inn—a proceeding which caused the gloomy Leek momentarily to brighten—had a long conversation with the doctor who had extracted the bullet—an old man, past sixty, who had lived in the village all his life.

On the way back to Monk's Abbey he had left a note for Inspector Winscon, the writing of which appeared to have given him a certain amount of satisfaction.

A well-laden tray was brought to them in a small smoking-room adjoining the library and both Mr. Budd, and the Sergeant ate their dinner with enjoyment.

"They haven't brought any red currant wine," said the "Rose-bud" sadly, "but this whisky is some of the best I've tasted."

Just as they were finishing the meal Sir Isaac came in.

"Well," he inquired. "Have you discovered anything?"

"I've discovered that you have a very good cook, Sir Isaac," replied Mr. Budd, and the flabby man clicked his teeth impatiently.

"I mean about the murder of my unfortunate butler," he said curtly.

Mr. Budd gently massaged his nose.

"He was unfortunate," he murmured. "But what is one man's misfortune is another's fortune. Are you workin' late tonight, sir?"

Sir Isaac shook his head.

"No," he answered. "It's Christmas Eve."

"So it is," said Mr. Budd, as though the information were a complete surprise to him. "Well, well. Could you make it convenient, sir, to meet me in the library at a quarter-past two?"

"I could," answered Sir Isaac. "But why?"

"I think I could show you somethin' interestin'," said the "Rose-bud".

"It's very late," grumbled the other. "Can't you make it earlier?"

Mr. Budd shook his head sadly.

"I'm afraid I can't, sir," he replied. "You see, ghosts haven't got any union, they work at all sorts of peculiar hours!"

*

The night was cold and frosty with a frozen moon like a bulkhead light set in a bowl of steel. The broken arch of the ruins cast a sharp shadow across the rime-covered grass—a shadow that was lost in the deeper blackness within the curved arch.

Clearly, on the rarified air, a clock in the village struck two and, as the last stroke vibrated to silence, Mr. Budd roused himself from a short nap in front of the smoking-room fire, yawned, stretched, and rose with a groan to his feet.

"Wake up," he said to the dozing Sergeant in the chair opposite. "It's time you got busy."

With a resigned look on his long face Leek got up and went out. The "Rose-bud" took a thin black cigar from his pocket, eyed it regretfully, and put it back, and then going over to the door that communicated with the library he opened it.

Sir Isaac Lewin was sitting at his desk reading through a long type-written document. He looked round as the big Superintendent entered.

"Well, I'm here as you asked," he said, "though I'd very much like to know what is supposed to 'appen."

"What I'm hopin' will happen," replied Mr. Budd, "is the ghostly manifestation."

Sir Isaac started.

"What? You mean—the Monk?" he asked a little nervously.

The "Rose-bud" nodded slowly.

"Yes, sir," he said. "I'm very anxious to see that spook who kills with a modern automatic pistol."

He put up his hand, and with a click all the lights in the room went out. Out of the darkness came a gasp from the man at the desk.

"Why have you done that?" he said sharply.

"You can't expect to see spooks in the light," said Mr. Budd. "It's one of the rules of the ghosts' association that members must only appear in the dark."

He groped his way over to the window and drew aside the heavy curtains. A glimmer of reflected moonlight lit the room dimly.

"I wish—" began Sir Isaac.

"Don't talk—watch!" muttered Mr. Budd, and peered across the circular patch of grass towards the picturesque pile of the ruins. Clearly defined in the cold moonlight they stood lifeless, deserted, and silent. Five minutes dragged slowly by, and the "Rose-bud" looked at the watch on his thick wrist. It was just on a quarter-past two. And then suddenly the silence was broken by the sound of a step on the crisp gravel outside. Sir Isaac Lewin at Mr. Budd's elbow drew a quick breath as he saw a figure slowly come into sight and begin to cross the lawn towards the ruins.

"My God!" he muttered huskily, for the figure was wearing his own heavy overcoat—the coat that Hewitt had been wearing when he was killed.

The man in the overcoat had reached the middle of the grass plot when the shadow beneath the broken arch seemed to come to life. A grey shape formed in the centre of the black patch and glided forward into the moonlight. They saw the long habit and cowled head, and then the right arm went up and the moonlight glinted on something in the thin hand. There was a sharp, whip-like crack, and the figure crossing the grass collapsed. At the same instant two men sprang from the conceal-ment of the broken masonry and gripped the grey figure by the arms.

Mr. Budd unlatched the window, flung it open, and ran towards the struggling group.

"Hold him!" he panted, and Inspector Winscon and the constable turned crimson faces towards him.

"We've got him," gasped the Inspector, "but he's as strong as a horse."

"Madmen always are," said Mr. Budd, and threw back the cowl that hid the man's face. In spite of the snarling lips and glaring eyes they recognized Lord Ruce.

★

"Poor old chap, he was as mad as a hatter," said Mr. Budd later, shaking his head sadly. "Of course, he was after you, Sir Isaac. He knew about your nightly constitutional and mistook Hewitt for you because of your coat—the same as he mistook Leek tonight. Leek was safe enough though, because I'd substituted blank cartridges in his pistol earlier."

Sir Isaac wiped his forehead with a trembling hand.

"Good God!" he muttered. "How did you guess it was Ruce?"

"I never guess, sir," said the "Rose-bud" slowly, "but when I learned in the village that there was madness in the family; that Lord Ruce was a crack shot; that you had tricked him out of his fortune by a piece of—shall I say, smart business—an' that he hated you, it wasn't difficult to put two an' two together an' make them four."

He turned to the door.

"Come on, Leek," he said. "You'll be in time to spend Christmas with your aunt after all. Good-bye, Sir Isaac. It's rather a pity you weren't wearin' that overcoat instead of your butler, isn't it?"

# WHO SUSPECTS THE POSTMAN?

## *Michael Innes*

In a light-heated prefatory note to his first detective novel, *Death at the President's Lodging* aka *Seven Suspects* (1936), Michael Innes wrote: "The senior members of Oxford and Cambridge colleges are undoubtedly among the most moral and level-headed of men. They do nothing aberrant; they do nothing rashly or in haste." In his novel, of course, things are rather different: Dr. Josiah Umpleby of St. Anthony's College is found murdered in the night before the end of the first paragraph. The book was a critical and commercial success and launched a long career in the mystery genre.

Innes was himself a distinguished academic who spent more than twenty years as a Student (i.e. fellow) of Christ Church College, Oxford, having previously taught at Leeds, Adelaide, and Belfast. His real name was John Innes Mackintosh Stewart (1906–1994) and he published mainstream novels and full-length literary studies of Joyce and Hardy among others as J. I. M. Stewart. When one reads *Myself and Michael Innes: a Memoir* (1987), it's impossible to escape the feeling that he would have preferred his "serious" writing to be remembered more fondly than his mystery fiction, which has not proved to be the case. He says rather wistfully: "The novelist lurking in Michael Innes has coped with this situation as he can: preserving always a certain lightness of air in his writing: aerating it with such wit as he can command; escaping from the artificial into the fantastical or farcical." John Appleby of Scotland Yard made his debut in *Death at the President's Lodging* and enjoyed an illustrious career, ultimately becoming Commissioner of the Metropolitan

Police. This story first appeared in the *Evening Standard* on 9 April 1958 as "Who Suspects the Postman?" but was later reprinted as "In the Bag".

PARTINGTON HOUSE PRESENTED A FORLORN APPEARANCE AS Appleby kicked the snow from his shoes and hurried in. The bleak thin light of a winter morning made the splendid rooms seem pretentious and uneasy, and the dismal effect was increased by the litter left over from the party of the night before. There were champagne glasses on the floor, and in the great green and gold drawing-room nobody had turned out the lights on the Christmas tree.

It had been very much a Christmas party. Lord Partington himself gave evidence of this when Appleby was ushered into his presence in the library. There was still a smear of red greasepaint high on one cheekbone. And—what made his appearance really fantastic— he had failed to remove two tufts of white cotton-wool from his eyebrows.

Lord Partington, clearly, had been representing Father Christmas. He did that at this fancy-dress party every year—making a spectacular appearance and disappearance, it was said, on a sledge, and present-ing his guests with presents conceived on rather a lavish scale. Lord Partington, in fact, had a showy side. And this annual party, given not to children but to bored grown-ups, was an expression of it.

"It was enormously valuable, you know," Lord Partington began abruptly. "The Whang Vase, it's called. An ancestor brought it from Pekin. Pretty well stole it, I dare say."

Appleby nodded. "And now it has been stolen from you?"

"Yes—during my party. And when I wasn't three paces from it, if you ask me. You saw that Christmas tree? The Whang Vase stood in an alcove just beside it. It's a large pot-bellied affair about three feet high. I can't say I ever saw much in it myself. But it's enormously valuable, as I say."

"But surely, Lord Partington, it could hardly be worth much to a thief? If he tried to dispose of it, it would be identified at once?"

"That's the deuce of it, my dear fellow. Those affairs go, it seems, in pairs. Somewhere in the world there's a missing Whang vase, identical with mine. So it's open to anybody who gets hold of mine to invent some cock-and-bull story about having picked it up in a junk shop."

"And when," Appleby asked, "was the disappearance discovered?"

"Quite late, when most of my guests had left. I must say your people were here in no time. They'll have told you how the thing was done?"

Appleby nodded. "I gather that your butler found a window open on a staircase at the back of the house, and a rope trailing down from it into a yard. It seems an odd way to make off with a large fragile object."

"Quite so." Lord Partington nervously lit a cigarette. "But nobody, you see, could have walked out of the front door with that great thing without being spotted by half-a-dozen servants. And the same goes for any route through the kitchens and so forth. But once down that rope and into the yard, the fellow could get away easily."

"I see. Well, I think I'll have a look at that window."

It was twenty minutes before Appleby returned to the library. "I'm afraid," he said, "that I must ask some questions about your guests."

Lord Partington was startled. "My guests? You think one of them made off down that rope?"

"I don't think that anybody did. The rope is a mere false trail. And whoever arranged it didn't reckon with the snow. There's an untrodden carpet of it in that yard. So that's that."

"But suspecting my guests just doesn't make sense. None of them could have got away with it."

"That may be so." Appleby paused for a moment. "But a few of them, at least, must be thoroughly familiar with your house?"

"Certainly."

"Then one of them may simply have hidden the thing until he—or she—can collect it on a favourable occasion. There must, after all, be a hundred hiding places in a great mansion like this."

Lord Partington stood up abruptly. "I can't believe it," he said. "That it should still be here isn't a possible solution at all."

It was only after close questioning that Lord Partington let slip the rather special position of his old friend Colonel Wain, who was an authority on Chinese pottery, with connections among collectors in many parts of the world. But Wain had never been a man of wealth. And now, Lord Partington believed, he was having difficulty in making both ends meet. "But that, you know," he said drily to Appleby, "doesn't necessarily make him a thief."

"Of course it doesn't. But we must keep an eye on him, all the same. Do you remember when he left your party? No? He wasn't conspicuous? What sort of costume did he come in to this fancy dress affair of yours?"

For a second Lord Partington hesitated. "I don't remember," he said.

Appleby found Colonel Wain in his flat off Piccadilly. He was an elderly hard-bitten man with keen grey eyes. Appleby was a little startled to find him sitting in the company of the Home Secretary. "You've come about this theft?" Wain asked.

"Yes, Colonel. But I mustn't disturb you when you are with Mr. Mellanby."

"Never mind Mellanby." Wain barked this out. "He and I are old friends. Go ahead. What do you want to know?"

"I want to know in what costume you went to Lord Partington's last night."

There was a silence—and then Wain gave an odd sigh. "I went as a postman," he said. "And you'll be quite right if you suppose that part of the outfit consisted of a large sack." He turned to Mellanby. "What do you think, Jim?"

"That you'd better tell the truth. Or shall I do it for you?"

"Please do." Wain looked curiously aged and broken. "I never thought it would come to this."

"The colonel and I left Partington's affair together." Mellanby was accustomed to waste no words. "And in our taxi he asked me to search that postman's bag. It contained empty cardboard boxes—nothing else. Can you take my word for that?"

Appleby smiled. "Yes, Minister, I think I can." He turned to Wain. "Just what had Lord Partington done?"

"He took advantage of some distraction to slip *his* bag—Father Christmas's you know—over the Vase. And then he gathered it up and had himself drawn out of the drawing-room on his ridiculous sledge. I was the only man who spotted the manoeuvre—in the East, you know, one gets into the way of keeping one's eyes open—and I was absolutely astounded. Then I remembered that Partington had made a great point of my coming as a postman, bag and all. It was a plot against me." Wain's voice faltered. "And he is one of my oldest companions."

"It was certainly a plot, sir. He arranged a very palpable false trail with a rope from a window, such as a not-too-clever guest might have contrived in order to suggest an outside job. And then, in talking to me, he managed to bring you, Colonel, into the picture in a thoroughly suspicious way. Nothing could ever be proved against you, of course. But, having left Partington House with that bulky bag, you would be a suspect to point to when the matter was being investigated by the insurance people."

Wain nodded slowly. "And that is what it was about?"

"Certainly. Lord Partington stole his own Whang Vase in order to collect the insurance on it, and subsequently to sell it quietly as the twin of the one that had ostensibly been stolen from him. There would be a double profit."

Mellanby stood up. "And Partington?" he asked. "Will he ever be more than a suspect?"

Appleby shook his head. "I'm afraid not, Minister. The first move we make will alarm him, and the vase will just unobtrusively turn up in Partington House again. A bad business."

Mellanby nodded, and turned to Wain. "A bad business, indeed. We can't even throw him out of the club."

Wain looked at his friend in sombre dismay. "Yet one couldn't belong to the same club as a fellow like that. We'll have to resign ourselves."

Appleby looked at the two perturbed gentlemen. "At least," he said, "a reflection of general usefulness emerges. One doesn't necessarily get away with a thing even when one is quite sure one has it in the bag."

# HERLOCK SHOLMES' CHRISTMAS CASE

## *Peter Todd*

Like many of the contributors to this book, Charles Hamilton (1876–1961) was a prolific and highly professional writer whose name featured regularly in a wide variety of magazines. He used numerous pen-names, most famously Frank Richards. His stories about Greyfriars School and the "Owl of the Remove" Billy Bunter entertained generations of younger readers. Bunter first appeared in a story in *The Magnet* in 1908 and took his final bow in 1965, having featured in a television series scripted by his creator which ran from 1952–61.

Writing as Peter Todd, Hamilton produced scores of Sherlock Holmes parodies, often with jokey titles such as "The Freckled Band". In 1976, an enterprising American publisher, Mysterious Press, came up with an anthology of the tales, *The Adventures of Herlock Sholmes*. This particular story was not included and it first came to my attention when I read one of my favourite anthologies of Yuletide mysteries, *Crime at Christmas*, edited by Jack Adrian thirty-five years ago. It first appeared in *The Magnet* on 3 December 1916.

"CHRISTMAS TOMORROW!" HERLOCK SHOLMES REMARKED thoughtfully.

I started.

"My dear Sholmes!" I murmured.

Herlock Sholmes smiled.

"You are surprised, Jotson, to hear me make that statement with such positiveness," he remarked. "Yet, I assure you that such is the case."

"I acknowledge, Sholmes, that I ought no longer to be surprised at anything you may say or do. But from what grounds do you infer—"

"Quite simple, my dear Jotson. Look from the window upon the slushy streets and the hurrying crowds, all indicative of the approach of Christmas!"

"True! But why tomorrow precisely?"

"Ah, there we go a little deeper, Jotson. I deduce that Christmas occurs tomorrow from a study of the calendar!"

"The calendar!" I exclaimed, in astonishment.

"Exactly!"

"As you know, Sholmes, I have endeavoured to study your methods, in my humbler way, yet I confess that I do not see the connection—"

"Probably not, Jotson. But to the trained, professional mind it presents no difficulties. Christmas, you are aware, falls upon the twenty-fifth day of the month!"

"True!"

"Look at the calendar, Jotson!"

I obeyed.

"It tells you nothing?"

"Nothing!" I confessed.

Sholmes smiled again, a somewhat bored smile.

"My dear fellow, the calendar indicates that today is the twenty-fourth!"

"Quite so. But—"

"And as Christmas falls upon the twenty-fifth, it follows—to an acute mind accustomed to rapid deductions—that tomorrow is Christmas!"

I could only gaze at my amazing friend in silent admiration.

"But there will be no holiday for us tomorrow, my dear Jotson," resumed Herlock Sholmes. "I have received a wire from the Duke of Hookeywalker, who—Ah, his Grace has arrived!"

Even as Sholmes spoke the Duke of Hookeywalker was shown into our sitting-room.

Herlock Sholmes removed his feet from the mantelpiece with the graceful courtesy so natural to him.

"Pray be seated," said Sholmes. "You may speak quite freely before my friend, Dr. Jotson!"

"Mr. Sholmes, I have sustained a terrible loss!"

Sholmes smiled.

"Your Grace has lost the pawnticket?" he inquired.

"Mr. Sholmes, you must be a wizard! How did you guess—"

"I never guess," said Herlock Sholmes quietly. "My business is to deal with facts. Pray let me have some details."

"It is true, Mr. Sholmes, that the pawnticket is missing," said the duke in an agitated voice. "You are aware that the house of Hookeywalker has a great reputation for hospitality, which must be kept up even in these days of stress. It was necessary for me to give a large Christmas party at Hookey Castle, and, to obtain the necessary funds, the family jewels were pledged with Mr. Ikey Solomons, of Houndsditch. The ticket was in my own keeping—it never left me. I kept it in my own card-case. The card-case never left my person. Yet now, Mr. Sholmes, the ticket is missing!"

"And the card-case?"

"Still in my pocket!"

"When were the Hookeywalker jewels placed with Mr. Solomons?"

"Yesterday morning!"

"And the ticket was missing—"

"Last night," faltered the duke. "I looked in my card-case to make sure that it was still safe, and it was gone. How it had been purloined, Mr. Sholmes, is a mystery—an unfathomable mystery!"

"No mystery is unfathomable to a trained mind," said Sholmes calmly. "I have every hope of recovering the missing pawnticket."

"Mr. Sholmes, you give me new life. But how—"

Sholmes interrupted.

"After leaving Mr. Solomons' establishment, where did your Grace go?"

"I had to make a call at the Chinwag Department of the War Office, and from there I returned to Hookey Castle."

"You made no other call?"

"None."

"It is scarcely possible that a skilled pickpocket is to be found in the Chinwag Department," said Sholmes thoughtfully.

"Impossible, Mr. Sholmes! Every official of that great Department is far above suspicion of being skilled in any manner whatsoever!"

"True!"

"There is no clue!" said the duke in despairing tones. "But unless the missing ticket is recovered, Mr. Sholmes, the famous Hookeywalker jewels are lost!"

"You may leave the case in my hands," said Herlock Sholmes carelessly. "I may call at Hookey Castle with news for you tomorrow."

"Bless you, Mr. Sholmes!"

And the duke took his leave.

Herlock Sholmes lighted a couple of pipes, a habit of his when a particularly knotty problem required great concentration of thought. I did not venture to interrupt the meditations of that mighty intellect.

Sholmes spoke at last, with a smile.

"A very interesting little problem, Jotson. I can see that you are puzzled by my deduction that the pawnticket was lost before his Grace had mentioned it."

"I am astounded, Sholmes."

"Yet it was simple. I had heard of the great social gathering at Hookey Castle," explained Sholmes. "I deduced that his Grace could only meet the bills by hypothecating the family jewels. His hurried visit to me and his agitation could have had but one meaning—I deduced that the pawnticket was lost or stolen. Quite elementary my dear Jotson! But the recovery of the missing ticket—"

"That will not be so simple, Sholmes."

"Who knows, Jotson?" Sholmes rose to his feet and drew his celebrated dressing-gown about him. "I must leave you for a short time, Jotson. You may go and see your patients, my dear fellow."

"One question, Sholmes. You are going—"

"To the Chinwag Department."

"But—"

But Herlock Sholmes was gone.

II

I confess that Sholmes' behaviour perplexed me. He had declared that the pickpocket could not be found in the Chinwag Department, yet he had gone there to commence his investigations. When he returned to Shaker Street, he made no remark upon the case, and I did not venture to question him. The next morning he greeted me with a smile as I came down into the sitting-room.

"You are ready for a little run this morning, Jotson?" he asked.

"I am always at your service, Sholmes."

"Good! Then call a taxi."

A few minutes later a taxicab was bearing us away. Sholmes had given the direction to the driver—"Hookey Castle."

"We are going to see the duke, Sholmes?" I asked.

He nodded.

"But the missing pawnticket?"

"Wait and see!"

This reply, worthy of a great statesman, was all I could elicit from Sholmes on the journey.

The taxi drove up the stately approach to Hookey Castle. A gorgeous footman admitted us to the great mansion, and we were shown into the presence of the duke.

His Grace had left his guests to see us. There was a slight impatience in his manner.

"My dear Mr. Sholmes," he said, "I supposed I had given you the fullest particulars yesterday. You have called me away from a shove-ha'penny party."

"I am sorry," said Sholmes calmly. "Return to the shove-ha'penny party, by all means your Grace, and I will call another time with the pawnticket."

The duke bounded to his feet.

"Mr. Sholmes! You have recovered it?"

Sholmes smiled. He delighted in these dramatic surprises.

The duke gazed with startled eyes at the slip of pasteboard my amazing friend presented to him.

"The missing pawnticket!" he ejaculated.

"The same!" said Sholmes.

"Sholmes!" I murmured. I could say no more.

The Duke of Hookeywalker took the ticket with trembling fingers.

"Mr. Sholmes," he said in tones of deep emotion, "you have saved the honour of the name of Hookeywalker! You will stay to dinner, Mr. Sholmes. Come, I insist—there will be tripe and onions!" he added.

"I cannot resist the tripe and onions," said Sholmes, with a smile. And we stayed.

### III

It was not till the taxi was whirling us homeward to Shaker Street that Herlock Sholmes relieved my curiosity.

"Sholmes!" I exclaimed as the taxi rolled out of the stately gates of Hookey Castle. "How, in the name of wonder—"

Sholmes laughed.

"You are astounded, as usual, Jotson?"

"As usual, Sholmes."

"Yet it is very simple. The duke carried the pawnticket in his card-case," said Sholmes. "He called only at the Chinwag Department of the War Office before returning home. Only a particularly clever pickpocket could have extracted the ticket without the card-case, and, as his Grace himself remarked, it was useless to assume the existence of any particularly clever individual in a Government department. That theory, therefore, was excluded—the ticket had not been taken."

"Sholmes!"

"It had not been taken, Jotson," said Sholmes calmly. "Yet it had left the duke's possession. The question was—how?"

"I confess it is quite dark to me, Sholmes."

"Naturally," said Sholmes drily. "But my mental powers, my dear Jotson, are of quite a different calibre."

"Most true."

"As the ticket had not been taken from the duke, I deduced that he had parted with it unintentionally."

"But is that possible, Sholmes?"

"Quite! Consider, my dear Jotson. His Grace kept the pawnticket, for safety, in his card-case. On calling at the Chinwag Department he sent in his card, naturally. By accident, Jotson, he handed over the pawnticket instead of his own card—"

"Sholmes!"

"And that ticket, Jotson, was taken in instead. That was the only theory to be deduced from the known facts. I proceeded to the Chinwag Department, and interviewed the official upon whom the duke called. There was a little difficulty in obtaining an interview; but he was awakened at last, and I questioned him. As I had deduced, the missing pawnticket was discovered on the salver, where it had lain unnoticed since the duke's call."

"Wonderful!" I exclaimed.

Sholmes smiled in a bored way.

"Elementary, my dear Jotson. But here we are at Shaker Street."

## A PRESENT FOR IVO

# *Ellis Peters*

Ellis Peters was the best-known pseudonym of Edith Mary Pargeter (1913–95), who was born in Shropshire and set much of her fiction in the borderlands between England and Wales. She achieved distinction in several fields before becoming renowned later in life as the creator of the medieval monk and detective Brother Cadfael, who featured in twenty-one novels published between 1977 and 1994 and was brought to the screen in 1994, with Derek Jacobi as Cadfael; the TV series ran for four series and fourteen episodes. She was awarded the CWA Diamond Dagger, recognizing her outstanding contribution to the genre, in 1993.

The success of the Cadfael novels has tended to overshadow the rest of her work in the crime and mystery genre, but her talents as a storyteller were evident in her early novels, including some written as by John Redfern and Jolyon Carr, and historical series published under her own name, such as The Brothers of Gwynedd Quartet. Her novella *The Assize of the Dying* was filmed in 1958 as *The Spaniard's Curse*, while her series about the detective George Felse and his family included *Death and the Joyful Woman*, which won the Edgar award for best novel from the Mystery Writers of America in 1963. With Sue Feder, I co-edited a posthumous volume of her previously uncollected short stories, *The Trinity Cat and other stories*, in 2006. That book included this entertaining bibliomystery, which originally appeared in *Everywoman* in two parts, from December 1958 to January 1959.

I F SARA BOYNE HAD NOT TAKEN HER DUTIES AS THE SECRETARY OF the Shelvedon Teachers' Christmas Committee so seriously, the curious affair at Shelvedon would probably have remained a mystery, a rankling reproach to the local police, to this day. But Sara, in addition to being very young and earnestly pretty, was conscientious, and new to the responsibilities of office.

The committee was collectively responsible for the organization of the great Shelvedon Christmas party, held annually in the castle on Christmas Eve for all the school children of the little borough; but in practice the onus fell fairly and squarely upon the secretary. And if Sara took on a job, she did it thoroughly.

The night before the party she lay awake half the night, checking over everything in her mind. Was there a present for each child, duly selected and wrapped by his or her class teacher? Did the tree look pretty enough?

In some towns it would have been unthinkable to hang all the parcels on the tree overnight, and stand the tree in the open courtyard of the castle, which was also the town hall and civic offices, at the mercy of any passer-by, and protected only by the occasional perambulations of a constable on his beat. But in Shelvedon it was part of a proud tradition, and nothing had ever been stolen, and no one entertained any fears that anything ever would be.

And the food for the party tea—was there really enough of it? Were Tom Fielding's decorations too adult to please? Roger Brecon had been sweet about the fairy lights, too—fancy a solicitor being so knowledgeable about electricity! Sara, who wasn't vain but knew that she was attractive, could not help wondering whether Roger's interest in the party was on her account.

She awoke with the first hint of dawn to the conviction that the carol sheets had been forgotten. Shelvedon parents, coming at half past six to fetch their children home, liked to stay for a final half-hour of carol singing. She must go along very early to the castle and bring down the leaflets from the cupboard upstairs, in case they should be overlooked later.

That was how she came to leave home immediately after lunch, though the party was not due to start until half past three.

On her way to the castle she bought an evening paper—the first edition was on the streets at noon—to see what it had to say about the junior school nativity play, in which some of her own hopeful pupils had starred. Not until she had sunned herself in the praise of her charges did she suddenly register the shock of the staring headlines which had the place of honour on the front page.

## SHELVEDON CHRONICLE STOLEN
*Daring midnight raid on town museum*

During the night the town museum, housed in one ward of the castle, has been broken into by means of the removal of a pane of glass from which the burglar alarm could be reached and switched off. An expert job, arguing a preliminary reconnaissance, and considerable experience of all kinds of safety devices. By chance the constable on his beat made a round of the buildings, found the window unfastened, and observed the vacant pane, whereupon he immediately gave the alarm, and kept close watch on the building until the arrival of reinforcements who could cover all exits from the castle.

The report went on to say that the museum had then been searched, but the thief must already have vacated this wing, and the search had to be extended to all the civic offices and the arcades of the castle, before a man was run to earth in the open undercroft of the rear gatehouse.

He was sitting on one of the benches, apparently asleep, and claimed that he had no recollection of how he had got there, though he admitted earlier he had been drinking in the Black Bull. The man had been detained and it was understood that he was well known to the police. However, nothing incriminating was found on him.

Examination of the museum premises had revealed that only one item was missing: the world-famous *Shelvedon Chronicle*, the most perfect fourteenth-century manuscript of its kind in existence, a local history written by the monk Anselmus of Shelvedon Priory, and particularly renowned for its beautiful illuminations.

The manuscript of the *Chronicle* had not been recovered. Enquiries were being pursued both in Shelvedon and elsewhere, as this was the latest of many such thefts of extremely valuable antiques and works of art during the last six months, and the police suspected what must be an organization of a national scale for their acquisition and consequent disposition.

Sara stood gaping at the improbable paragraphs with all the consternation and disbelief of a Londoner reading of the theft of the Crown Jewels. *The Shelvedon Chronicle* lay alone in a black velvet-lined case in the museum, with a small strip-light shining upon its exquisite, jewel-like initial letters and minute pictures.

A steel frame closed down over the glass case at night. How could it be stolen? Only an expert could have done it. A national scale? International, more likely, thought Sara, impervious for the moment to the frosty sharpness of the air and to a rapid ring of footsteps crossing the glazed cobbles.

\*

A tall young man in a duffle coat was reaching up into the branches of the tree, setting the chains of lights tinkling.

"Hallo!" said Sara, embarrassed and delighted to recognize her helpful amateur electrician. "Have you got this affair on your mind as badly as that, too?"

Roger Brecon swung round, the needles showering down over him as he turned his head. "Oh, hallo, Sara! My goodness, you startled me!" But his surprise struck her as slightly overdone. "Where did you spring from?"

"I didn't spring. I was here. I was reading the paper."

"Whatever brings you here so early, anyhow?"

"I just couldn't rest. I wanted to make sure everything was all right. I forgot to bring down the carol sheets yesterday. Anyhow, what about you? It isn't even your headache, really."

He laughed, twitching a bright red parcel into a better position, and stepped back to observe the general effect. "I just wanted to make sure they really light up. After all, I was the one who fixed them up. I'd look a fine fool if they didn't work."

But they did work; the whole tree leaped into brilliance and colour at a flick of his finger. He stared up at it delightedly, and then bestowed upon Sara the most radiant and intimate of smiles.

They were silent, looking at each other with slightly flushed faces and slightly dazzled eyes, when Tom Fielding came slithering across the cobbles with casual skating strides of his long legs, a newspaper crumpled up under his arm. His black forelock bobbed over the broad brown forehead, and his lean cheeks were red from scurrying through the frost after Sara.

"Hi!" said Tom, pulling up in a long glissade, Roger still hidden from him by the tree. "Your sense of duty will be the death of you. Did you remember to eat any lunch, or were you too worried about the ice-cream for the kids? Seen the news? Crime marches on!"

"I was just reading it. Isn't it terrible? Somehow you never expect that sort of thing to happen in your own town."

She was annoyed with herself for sounding embarrassed, and her rising colour caused Tom to scowl suddenly in suspicion. He took a couple of steps to the right, and his line of vision embraced Roger Brecon.

"Oh, it's you!" Tom remarked, with no enthusiasm at all. His lowering brows added: It would be!

"Hallo, Fielding," said Roger, with more civility but no more warmth. "A bad business, this museum affair!"

"Oh I don't know, might be quite good business for you. I heard you'd stalked out of the police station—don't tell me you're turning the client down? Think of the capital there must be behind an organization big enough to market stuff like the *Shelvedon Chronicle*!"

"Did this man you're talking about really want you to be his solicitor?" asked Sara, fascinated.

"They charged him, and he asked for a solicitor." It was clear from his flush of annoyance that Roger had no wish to talk about it. "He didn't seem to care who it was—said a local man would do, and picked me out at random. I didn't know anything about the case until they notified me he was asking me to act for him."

"And are you going to?" Sara couldn't help asking.

"No, of course not, how can I? You'd have thought the police would have seen that for themselves. I'm a councillor, and the *Chronicle* is municipal property. I'm even on the museum sub-committee. It wouldn't be proper for me to involve myself in the case legally." He was red with irritation now. "Hadn't we better get those carol sheets down, Sara?"

"Didn't you take a good look at him?" asked Tom, happily pursuing what he saw to be an unwelcome subject. "Surely you wanted at least to *see* the one that got away?"

"I didn't even know what it was all about until I was there. It was only decent to see him, and explain why I couldn't act for him. Sara, I'm just going to straighten that one chain—you go ahead, I'll follow you in a moment."

"I'll hold the steps for you," volunteered Tom, maliciously obliging. Even willing to let me out of his sight, thought Sara, as she scurried indoors and through the entrance hall, rather than stop baiting Roger. Well, let him get on with it. Roger could hold his own.

The decorations leaped into beauty as she switched on the lights, and the laden tables shone with jellies and trifles and cakes. She ran up to the small committee-room in the gate tower, unlocked the cupboard and brought down her carol leaflets. There was really nothing else to be done.

Surprised that the two young men had not yet followed her indoors, she took an apple from the bowl of fruit on the nearest table, and went out, peacefully munching it, to see what they were up to.

"Well, well!" said Tom, observing the apple. "Eve in person! Now which of us two, Brecon, old boy, would you say was cast for the serpent?"

"Which of us," snapped Roger bitterly, "looks more like a snake in the grass?" And he strode away from the tree and took Sara by the arm, turning her back towards the hall. "Come on, Sara, let's get inside. Here come the others."

Paul Hartland and two of his juniors from the Modern School were just unloading a car on the pavement outside the gatehouse, and little Miss Price from the infants department was trotting across the courtyard with her arms full of sheet music.

Then, quite suddenly, came the first of the children, with dazzled eyes fixed on the tree. And the tenth great Annual Joint Christmas Party for the schoolchildren of Shelvedon began.

*

Everybody agreed the party was the most complete success so far, and the best organized. They played games first—active games and quiet games alternately—then they ate an enormous tea, and after it came the puppet show, the conjurer, and the ventriloquist, to keep the guests reasonably still and engrossed while the tea settled; while the helpers snatched a brief rest, too, and Tom Fielding sneaked away and clambered into his beard and his scarlet gown, ready for the climax.

Then out they all trooped, already warmly packed into their outdoor clothes, to cluster round the lighted tree. Tom's assistants climbed about the tree handing down parcels, while he called up eager owners to receive them. He was a voluble and effective Father Christmas. The one real consolation, he claimed, was that inside all that red flannel he didn't feel the cold.

Then the parents came, and the town band, and the time-honoured half-hour of carol singing began, under the coloured lights and the floating balloons; and before anyone was really ready for it—which was the right time for it to happen—the party was over. With a noise like the descent of the evening starlings upon Trafalgar Square the children of Shelvedon were on their way home.

Sara stood under the ravaged tree, speeding the departing guests as they withdrew.

"Goodnight, Jimmy! Happy Christmas! Goodnight, Alison! Goodnight, Pat! Did you have a good time? A happy Christmas…"

"You seem to know every kid in Shelvedon personally," said Roger, grinning from behind her shoulder.

An under-sized boy in a navy flannel duffle beamed up at her demurely over his large, flat parcel and gave the string an extra twist round his wrist. "Miss Boyne, I got a book!"

"You haven't opened it yet," she said, smiling. "How do you know it's a book?"

"Oh, yes, Miss Boyne, I have. I did it up again carefully, so it won't get wet even if it snows. The man on the wireless said it would snow."

Plainly he hoped for the prophecy to be fulfilled. "And do you like your present, Ivo?"

Large eyes, black-fringed, shone in the shadow of his hood. "Miss Boyne, it's *beautiful*! It's a *beautiful* book!"

"Funny little thing," said Roger as the small figure trotted away over the scintillating cobbles. "Who is he?"

"He's an orphan, in the county's care—name's Ivo Jenkins. He's boarded out with old Mrs. Freeman—you know, at Cross Farm Cottage. She's very good to him, but she's rather old. I wish he had more young, stimulating company, he's such a reserved, serious child."

"One of yours, I see," said Roger, gently laughing at her. He stretched and sighed, looking after the last stragglers as they withdrew under a barrage of dancing balloons, leaving the courtyard suddenly quiet and desolate. "I should have liked to stay and help you tidy up, Sara, but I've got to go to a dinner tonight, and I promised I'd go home first."

"You've done enough," said Sara. "You've been most helpful. Thanks for everything!"

She had almost hoped that he would make some tentative reference to the New Year's Eve dance, but he didn't. He simply smiled, wished her a happy Christmas, and fled.

She turned away with a sigh, and went to join her weary fellow-workers who were clearing up the debris. Just then Tom emerged, scarlet and perspiring, from his beard. He stripped off his robes, and began to gather up the coloured heaps of tinsel and wrappings under the tree. "Hallo, what's this? There's something buried in the soil here!"

Sara went to his side. The earth in the tub had certainly been disturbed, and Tom's vigorous gesture had swept aside the fallen needles and exposed a corner of brown paper.

"It's a box—no, a book!" He tugged it clear and brushed away the needles that clung to it. An oblong package wrapped loosely in a single fold of stiff paper, which fell away as he turned it in his hands, revealed the vividly coloured dust jacket of a book. "*Boys Gigantic Adventure Annual!* Oh, lord!" said Tom blankly. "Has somebody been forgotten? One of the absentees?"

"No, I'm positive! Besides, this was for one of my boys. I remember it perfectly. But how on earth did it get there do you suppose?"

"Sara!" Tom stared at her reproachfully. "*You* didn't choose this for some poor kid, did you?" Just because he taught art at the Secondary Modern and the Technical College, she thought indignantly, he didn't have to be so damned superior about other people's taste.

"Yes, I did! What's the matter with it? But—" She gaped helplessly towards the gateway, through which young Ivo Jenkins had vanished some ten minutes ago. "But he *had* his book! He just told me he'd looked at it, and it was beautiful."

"Couldn't have meant this," said Tom, averting his eyes from it. "Anyhow, he buried it decently. Probably disapproved of the art work—and who could blame him? Obviously he was just being nice to you—thought you didn't know any better."

Sara experienced an urge, by no means new to her where Tom Fielding was concerned, to box his ears. "I tell you he *liked* it! A beautiful book, he said!" She heard him saying it again, and knew that he had meant it; and quite suddenly the confusion in her mind was all blown away by a staggering thought.

This annual was undoubtedly the book she'd chosen for him; what, then, had he been clutching so tightly under his arm as he took leave of her? What was the beautiful book that had caused his serious eyes to shine so brilliantly in the shadow of his hood?

She clutched at Tom's arm, forgetting all her irritation with him. "Tom!—*how big* is the *Shelvedon Chronicle?*"

Tom turned a face stricken into ludicrous consternation, and stared at her wildly, making the same mental leap she had just made. *"Just about as big as this thing!"*

They stood gaping at each other, trying to grasp the monstrous implications. "It couldn't be! Things like that don't happen!"

"But they have happened! It disappeared from the museum, didn't it? And the police closed all the ways out of the castle, and then made a thorough search for the thief, didn't they? And found a man with a criminal record in just that line—"

"Right here inside the courtyard!"

"But without the *Chronicle*," said Tom. "You realize what that means? They had him penned inside here, unable to get clean away with the goods, but with a few minutes respite while they combed out the museum buildings.

"Long enough for him to swop his loot for a similar-sized parcel on the Christmas-tree, wrap it and leave it to be collected later—by himself or someone else. Without it, he stood a chance of getting off. He'd only to hang the *Chronicle* on the tree, and hide it, and let himself be picked up. What else could he do?"

"But how could he get a message through to anyone else?" protested Sara breathlessly, swept away by this reconstruction.

"I don't know. There are ways; maybe he had a confederate outside the enclave, maybe he managed to get some sort of signal through."

"Then one thing's certain," said Sara. "He'd let them know the name on the parcel, otherwise they could hunt all day. And if he did manage to get word through, why haven't they collected it?"

"Maybe they have. Maybe that's some fresh substitute young Ivo's carrying home now. Or perhaps they simply didn't get here in time. The precincts would be rather popular this morning, while the offices were open. And this afternoon conscience brought us along so early—"

"Then they'll be looking for Ivo now," said Sara with fierce finality, and grew pale at what she herself had said. It wasn't the *Shelvedon Chronicle* she was thinking of, it was that funny, old-fashioned little boy with the quiet manners and the impenetrable reserve, trotting home through the frosty evening with thousands of pounds worth of skill and beauty and devotion under his arm.

"A beautiful book!" said Tom with awe. "My God, he was right!"

They exchanged one bemused, incredulous glance.

"Come on!" said Tom, seizing her by the arm. "At least, we've got to make sure. See him safely home, and beg a look at his book, just in case."

"And take him this!" Sara grabbed up the *Boys Gigantic Adventure Annual* as she was towed away at the end of Tom's long arm.

"*That!*" Tom snorted as he slid into the car and reached for the starter. "A boy who falls for the *Chronicle* won't think the *Gigantic Adventure Annual* a fair exchange."

"This is entirely appropriate for his age group," said Sara indignantly, slamming the door on her side as the engine obediently hiccupped into life.

"Only unfortunately he doesn't seem to be entirely appropriate to it himself."

"You don't know him! I do! I chose it specially for him, because he's far too prim and quiet. I want to encourage him to think adventurously," she said, all the more aggressively because Tom always made her feel self-conscious about her beliefs.


Tom swung the car out through the gateway. They threaded their way rapidly through the late Christmas shoppers and the lighted windows fell behind them. Through the archway in the town wall the black sky lowered at them, heavy with cloud. The first desultory flakes of the promised snow were already falling.

"Perhaps there's no one to collect," said Sara. "Perhaps there wasn't any message. Maybe he's just been hoping they couldn't hold him, so that he could pick it up himself. It may be just a one-man job, after all."

"Not a chance! He can't be any more than a very small cog in a very large system of wheels. What would an ordinary thug want with a thing like the *Chronicle*? No, this is no one-man job. It ties in with all those other thefts of works of art, just as the newspaper said."

"Isn't it queer," she said, "to think there are people willing to spend a fortune on a thing they'll never be able to show off to anyone? What do they get out of gloating over them in secret?"

"If I had the chance to gloat over the *Chronicle* in secret, and feel I owned it, I might be able to tell you. They exist, all right. Plenty of them, if you know where to look."

He put his foot down hard as soon as they were well out of the shopping streets and through the gate. The high, windy road, fringed with semi-detached houses at first, soon fell into darkness between the occasional older cottages. Not three miles away to the right, keen in the strong salt scent of the wind, was the sea.

"Wouldn't Ivo be with some of the other children? The little Grettons have to come out this way, nearly as far as Cross Farm."

"They left well ahead of him. No, I'm afraid he'll be alone." He was so often alone, partly from habit, partly from choice.

She wished he lived with some large, cheerful family in the town, where he'd be jockeyed into mixing with other children whether he liked it or not. But foster-homes are where you can find them. And the old lady was very good to him. Sara found herself thinking of Ivo with an indignant, anxious affection, as though she had only become aware of his deprivations when danger was added to them.

The road ran between hedges and fields now, and the street lighting was all left behind, but it was only a quarter of a mile to Cross Farm. And suddenly Sara gave a breathless laugh of sheer relief, and pointed ahead. "There he is! He's all right!"

The small figure, bent purposefully forward in an old man's trotting walk, scurried along the footpath with his parcel tucked under his arm.

Tom heaved an audible sigh, and relaxed the pressure of his foot on the accelerator. The next moment he had to jam it hard upon the brake, for out of a side road on the right a large, old, dark-bodied car drove suddenly across his path, and turned into the road ahead of him, cutting off his view of the child trotting briskly into the distance.

It all happened in an instant. The big car drew alongside the hurrying child, and slowed there smoothly, and an arm and shoulder, no more than a vague black movement in the murky dusk, leaned out and plucked the parcel from under his arm.

Ivo's scared squeal sounded thinly through the moan of the snow-laden wind, and sharpened into a yell of pain as the strong cord dragged sharply at his wrist. Sara remembering how tightly he had wound the string round to anchor his treasure, gasped in sympathy. It must have been the sound of Tom accelerating furiously that decided what happened next. If only the string had broken Ivo would have been safe, but the string did not break, and delay was impossible.

The man in the passenger seat transferred his grip suddenly from the book to the boy's arm, and hoisted him bodily into the car, which shot away into the night with a roar of a powerful engine, Tom's old Morris throbbing on its tail.

Sara heard herself repeating the car number breathlessly, memorizing it because she had no opportunity of writing it down.

Tom said nothing at all. His jaw was set, and his foot had the accelerator pedal flattened to the floor of the car, and every ounce of energy he possessed was devoted to hurling them along after the kidnappers. Sara hooked an arm over the back of the seat to steady herself as they rocked round the corner into the Westensea road, and met the squalls of thin, sharp snow head-on.

The rear light ahead winked at them through the murk, and seemed if anything a shade nearer. The speedometer needle was wobbling furiously around sixty-five; it crept up towards seventy, in a flash of desperation lunged above seventy, and lurched back shuddering at its own temerity.

Past the Mitre Inn now, and round the long curve, turning with the curve of the coastline. Two miles or so more, and they'd be entering the suburbs of Westensea, and the big fellow would be forced to slow down. They'd get him there, if they had to ram him to do it. If he kept up this speed the police would join in the chase, and he wouldn't risk that, with what he had on board.

"He's stopping!" panted Sara. The big car seemed to have drawn into the hedge and slowed considerably, if not stopped. The driver opened his door, and seemed to be getting out, though he clung close to the body of the car.

Tom didn't lift his foot until the first tiny flash against the blackness of the night and the deeper blackness of the car warned him. The report was lost in the protests of his own sorely tried motor, but he recognized the signs, and slowed for an instant, then, realizing that if he stopped he would merely present a sitting target, he gritted his teeth, trod hard down again, and wrenched the wheel round to drive full at the enemy. Head-on he'd have a better chance of upsetting the marksman's aim.

The second shot, by luck or skill, got their right front tyre, and brought them round with a horrible, lurching plunge towards the ditch.

Tom, wrestling frantically with the wheel, wrenched the Morris back on to the road, and somehow managed to pull it up without disaster on a front tyre slashed to ribbons; but by the time they had tumbled, panting and trembling, out into the snow the big car was pulling away at speed, and before they had breath enough to speak it had vanished completely in the direction of Westensea.

Tom caught Sara by the shoulders, and held her for a moment against his heart. "Sara, you're all right? You're not hurt?" The alarm and ardour in his voice hardly registered until later, she was so intent upon the chase.

"I'm all right! A bit shaken, that's all. Now what do we do? We *can't* let them get away!"

"We're not going to. I've got to change this wheel. Thank God the spare's all right! I can manage alone—only a twenty-minute job! Sara, darling, could you run on alone? You're not afraid? We can't be far out of the town, there must be a call-box soon, or a house with a phone.

"Call the police, tell them the car number, and where it's headed. As soon as I've changed the wheel I'll come on after you and pick you up, and we'll go on together and report, see if we can help at all. After you've called them, walk back towards me. Or if the snow gets bad stay in shelter somewhere by the side of the road and watch out for me. Can you do that?"

"Yes, of course!" She was glad to have something active to do, glad to be still in the hunt. She set off at a rapid run, head-down into the snow. Not until she had left Tom and the Morris well behind did she realize that she was still clutching the *Gigantic Adventure Annual* under her arm. She tucked it inside her coat to keep it dry, and ran on.

The first larger house, after several isolated cottages, lay back from the road behind a screen of trees and shrubberies. There was a wide carriage-gate, and a small wicket beside it, and the overhead wires, thrumming angrily in the wind, turned inward with the drive towards the house.

As she pushed open the wicket gate she thought it might be wise to leave Tom an indication of where she had halted, in case he came along before she was back on the road. No use leaving boy scout's signs in this obliterating blizzard. She detached the gaudy cover of the *Gigantic Adventure Annual* and impaled it firmly on one of the top spikes of the iron gate, so that it stood up and faced the road like a professional sign.

Then she ran up the drive, and rang the bell at the front door of a large, complacent Victorian house in two-coloured brick.

There was what seemed a long interval before a light came on inside the porch, and high heels tapped up to the door. The woman who opened it was dressed in a smart black suit, and had the cool, noncommittal manner of a housekeeper or a secretary.

At Sara's request to use the telephone she raised her eyebrows very slightly, but waved the intruder civilly into the porch out of the snow.

"It's urgent," Sara found herself saying, "or I wouldn't trouble you." Possibly the eyebrows had intimidated her a little. "I want to call the police," she added breathlessly.

"Not an accident?" the woman in black asked, with quick sympathy.

"Well, no, but—"

"I'm sorry, of course you mustn't lose any time. One moment, I'll tell Professor Brayburn." And she left Sara standing in the hall, and vanished through one of a bewildering array of doors.

After a few minutes the same door opened once again, and out bustled a small, benevolent, grey-haired man, peering kindly at Sara over the rims of bifocals.

His face was rosy and elderly, and instantly familiar though it took her a moment or two to relate both face and name to her memories of three or four summers ago, when she had last seen him.

It had been at a rally of adult educationalists, at the University of Westchester, and the Professor of English Literature had moved benignly among guests at tea. She felt herself suddenly back among known, safe, comforting things; the lurking car and the gunman on the lonely road seemed as remote as the moon.

"My dear young lady, of course, of course, come into my study, you'll be more comfortable at the extension in there. Such a night! Terrible!" He waved her before him into a brown, book-lined room full of deep leather chairs, and indicated the telephone.

Sara lifted the receiver. The line was quite dead. She tried dialling the operator, joggled the rest, waited, tried again. But nothing happened. The heavy, dead silence closed on her hearing like a vice.

Professor Brayburn, surprised by the delay, looked in from the next room. "Dear, dear, is there some trouble on the line? It was all right an hour or so ago."

"It seems to be dead. No response at all."

He bustled across with a concerned face to try it for himself, and had to admit defeat. "That's extraordinary—surely there's not been enough snow to bring down wires? My dear child, I'm so sorry! Can I—"

"Oh, I can't put you out any more. You've been most kind. My friend will soon be along to pick me up, and we can go on into the town."

"But my dear, you can't possibly go out again in this, it's still snowing heavily. Won't you at least let me give you a warm drink, and wait a little, and see if it stops?"

"It's most kind of you, but I can't. My friend might miss me if I don't go to the road. He won't know where I am, you see—"

She was moving steadily towards the door as she spoke, preparing to bow herself out as gracefully as she could, when she stepped upon something that felt sharp and hard in the pile of the Persian carpet, something that stabbed through the sole of her shoe. She withdrew her foot and looked down, quite involuntarily, to see what she had trodden on. A button. A wooden toggle button from a duffle coat, with a girdle of red string still circling its middle.

The thick, strong cord by which it had been attached to the coat had torn loose, bringing with it a few threads of dark blue flannel; and the button was not big enough to have come from a man's coat. A child's, then; a navy blue one—*Ivo's*!

She tore her eyes from it instantly, but she was too late. Across three yards of charged air they encountered Professor Brayburn's old, faded, benevolent blue eyes, and she knew that he had followed her glance, and understood all its implications.

She made a gallant attempt. She took another tentative step towards the door, and said, "Goodnight, and thank you very much. I'm sorry I've troubled you for nothing."

But with that the door opened, and the black-clad secretary slid through it, and after her, circling gently, one to the left and the other to the right, like dancers, two large and silent men in dark overcoats.

They drew into a tight semicircle between Sara and the door.

"What a pity!" said the Professor sadly. "Such a nice young lady, too! But we can hardly let you go running off into the night now, knowing what you know—can we?"


The door closed behind her, and she heard the key turn in the lock. The soft footsteps of the man with the gun receded down the staircase.

The room, heavily furnished but with that impersonal look of a bedroom which is seldom slept in, was dimly lit by one inadequate electric bulb under a fringed shade. On the big bed, draped with a dark tapestry cover, Ivo sat staring at her in astonishment and uncertainty through the tears he had just hurriedly scrubbed away.

"Miss Boyne, you mustn't be scared. I'll look after you! Was it you, Miss Boyne, in the car with Mr. Fielding, following them? They haven't got him, too, have they?" He slid off the tall bed and stood in front of her, quivering gently like a terrier on a scent. "Was he hurt when they fired the gun? What happened?"

She told him. Putting the whole crazy sequence into words somehow clarified it for her, too, and she found in it more to reassure her than she had expected. "So you see, he's sure to come, as soon as he's changed the wheel. Even if he misses seeing my sign as he comes by, he'll go straight to the police when he doesn't find me. And once they start looking for us properly, they're sure to start from where the car was halted, so they'll soon be here. They can't miss us, really Ivo."

"But suppose Mr. Fielding sees it the first time, and comes here by himself?" asked the all too-knowing child, staring at her with those unblinking eyes of his. "There's at least *four* of them. I think there may be more."

"Mr. Fielding will almost certainly call the police first," said Sara, all the more firmly because of the sinking feeling he'd given her. "Why, *all* your buttons are gone!" she said, surveying the duffle coat that hung open over Ivo's Sunday suit.

"I pulled them off. I left one in the car, in case we ever have to identify it," he explained simply, "because there might be a lot of big black cars like it, and they could change the number-plates, couldn't they? And one in the garden here—"

Somewhat staggered, Sara sat down on the bed, and drew him down beside her. "Ivo, I want to ask you about the book you had from the Christmas tree."

His face burned up into indignation. "They took it away from me! They can't do that, it's stealing. It's *my* book!"

"Ivo, dear, I'm afraid it may not be. You see, I think it was stolen already, from the town museum, and put in the place of the book that was meant for you. Tell me what it was like."

He gave her one dismayed glance, and then obeyed, shutting his eyes the better to see it again. "It was in a folding leather case, without any fastener. Inside it had a beautiful leather cover, and the paper was funny, but nice to feel. I couldn't read the letters, they were funny, too, but they made lovely patterns, and the big ones were done with colours, with birds, and animals, and people. And there were lots of little pictures, with people with queer dresses like in the history books."

"It is a history book, Ivo, a wonderful one, made hundreds of years ago. Somebody stole it from the museum, and then he wanted to hide it because the police were after him, and he hid it in the parcel meant for you."

"What will they do with us?" asked Ivo.

That was what Sara was wondering, too. She hoped he had not realized the full implications of their position, but she was afraid he had.

"Oh, take us and leave us somewhere miles from home, while they make their getaway. Or leave us locked up here—that would give them time to vanish, too, before anyone finds us."

"But if that old man who lives here has got to vanish," said the disconcerting child after a moment's thought, "that means he'll lose his house, and his job, and everything. And then he wouldn't be any use to them again, would he? I mean, if the police knew who he is, and are looking for him, and all that? I don't think he'll like that. And the people he's working for—they won't like it, either, will they?"

They would not, and she knew it. There was too much at stake. To leave Ivo and herself to tell what they knew, however much later, meant to sacrifice at least all this local part of a carefully-built organization. No, the game was far too big. They would be quietly disposed of. Not here, though! This house was too close to the scene of the latest theft.

Furthermore, it would be very much easier and safer to remove them to some more discreet place for disposal alive. They would be taken away from here, she felt sure. In this blizzard? There was too great a chance of a car getting stuck in the drifts. No, nothing would happen until the snow stopped. Tom and the police had a little grace in which to find them, and she and Ivo a short respite in which to help themselves.

She was uncomfortably aware that Ivo was adding up the prob-abilities no less accurately than she, and it was largely to distract him if she could, and avoid confirming his conclusions at all costs, that she jumped up briskly, and began to look round their prison.

First of all she crossed over to the window, pulled back the thick, dusty curtains, and hoisted the heavy lower sash. Its weight was greater than she had expected, and as soon as she relaxed her upward pressure she saw why, for instantly it surged down again, and she had only just time to catch it before it crashed.

Both sash-cords were broken so she let it slide down the last few inches, quietly, and looked round for something with which to prop it open.

There was an enormous book on the old-fashioned table in the corner, a family Bible. She propped it under one end of the sash, and through the opening the snow blew in thinning eddies.

Sara hoisted the sash of the heavy window cautiously higher, inserting her shoulder under it, and stacking the *Boys Gigantic Adventure Annual* on top of the Bible. When she gently lowered the weight upon this precarious erection it settled and held fast, giving her reasonable room to lean out and inspect their position.

"We're on the garden side," said Ivo apologetically. "I looked. We couldn't signal to the road from here."

Sara looked down upon a depressingly blank wall. "We're only on the first floor," she said strenuously.

"The bed isn't made up," said the practical child, even more sadly. "No sheets or blankets, only that big cover. And the curtains!"

The curtains were old brocade, far too thick to knot successfully with-out losing half their length. And even if curtains and bedcover could be joined together, how were they to be anchored? The furniture offered no help, the bed had no posts, only a solid footboard.

Then, looking round with more optimism than she felt, she perceived for the first time in her life the true beauty and utility of Victorian furnishing. Instead of a neat little track and plastic runners, the curtains were slung by metal rings from an enormous mahogany pole, as long as a tilting lance and as thick as her wrist.

This pole, she discovered, was at least three feet longer than the width of the window frame, and the very pins by which the rings were secured to the fabric of the curtains were of solid brass, and thick as skewers.

She began almost to believe in what she was doing. She hoisted a chair across to the window, and piled several volumes of a discarded encyclopaedia on top of the chair, and climbed precariously to the swaying crest. Large curved brackets supported the curtain pole.

She had to exert all her strength, thus straining upward, to lift clear one end, and then the sudden shifting of weight sent all the rings rattling and chiming down the pole in a fine shower of dust and almost toppled her from her perch. Ivo flew to prop her up, and stretched up his puny arms to nurse the weight while she climbed down and moved her ladder to the other end. There was no need to explain anything to him, he was already ahead of her in spirit, his eyes glittering with excitement.

The pole, braced across the open window to take the weight upon those huge, solid rings, was the safest anchorage they could have found anywhere. Sara stripped off one of the heavy curtains, rings and all, and with the brass pin attached to the rings secured it firmly to the curtain which still dangled in place. She pulled at the join, first gingerly, then more confidently. A few threads strained warningly, but nothing gave.

Then Ivo dragged the tapestry cover from the bed.

Attaching that was not so easy. There were no more spare pins, and after one attempt she gave up the idea of tying it on. There remained only the two looped curtain cords. She used them to bind the thick fabrics together as tightly as she could, and hoped they wouldn't slip. The thickness of the hems would certainly help to hold them fast.

By that time she really believed in the machinery of escape. She had the awkward bundle coiled in her arms on the snowy window-sill when she checked for a moment to say: "Turn out the light!"

When it was out, the whole face of the house below her lay black and unpeopled. The Professor and his henchmen were all at the front, there was no one to observe the dangling curtains snaking down the wall and past the ground-floor window.

Past it? She was afraid that even when the whole length was paid out the end still swung only just level with the upper panes of the downstairs window. From above it was difficult to tell by how many feet it hung clear of the ground, but she was afraid it must be almost six feet.

"All right, Ivo, put the light on again. It looks a long way to drop. Do you think you can manage? Are you good at climbing?"

The snort he gave was the most contemptuous sound she had ever heard! He leaned out and peered down the wall. "Do it on my head! Plenty of snow to drop in!" He was already balanced on his stomach with both legs waving out of the window, and both hands locked fast on the pole, when he checked. "Sorry, Miss Boyne," he said, abashed. "Ladies first!"

Sara looked at the distant ground, and the absurd rope, and shut her eyes. "I'm not sure it will bear me. You go, quickly! When you get down, get into cover at once, and go down the drive to the road. You must go into the town, to the police, and tell them everything, do you understand?"

"But what about you?" His solemn eyes stared anxiously across the window-sill.

"Never mind me, I shall be all right until the police come. Go on down, quickly!"

She was so intent on seeing him safely down that she never heard the door of the room open behind her. The first she knew of it was the sudden pull of the ice-cold wind surging more strongly into the room, and a bellow of alarm and indignation that made her leap round wildly to face the doorway. One of the two gunmen, the taller, came plunging across to the window in three great strides. She saw the dark-blue gleam of the revolver barrel in his right hand, and screamed, "Quickly, Ivo!" Then the man swung his left arm and struck her out of his way, and she was flung against the wall, and slid to her knees, shaken and dazed.

It took her a moment to realize what he meant to do. In her world such things had never happened before. It took time to adjust herself to them. He was leaning well out from the open window, looking down the still jerking rope. He took hold of it for an instant as if he meant to try and haul it up again with its burden, then abandoned the idea, for Ivo was now so near to the end of it that he had only to slither down the last foot or so and let go. Instead, the right hand that held the gun steadied deliberately, pointed the barrel downwards and took aim.

She flung herself forward on her knees, gripped the spine of the *Boys Gigantic Adventure Annual* in both hands, and wrenched it from its place. The family Bible, pulled askew with it, toppled majestically to the floor, just before the falling window could strike it. Instead, it struck the leaning man across the small of the back with a crunch like that of a tree falling, just as he fired. Shot and scream, and the awful, crushed sound of the sash thudding into his ribs, all came together. Where the shot went nobody knew, but the gun flew out of his paralysed hand and dropped into the snow and one muted yell of triumph from the invisible garden eased Sara's heart once for all of any terror that Ivo had been hit.

His movements were so implicit in that joyful shout that she almost saw him drop like a hunting cat upon the fallen gun, and dive with it into the snowy shrubberies, that threshed for one moment after his vanishing, and then were still.

She stood petrified in the middle of the room, clutching the battered annual, and staring at the trapped man in fascinated horror.

He had left the door wide open. Sara turned and darted through it. Instinctively she turned towards the staircase, and scurried down it. At the foot she suffered a moment of terror, because the woman in black was standing by the hall door, peering out into the drive. No quick way out there. She drew back hastily, and backed through the nearest doorway in the shadow of the stairs, into an unlighted room. Somewhere she could hear the humming of a car.

The curtains of the room were not drawn, and her eyes, aided by the reflected glow from the snow outside, gradually grew accustomed to the darkness. The place seemed to be a little rear parlour, looking on to the same silent, bushy garden she had seen from above. She felt her way to the window, and put down the *Boys Gigantic Adventure Annual* while she quietly eased back the catch and freed the lower sash. Before she could raise it there were rapid footsteps at the door, and the rattle of the knob turning.

She had no time to think or plan. She dropped to the carpet and crept under the chenille-covered table, just as the door opened and the light was snapped on.

The neatly-shod elderly feet entering could belong to no one but Professor Brayburn. Sara cowered in her hiding-place, and watched him approach her across the room; and for one awful moment she believed he had seen her and was coming to coax her out of cover with his gentle, regretful, almost apologetic voice.

But she saw he was only making for the window, just as she had done. When he reached it she was even able to peep from under the

chenille folds, and watch him. He had a leather case under his arm,
something like a flat briefcase. Her heart gave a lurch as she realized
what it must be.

A folding case minus fastener, Ivo had said. Was the Professor just in
the act of putting his plunder safely away somewhere in this room? It
didn't look like that. He had laid it down on the edge of the table—she
heard the tiny, dull sound it made on the chenille pile.

Now he had left the table and gone back to the door for a moment.
He opened it a crack, and curious sounds came in. Wasn't that a car
again? More a roar than a purr this time, surely, in the drive. It sounded
like more than one car. Then suddenly a shot, or at least something
that sounded like a shot.

She no longer understood anything that was happening, it was all
a terrifying confusion. The Professor was quietly closing and locking
the door.

Now he had turned his back on her, and was bending over the
drawers of a writing-desk across the room. Sara reached up a timid
hand, and groped along the edge of the table until she found the
leather case. She lifted it gently down, and drew it into the shelter of
the tablecloth with her.

The flap opened quietly, the vellum, supple as velvet, slid softly
out upon the floor. She slipped the battered annual into the case,
and gingerly hoisted it back on to the table. They'd reckoned it a fair
exchange once, so why not a second time?

The Professor had not turned. He was busy stuffing his pockets
with small, rustling bundles from the drawers of the desk. Sara retired
undetected into the darkest corner under the table, hugging *The Shelvedon
Chronicle* to her heart. Now it only remained to get safely out of here!

But that, it appeared, was just what the Professor was doing. She
ought to have known. Why else should he be wearing a long black

overcoat and a scarf? And why else should he be methodically filling his pockets with money, and quietly withdrawing into a locked back room with the *Chronicle*?

The cars, then, and of course the shot—these were wonderfully relevant. They must mean that Tom had got through to the police, that the hunt was up, and this house written off—at least by the Professor.

His underlings, apparently, were expendable. For now he was hoisting the creaking lower sash of the window, and picking up his precious leather folder, and sliding, with an agility surprising in one of his sober years and appearance, out into the snowy garden.

Sara crept from under the table, and clambered resolutely over the sill in his wake. She waded through the deep snow under the window, and followed his track into the thick darkness of some fir-trees.

Behind them, from somewhere on the other side of the house, came a few brief, staccato shouts, a shot, a confusion of sounds.

Then there were other sounds, much nearer, the snapping of a twig, trodden inadvertently under the snow, a soft, slithering fall from other branches, behind her now. She was following the Professor, but someone else was following her.

Frightened of what this might mean, she began to hurry and then, remembering how precious and how dangerous was the thing she carried, she took off the scarf, wrapped it about the unprotected leather cover, and halted for a moment to thrust it into the middle of a big, round hollybush at the side of the path.

She was not ten yards past the hollybush, and hesitating in momentary panic, unsure of her direction, when hands reached out of the obscurity behind and grasped her by the shoulders. She opened her lips to scream and her captor clapped one palm over them and hissed frantically, "Sara, darling, don't! It's me, Roger! Don't make a noise!"

He withdrew his hand and she gasped in a quavering sob of relief, "Roger, thank goodness! I thought it was *them!*"

Sara clung to him, trembling with reaction, looking up at his strained and anxious face, so close to her own. "How did you get here? How did you know where we were? Where's Tom?"

"Later!" he whispered back urgently. "No time now to tell you. Come on, this way, quickly!" And he folded his arm round her, and dragged her on through the bushes, away from the house. She hung back for a moment. "But the police—I heard cars—"

"Not police cars! It's more of the gang. They're in trouble, but so are we if we run into them before the police arrive. Come on! Let's get out of here, quick!"

"And Ivo—" panted Sara, almost swept off her feet by the masterful and most reassuring arm about her waist. "He got out safely—I told him to get to the road and go on into the town—"

"I know! We'll take care of Ivo. Let's get you safely out of here first. Come on, run for it! My car's down here."

She had neither breath nor time to say a word more, or she would probably have told him what she had done with the *Chronicle*.

Round the curve of the path, shrouded in trees, there was a long, low, creosote-brown shed. Open garage doors had scooped new arcs out of the piled snow, and someone was hurriedly shovelling away the remains of the drift which had formed in front of them. With a sudden sickening downward lurch of her heart she recognized Professor Brayburn. The old man had imposed upon Roger!

He possibly thought they were all escaping from the same alien danger, carrying the rescued *Chronicle* with them. She tried to halt, but Roger dragged her onward.

"Roger, stop! The Professor—he was with them—he's in it! Don't let him—"

He must have heard, he must have understood, but he didn't stop. His grip tightened upon her arm, he drew her into the shed, and held her hard against the side of his familiar grey Jaguar. He looked over her shoulder at the Professor with a white, strained grin and said, "Insurance! The kid's evidence won't be worth much."

"Admirable!" said Professor Brayburn, giving her a brief glance bereft now of all benignity. "She'll come in handy if there's any bargaining to be done, too—but I hope it won't come to that." And he opened the rear door of the car, and slid rapidly into it, fastening a hand on her wrist to draw her after him.

She hung back, trembling, too dazed to understand what was happening.

"Roger, what are you doing? Roger, you can't—"

"Get in!" he said peremptorily, and thrust her bodily into the car. She fell against the Professor, and he took her by the arms and held her fast as she fought to reach the handle of the door. Roger got into the car, and started the engine.

Bitterly through all her rage and hurt she remembered how she had admired and envied the car's rapid getaway and breathless acceleration when he had driven her home from the Hallowe'en dance.

They lunged forward out of the garage, and crunched into the snow, turning away from the house. Down the steps, down the path, shouts echoed distantly, and small black figures came running, too late. The nearest of them, tall, long-legged, running like a hare and shouting like a maniac, was already recognizable. She screamed, "Tom!" "Tom!" But he couldn't possibly reach them—she might never see him again.

The car heeled round the curve of the narrow drive, gathering speed. Far behind, another car roared into action. Close at hand, Tom Fielding took a flying leap at the rear door, and was flung off and sent sprawling into the snow by the wing. Nothing could intercept the Jaguar now.

Between the enclosing trees the shot was flung back and forth in a loud, stammering repetition. The car swerved violently to the left, plunging like a wild horse under Roger's startled hands. Sara heard the squeal of the front tyre, the horrid scraping of wings against branches; then with a shattering crash the Jaguar flattened its nose against a tree, and settled sideways into the snow.

By the time Sara had got the door open and tumbled out into Tom's arms the police were all round them, and everything was under control. The Professor emerged unhurt into the welcoming hands of constables. From the driving seat they lifted out Roger Brecon, stunned, shaken and bruised, but without more serious injuries. And then, as though by common consent, everyone looked round for the source of the shot.

Ivo Jenkins came swaggering out of the bushes, glowing with excitement and pride, and brandishing his captured revolver in a manner which caused the policeman to exclaim in horror.

"Give that to me!" Tom said.

Ivo looked mutinous for one moment, but he was resigned to the fact that the scales are loaded against the young. "Sorry!" said Tom. "Very hard, I know, but the law's the law." And discreetly ignoring a muttered comment which had sounded to him like: "Just like a bloomin' teacher!" he added generously, "Jolly good shot, all the same, had you been practising Ivo? Congratulations!"

"I *am* a good shot," said the marksman, expanding into good-humour again. "Did you find my book? Did they have it in the car with them, Miss Boyne?"

Sara had almost forgotten the *Chronicle.* She smiled for the first time, rather wryly, as she saw the sergeant lift the leather case triumphantly out of the car, and laughed aloud at his dumbfounded face as Tom drew from it the *Boys Gigantic Adventure Annual.*

"It's all right," she said, suddenly, ceasing to laugh because of the childlike disappointment in Tom's face. "It's all right, I know where the real *Chronicle* is. I hid it myself."

Her only regret, and for personal reasons it was admittedly a vindictive one, was that Roger Brecon wasn't present to see her draw the precious bundle from its refuge and put it safely into the hands of the police.

"They wouldn't use Brecon's car or him for the snatch job, naturally," said the police sergeant as they stood in the main garage a little later. "It was far too conspicuous, and he was too well known in the district. He had to rush out here and send someone else to get the book back from the kid. An old, unobtrusive job like this of Brayburn's was much more the mark. Once the London registration was whipped off again, a big, dark, elderly car could be any one of hundreds.

"I know one thing, if it hadn't been for Buster here, with his toggle buttons, we couldn't have proved this was the right car without digging up the number plates—unless the other two or the girl choose to talk. I don't imagine they will. Organizations as big as this take care of their pensioners, as a matter of business, and besides, selling them out would be suicide. On the other hand, they're not likely to hold out anything that can shop the Professor for years, once they know he was leaving them to rot. Well, one centre of the organization's wiped out anyhow, and one of their experts immobilized, and we've got *The Chronicle* back.

"Well, young man, we'd better see about that telephone extension that so conveniently wouldn't work. I bet it will for us. The sooner we get in touch with your folks, and send you safely home, the better."

"I'm not tired, thank you very much," said Ivo politely, if not very truthfully. But he climbed contentedly into the back seat of Tom's car when he was told and curled up in the corner with his marvellous memories.

"I tell you what," said the sergeant in a low voice, looking warily after him, "that one may have pulled off all his buttons in a good cause, but take it from me, I never saw a kid who more certainly had his buttons *on*!"

Ivo fell asleep on the drive home, and only opened his eyes again when Tom lifted him gently out of the car and carried him into the cottage, where Mrs. Freeman was waiting to fuss over him and put him to bed. "I shall have something for Christmas instead of the beautiful book, shan't I? Something just as nice? But I wanted that!" And his mouth drooped for a moment.

"You'll have two somethings. And you shall choose any book you like, or anything else within reason."

"Can I have a gun?" asked Ivo, waking up fully for a moment.

"No, you certainly can't!" said Tom very firmly indeed "You've cost me ten years of my life tonight with the one you borrowed. Suppose Miss Boyne had been hurt badly when the car crashed?" But remembering what might well have happened to Sara if the car had not crashed, he was not disposed to dwell upon that.

"All right," conceded Ivo, recognizing one of those blank walls in which the young cannot yet hope to find a convenient door, "I'll have a book, if I can pick my own."

They were silent as they drove on towards Sara's home. Too much had happened too suddenly. They sat side by side in the car, and couldn't think of the right things to say.

"*Boys Gigantic Adventure Annual*, indeed!" said Tom abruptly. "I told you he didn't need any stimulants, he's an adventurer born. Took to it like a duck to water."

"Yes," said Sara in a low voice. "I was wrong about a lot of things, wasn't I?"

"I'm sorry!" Tom said hastily, "I didn't mean to say *I told you* so— really I didn't." And he added hesitantly: "Sara, I *am* sorry! I never thought Roger could be crooked. They think he must have been the one who provided all the necessary information about the burglar alarms, you know—he's on the museum committee. And the burglar got his message out by asking for a local solicitor, and then choosing him, of course. That's why he came rushing to the castle as soon as he got away from the police station. But you were earlier still, and he never had a chance to pick up the loot."

"You know what I thought, don't you?" said Sara, turning her brown, honest eyes upon him and blushing to the roots of her hair. "I thought he'd followed me because he—liked me. I was nearly as wild with you for butting in as he was. And all the time he was only exasperated with both of us for getting in the way."

"We did it jolly effectively, anyhow," said Tom, scarlet in his turn. He coasted to a stop outside Sara's front door, and the quiet, snowy darkness of the street folded round their mutual embarrassment. "Sara," said Tom huskily. "*He* may not have been following you because he—liked you—but *I* was! I've been doing it for months!"

By that time she was in his arms, without any clear idea of how she had got there, without any clear idea of anything, except that the castle clock had just begun to strike midnight, and all the bells of Shelvedon had burst into a triumphant and entirely appropriate peal of exultation. In the clamour his words were lost. He gave up the attempt to talk, and kissed her instead.

Some time later, between the loud reverberations of the bells, she heard him mumble happily, "Bless that kid! We'll adopt him for this!" Not that he was expressing a serious intention at that stage, of course. Still, Mrs. Freeman was old, and Ivo was very young, and it was at least the germ of an idea. She put it away somewhere at the back of her mind, to be pondered over later.

"Happy Christmas, dear Tom! Happy Christmas!" she murmured, and settled her cheek more comfortably upon his shoulder.

# ALSO AVAILABLE

"The 'impossible situation' here is the best Mr Dickson has given us"
– Torquemada in *The Observer*, 1935

"Sir Henry is at his best in this baffling yarn, and so is Carter Dickson."
– *The New York Times*, 1934

James Bennett has been invited to stay at White Priory for Christmas among the retinue of the glamorous Hollywood actress Marcia Tait. Her producer, her lover, the playwright for her next hit and her agent are all here, soon to become so many suspects when Tait is found murdered on a cold December morning in the lakeside pavilion. Only the footprints of her discoverer disturb the snow which fell overnight – and which stopped just shortly after Marcia was last seen alive. How did the murderer get in and out of the pavilion without leaving a trace?

When Bennett's uncle, the cantankerous amateur sleuth Sir Henry Merrivale arrives from London to make sense of this impossible crime, the reader is treated to a feast of the author's trademark twists, beguiling false answers and one of the most ingenious solutions in the history of the mystery genre.

*"Ahoy, my lad!" he bellowed back. "I didn't expect you so early.*
*Come for a dip! The water's fine. Everything is—"*
*Then it happened.*

Mystery and murder run amok amidst ominous peaks and icy lakes. In hushed valleys, venom flows through villages harbouring grievances which span generations. The landscapes and locales of Wales ("Cymru", in the Welsh language) have fired the imagination of some of the greatest writers in the field of crime and mystery fiction.

Presenting fourteen stories ranging from 1909 through to the 1980s, this new anthology celebrates a selection of beloved Welsh-born authors such as Cardiff's Roald Dahl and Abergavenny's Ethel Lina White, as well as lesser-known yet highly skilled writers such as Cledwyn Hughes and Jack Griffith. Alongside these home-grown tales, this collection also includes a handful of gems inspired by, or set in, the cities and wilds of Wales by treasured British authors with an affinity for the country, such as Christianna Brand, Ianthe Jerrold and Michael Gilbert.

# ALSO AVAILABLE

*"… and what a motive! Murder to save one's
artistic soul… who'd believe that?"*

Behind the stage lights and word-perfect soliloquies, sinister secrets are lurking in the wings. The mysteries in this collection reveal the dark side to theatre and performing arts: a world of backstage dealings, where unscrupulous actors risk everything to land a starring role, costumed figures lead to mistaken identities, and on-stage deaths begin to look a little too convincing. . .

This expertly curated thespian anthology features fourteen stories from giants of the classic crime genre such as Dorothy L. Sayers, Julian Symons and Ngaio Marsh, as well as firm favourites from the British Library Crime Classics series: Anthony Wynne, Christianna Brand, Bernard J. Farmer and many more.

Mysteries abound when a player's fate hangs on a single performance, and opening night may very well be their last.

## ALSO AVAILABLE
## IN THE BRITISH LIBRARY
## CRIME CLASSICS SERIES

| | |
|---|---|
| *Death of a Bookseller* | BERNARD J. FARMER |
| *Death of an Author* | E.C.R. LORAC |
| *The Progress of a Crime* | JULIAN SYMONS |
| *Green for Danger* | CHRISTIANNA BRAND |
| *The Port of London Murders* | JOSEPHINE BELL |
| *The Seat of the Scornful* | JOHN DICKSON CARR |
| *Death on the Down Beat* | SEBASTIAN FARR |
| *Murder's a Swine* | NAP LOMBARD |
| *Two-Way Murder* | E.C.R. LORAC |
| *Due to a Death* | MARY KELLY |
| *The Chianti Flask* | MARIE BELLOC LOWNDES |
| *The Edinburgh Mystery* | ED. MARTIN EDWARDS |
| *The Widow of Bath* | MARGOT BENNETT |
| *Murder by the Book* | ED. MARTIN EDWARDS |
| *Till Death Do Us Part* | JOHN DICKSON CARR |
| *These Names Make Clues* | E.C.R. LORAC |
| *Murder After Christmas* | RUPERT LATIMER |
| *Murder in the Basement* | ANTHONY BERKELEY |
| | |
| *The Story of Classic Crime in 100 Books* | MARTIN EDWARDS |
| *The Pocket Detective: 100+ Puzzles* | KATE JACKSON |
| *The Pocket Detective 2: 100+ More Puzzles* | KATE JACKSON |
| *How to Survive a Classic Crime Novel* | KATE JACKSON |

Many of our titles are also available
in eBook, large print and audio editions

## INTRODUCING THE
## CRIME CLASSICS SUBSCRIPTION

Signing up to the Crime Classics Subscription Service automatically ensures you'll receive each new title in the series as soon as it's published – perfect for gifting stories from the Golden Age of crime, or if you're looking to treat yourself to some best-selling mysteries. You'll also receive a bookmark for the title and exclusive ephemera such as postcards, prints and presents all curated to match that month's book using the British Library's collections.

Subscribe at shop.bl.uk or by scanning this QR code: